TEN-NO-HEIKA! EMPEROR!
BANZAI! BANZAI! BANZAI!

EMERGENCY BULLETIN: Air attack made on Oahu . . . enemy planes shot down . . . airplanes definitely identified . . . Rising Sun of Japan on wings . . .

HAWAII, DECEMBER 7, 1941

To Kama Gusuda, loveable old drunkard, the news was almost too good to be true. He painted the Rising Sun on his roof and started brewing saki for the triumphant arrival of the Japanese Army. To his children, the beautiful Kimiko who was studying to be a doctor, and his son Saburo, the gambler, in love with an American teacher, the news was a disaster, foreboding a return to the rigid old customs of the past. With their world crumbling in flames all around them, brutalized by American soldiers who treated them as dangerous enemy spies, they fought desperately to survive.

LUCKY COME HAWAII

A REMARKABLE FIRST NOVEL OF PEOPLE AND WAR BY A BRILLIANT YOUNG JAPANESE-AMERICAN WRITER!

LUCKY
COME
HAWAII

by Jon Shirota

This book is a work of fiction. Any
character's resembling anyone living
or dead is absolutely coincidental.

LUCKY COME HAWAII
A Bantam Book / published December 1965

Library of Congress Catalog Card Number: 65-28053

Published simultaneously in the United States and Canada.

Bantam Books are published by Bantam Books, Inc., a subsidiary
of Grosset & Dunlap, Inc. Its trade-mark, consisting of the words
"Bantam Books" and the portrayal of a bantam, is registered in the
United States Patent Office and in other countries. Marca Registrada.
Bantam Books, Inc., 271 Madison Avenue, New York, N. Y. 10016.

PRINTED IN THE UNITED STATES OF AMERICA

In Memory of Lowney T. Handy

ACKNOWLEDGMENTS

Very deep and sincere gratitude is expressed to the following: The Handy Colony of Marshall, Illinois, for providing me with the necessary environment to finish this novel; Ned Brown, my agent, for his constant encouragement and perceptive suggestions; Marc Jaffe of Bantam Books, for his faith and belief in my work; Marilyn M. Owens, for her rare friendship and understanding; and my sister, Evelyn Y. Tan, without whose contributions this novel would never have been written.

1

It was just another sunny, lazy Sunday morning, but for Kama Gusuda, driving to Wailuku in his light green 1938 Ford pickup with a slaughtered pig and three empty slop cans in the back, it was a day of much happiness. Only last night he had listened to his number one son, Ichiro, speak all the way from Tokyo. Ichiro had been chosen the guest speaker for the 1941 class of Waseda University.

There must have been thousands of Japanese in Hawaii who had also listened to his son over the radio, Kama told himself proudly. He kept driving the pickup at crawling speed, rubbing his craggy, unshaven chin with his free hand, feeling slightly hungover from drinking too much sake. And the Nippu Ji-Ji was bound to have an article about it in next week's issue. Perhaps, even have Ichiro's picture on the front page. His eyes behind the steel-rimmed bifocals beamed wistfully. After all, his number one son was the first Nisei to graduate from Waseda with such honors.

It was good to know that Ichiro had at last gotten through school. His education had been very costly. But it had been worth it. He was a wonderful boy. A credit to the family. The number two boy, Niro, was also a credit to the family. He was attending the University of Hawaii in Honolulu. Of course, it would have been much better had Kama been able to afford a Japanese education for Niro, too. But Niro had always wanted to go to America someday and become a dentist, and was willing to work his way. Kama was proud of these two sons.

But the third boy, Saburo, who was still in high school —what happened to him? Why was he so different from the other two? He was lazy; didn't care for school; had no ambition at all. The worst part about him was that he had no respect for his father and mother anymore. Kama had even caught him in a pool hall in Wailuku one day when he should have been in school. Something definitely must be done about that boy, or he might end up a good-for-nothing bum.

And there was Kimiko, the only girl in the family, just above Saburo. She, too, was hard to understand. At times she acted like a Kanaka girl. She cared nothing about the Japanese traditions. Good god! there was no telling! If he had not put a stop to her going to those awful dances where men and women practically went through the sexual act while embracing each other on the floor, she might have married one of those lazy Porlegee or Kanaka boys from around those places.

Moving slowly on the narrow macadam road bordered by green cane fields, Kama thought Kimiko would one day meet some nice Japanese boy and get married. She was already eighteen so it would not be long before she had a family of her own.

The best thing for the Gusuda family—now that Ichiro had graduated—was to move back to Japan. That way, the two younger children would be under Ichiro's influence and would have a closer tie with the customs of the old country. But moving to Japan was expensive. Maybe, in a year or two it might be possible.

Pushing his sweat-stained straw hat to the back of his head, Kama gazed out to his right beyond the green spread of fluttering sugar cane leaves, noting that the sky was a calm blue without a speck of cloud over the blue-green West Maui mountains. To the left, about a half a mile away, the normally sunken coral reefs of Waihee Beach were sticking out of the low-tide sea like tiny islands, and farther out beyond the white waves, several early-morning skin divers were already spearing for tropical fish and octopus.

He stretched and yawned, hoping to get home as soon as possible. He wanted to listen to the local Japanese program on station KGMB in Honolulu. They might mention Ichiro's speech.

He had tried to waken Saburo, but that lazy boy was still sleeping when Kama loaded the slaughtered pig and slop cans on the pickup. He would be on his way back now if that boy had gotten up to help with the morning chores. No way to control that sonnabagun boy anymore! he thought, fuming. He passed the Chinese cemetery, approaching the mile-long slope that went up the Wailuku bend. What to do with a boy like that who was going to be seventeen next month!

After another ten minutes of slow, monotonous driving he came to the abrupt bend where Market Street began in Wailuku town. On the west were the towering green peaks of Iao Valley with spots of red tainted dirt.

Heading down the short slope, he could see the big white homes on Sand Hills glittering under the warm tropical sunshine. Sand Hills, of course, was the exclusive residential district for the rich haoles. Until recently, the entire area had been restricted. Now there were several oriental families living there, too. One of them was Lin Wo, the wealthy Pah-ke whose restaurant Kama would be going to in a few minutes to pick up pig slops. Lin, who always offered Kama a cup of coffee as they sat in the kitchen and chatted several minutes every morning, was a nice Pah-ke. He was one of the few non-Japanese that Kama considered a good friend.

Wailuku, the county seat for the islands of Maui, Molokai and Lanai, was a small cosmopolitan town of about ten to eleven thousand people. Barely able to read English, Kama could remember only two streets by name: Main and Market. They intersected in the heart of town. The rest were mostly back streets, hardly worth remembering.

Driving past the iron bridge on lower Market Street, he noticed that the big clock above the Japanese jewelry store said eight-thirty. Ai-yaya! He was supposed to have delivered the pig at eight, he thought cringingly, picturing the loud Filipino butcher screaming at him again. Just because Kama couldn't understand English too well. That sassy bugga!

He drove around to Main then back to Market from the opposite direction. He would have liked to drive straight down Market and ignore the foolish one-way regulation that started two blocks away from Main. But there was a policeman standing on the corner. He parked in front of the Wailuku Market, and as expected, Pablo, the butcher, was waiting impatiently for him.

"Wheredahell you been!" Pablo yelled out from inside the market, sauntering around the counter towards the pickup. "When I said eight o'clock, I mean eight o'clock. —Not eight-thirty. Goddamn stoopid Jap-anee!"

"Aw-w, shut your big mouth," Kama mumbled silently to himself, then apologized: "Please excoose me, Pablo. Me havo to feed pigs behore comin' to Wailuku t'is mornin'," grinning toothily, avoiding the disgruntled butcher's piercing eyes.

"Never mind making excuses. My customers been waiting since seven-thirty," Pablo grumbled, pointing to several cold-faced women standing around the counter.

"Al' righ', al' righ'," Kama bowed several times and helped the butcher carry the pig into the ice box.

After receiving a check, he was glad to get away from the market, and drove down Market Street to collect pig slops from two small Japanese restaurants, then headed back to Main Street where he made his last stop at Lin Wo's, across from Kress Store where Kimiko worked.

The restaurant was completely empty although usually it was filled with servicemen on Sundays. He carried the slop can all the way around through the alley so he could enter from the kitchen. Before Clarence Wo, Lin's lanky, half-Kanaka son began running the place, Kama used to go through the front entrance. That fresh boy had threatened to throw him out of the place if he ever came through the front with the stinking slop can again.

He turned the alley corner and came to the kitchen screen door. If it weren't for that boy he could save the long trip through the narrow alley.

A warm wave of delicious, Chinese food aroma brushed past him as he opened the door.

"Good-u mornin', Lin," he greeted the stout, back-stooping, white-haired Pah-ke who was standing beside his half-Kanaka son at the serving counter.

Lin said nothing. As though not having heard him. Lin and his son were listening to their small table radio on the top shelf of the counter.

Some kind of concert music was going on.

Kama dropped the empty slop can on the wet, lumpy concrete floor beside the two large galvanized sinks. As usual, dirty, half-sunken aluminum pots and pans and utensils of all sizes were in the greasy dish water of the sink, the hot water faucet leaking rhythmically.

"Oi, Lin," he called teasingly, going around the other end of the counter and standing next to the huge black oil stove, "whassamattah, you listen radio? You no sabey t'is music."

Lin gave him a stern, unfriendly look through thick, horn-rimmed glasses. Then, still saying nothing, he turned his head and kept listening to the radio. Somehow, the old Pah-ke did not seem his usual pleasant self this morning.

Kama gazed at the electric clock above the kitchen door. Eight forty-five. He looked over towards the stacks of plates, cups, bowls and serving utensils on the two shelves of the long counter that extended to where Lin and his son were standing. What was the old man doing?—listening to some crazy music, he wondered, puzzled. Lin could no more understand that kind of music than he could.

He tried to humor the old man once more. "Whassamattah you, t'is mornin', Lin? Too muchee nice day. Why you angry?"

"Goddamnit! Shut up!" Clarence Wo burst out balefully, giving him a menacing look.

Now, what's the matter with that boy? He wasn't even talking to the boy.—What's the matter with those two this morning anyway?

Finally, unable to restrain himself any longer, Lin Wo, his old wrinkled face pulling tight, turned towards Kama and said: "God-tam Jap-anee! Kill 'em loisa 'Melican sailah and soldiah, Pear' Har-bah!"

"Huh?" Kama uttered, not having the slightest idea what the old man was talking about—Pea-ru Har-bah.

"You no heah radio, Gusuda? You don' know Jap-anee

[5]

ai-plane attack Pear' Har-bah?" Lin said, pointing furiously at the radio.

"Pea-ru Har-bah?" Kama said, even more confused. The poor Pah-ke man. He must have smoked opium again. And so early in the morning, too.

The loud concert music suddenly stopped.

Lin, his shabby white hair hanging loosely over his wrinkled forehead, quickly turned his head then, studying his son's face for a second, stared at the small radio.

Kama walked curiously over to the radio and stood beside Lin. In a second or two a grave, dramatic voice came on in place of the music. Although he could hardly understand what the announcer was saying, he thought he heard:

"Air attack made on Oahu . . . enemy airplanes shot down . . . airplanes definitely identified . . . Rising Sun of Japan on wing tips . . . no maneuver . . . real McCoy! . . . listen to more news later . . . will keep everyone informed . . ."

The concert music came on again.

"Wha' he talk abou', Lin?" Kama felt flesh bumps rising on his arms and face, ears still ringing with the startling voice of the announcer.

Before Lin could answer, his son blurted out viciously: "Those goddamn Japs! I'd like to get hold of every one of them bastards and shoot 'em full of holes!"

Lin and Kama kept eyeing Clarence.

"Wha' him say? Clalence, wha' radio man, him say?" Lin asked his son.

"Dirty sonofabitches! Those goddamn bastards!"

"Wha' radio man say?" Lin questioned once more.

"It's war, Pop! War! And those no-good bastards in Washington pretending they want peace."

"T'at's why all servicemen go back base?"

"Yeah, Pop. That's why they all took off from the restaurant few minutes ago."

Both of them now turned to Kama with scorning looks.

Kama looked away. Nihon airplanes attacking Pea-ru Harbah! No. Mistake. He kept shaking his head with disbelief.

"God-tem Jap-anee!" Lin hissed between brown teeth, wiping his hands on the grease-stained apron around his portly belly. "Al' time, kill, kill. Kill 'em lotsa Chinee in China. Now, kill 'em lotsa 'Melican soldiah and sailah."

Kama remained silent. He kept looking away from the two pairs of accusing eyes. Could it be true? Japan had really attacked Pea-ru Har-bah? "You suah, radio man, him no bull-u shit-up?" he finally asked, forcing a toothy grin.

"Bull shit—hell!" Clarence Wo burst out.

War! Japan going to war with America. This was serious. Very serious, he told himself, the overwhelming immensity of the news slowly sinking in.

They stared at him with hate-filled eyes.

Why should they be angry with Japan? They weren't Americans, Kama told himself. Old Lin was a pure Pah-ke from China and his dark son was a Kanaka-Pah-ke. Why should they concern themselves with a war that had nothing to do with them? "Whassamattah you angry with Japan?" he asked sheepishly, a good-natured laughter ringing in his voice. "Japan fight 'em 'Merica. You no 'Merican. T'is no your business."

"Why you—!" Clarence Wo came charging around the counter. He grabbed Kama by the arm. "You lousy, no-good Jap-ance, you! If you weren't so old I'da kicked the living shit outa you. Getahell outa here!" he screamed into Kama's aghast face, pushing-shoving Kama towards the screen door, heaving him out with a swift kick. "And take this stinking can out of the restaurant!" He threw the empty slop can past Kama who had stumbled hard on the ground.

Rubbing his knee gingerly where it had struck a rock, Kama dragged himself up slowly. He straightened his glasses on his nose, wondering what he had said to provoke that sonnabagun boy. As he limped over to the slop can that had rolled against the wooden fence, he heard old man Lin and his son arguing in the kitchen:

"I'at not ligh'. Not ligh' you kick Gusuda like t'at."

"Aw, Pop. They're all the same. You can't trust a single one of 'em."

Kama carried the slop can back to the pickup, angry.

He began speculating where the Nihon airplanes had come from: Aircraft carriers? Japan? One of those Japanese islands near Hawaii?

Will they be landing troops? Are they planning to take over Hawaii? It was staggering—Hawaii captured by Japan. Too good to be true. He'd have to hurry home and tell

Kimiko or Saburo to listen to the radio for the latest news. He was quite sure the Japanese programs would be off the air. At least, until the troops secured the islands.

Then, it suddenly struck him! Honolulu, where his number two son, Niro, lived was very close to Pea-ru Har-bah. Was Niro all right? Was Niro in danger? he questioned himself, alarmed. But why would the Japanese airplanes bomb Honolulu? he told himself assuringly. They would only be interested in destroying the military installations; not the city.

He hurled the can on the pickup and quickly got up front.

Driving through Main Street, then down Market, he noticed that the streets were completely deserted now. In a few minutes, he passed the bend at the end of town and was heading for home, still not entirely convinced that Japan had attacked Hawaii.

He pressed down on the gas pedal until the speedometer reached forty, then realizing he was going too fast, released the pressure on his foot and resumed his speed at thirty miles—a little faster than he normally cared to drive. He was approaching the reservoir in the cane fields and was only a short distance from the downgrade slope. Gazing out to the right at the high Haleakala mountain top, he could see puffs of white clouds floating in the blue skies. It sure was hard to believe that a part of Hawaii was being ravaged by war.

Just as he drove up to the head of the slope, before his view was obstructed by the brown-gray sand hills between him and Kahului Harbor five miles away, he thought he saw an American destroyer cruising out of the harbor with thick black smoke trailing behind.

How can one tiny ship defend Maui against the mighty Japanese Navy? he scorned, already concluding that the Hawaiian islands were surrounded by the invincible naval armada of Japan.

Rather than shifting into neutral and turning off the ignition to save gas as he usually did whenever coming to the slope, he kept his foot down on the gas pedal, maintaining his speed. He pushed back his hat, asking himself: Why did Japan attack Hawaii? What was their plan?

What a brave country to embark on such a daring mission. So clever of them to have sent Nomura and Kurusu to Washington to negotiate for peace when they had been planning to attack Pea-ru Har-bah all the time. What ingenious strategy! You just cannot beat them. They caught the Americans with their pants down again.

And that Shintoku Maru, the Japanese naval cadet ship that came to Hawaii last year on a goodwill mission! It must have been part of the plan. They must have been here to map out the exact location of Pea-ru Har-bah and other military installations.

Thousands of Japanese on Maui had boarded the ship when it had docked at Kahului Harbor for a week. Most of them had contributed something to help win the long, costly war with the stubborn Pah-kes in China. Kama, himself, had made a generous contribution. He had loaded his pickup with old, discarded tires gathered around Waihee and Kapuna, and had hauled them down to the ship. The tires, he was told by one of the naval officers, were badly needed for the trucks in the China front. Other patriotic Japanese families had brought loads of blankets, steel parts of automobiles, lead plates from auto batteries and bags of American rice. Thousands of children had lined up the length of the pier behind their Japanese school teachers with rolls of tinfoil wrappers from cigarette packages to offer the captain of the ship. The tinfoil were to be melted and made into bullets.

In addition to the truck load of old tires, Kama had donated two big pigs, cleaned and dressed, for the tremendous farewell gala that had taken place at the Kahului Buddhist Temple. For his generosity, he was presented a huge silk Japanese flag autographed by all the officers of the Shintoku Maru. The flag became a prize possession in the family trunk.

That day, when the ship had sailed away from the harbor, thousands of patriots had stood at the pier to bid sayonara to its gallant crew. As throngs of children had begun singing Hotaru-No-Hikari (Auld Lang Syne), the older folks had kept yelling: "Ten-No-Heika! Emperor! Banzai! Banzai! Banzai!"—stiff arms jerking up and down over their heads.

Who knows? Kama thought, feeling the pickup bouncing up slightly as it rolled over the familiar dip mid-way down the slope, those very same cadets could have come with the attacking forces. Furthermore, he was certain that some Hawaii Nisei had led the attack. The Nisei would know the exact position of Pea-ru Har-bah.

Ichiro!

A cold shiver shot through the marrows of his bones. No! Ichiro could not possibly be with the force. What did he know about flying? Besides, he had spoken from Tokyo only last night.

—But wait a minute. That telegram that Ichiro had sent from Tokyo to tell everyone of his forthcoming speech could have been a deception: A decoy: A way to fool the Americans—give them the impression that nothing unusual was taking place in Japan. And Ichiro could have spoken from one of the naval ships.

He shook his head vigorously. He shuddered and straightened his hat. It was ridiculous to think that his number one son was with the attacking force, he told himself. He would be needed in Japan. Japan was badly in need of electrical engineers for the war effort. It would be terrible if Ichiro was sent to war after all those years of going to school. He might get killed.

Directly above him, flying in close-order formation, were three American fighter planes from the Puunene airport. He leaned forward against the windshield and peered up into the sky. Three American planes against the powerful Japanese Air Force, he scoffed. They wouldn't stand a chance. He suddenly thought how terrible it would be if there should be an air battle over Maui and the Japanese planes accidentally killed their own people on the ground.

What's going to happen after Japan conquered Hawaii? he asked himself, picturing hundreds of Japanese flags waving all over Maui. He could picture an extra large one fluttering gloriously on the tall flag pole in front of the Wailuku Courthouse. And he envisioned a long, welcoming parade down Main and Market Streets (the one-way regulation on Market at last ignored): A Japanese General in immaculate, beribboned uniform, riding on a spirited white horse; Japanese military bands playing familiar, heart-warming war marches; and sitting in one of the long, black shiny Cadillacs for the civilian dignitaries:

Kama's number one son, ICHIRO! Banzai! Banzai! Banzai!

Ichiro, one of the diplomats on Maui! Maybe, Governor! He would live in that big, white mansion in Wailuku now occupied by that fat, red-faced, haole plantation manager.

Kama was coming to the end of the decline where the Chinese cemetery was. He reached down under the dash and rubbed his swollen knee again. That goddamn Pah-ke boy! He was like a poi dog without a single ounce of civilized blood in his veins. As soon as Japan took over the islands that boy will have to be reported to the General for mistreating a Nihon-jin. As for the old man, well, under normal circumstance, he was a fine person despite Kama's failure all these years to convince him that China would be better off under Japan.

As he approached Waihee Village, he wondered whether Mr. Fukunaga, the Japanese school teacher, knew what was happening. He'd stop by and inform the teacher just in case. Won't the teacher be surprised if he was the first to tell him!

After passing the ball park where several children were playing football, he slowed down, then made an abrupt right turn beyond the theatre; went over a dilapidated wooden bridge; down a bumpy, rocky dirt road, finally stopping at the teacher's cottage, a white building, beside the green, two-room Japanese school house.

He hurried over to the front door, hoping he was the first to bring the great news.

"Sensei! Sensei!" he called, knocking repeatedly on the fragile wooden door.

In a few seconds he heard someone coming up to the door with short, shuffling steps.

It was Mrs. Fukunaga. "Ah-h, Gusuda-san, good morning," she greeted, bowing.

"Has your husband heard about the attack?" he asked without preamble.

"Attack?" youthful Mrs. Fukunaga, dressed in a faded light blue cotton dress, uttered. She looked at him, stupefied.

"Yes. Nihon airplanes have attacked Pea-ru Har-bah in Honoruru."

Mrs. Fukunaga's dainty hands jumped up to her cheeks, her pale, unpainted lips quivering. "Gusuda-san, are you sure?"

"Where's your husband?" he asked, refusing to speak any longer with the dumb-struck woman.

"He's in the back. Come in. Please come in," she invited, holding the door open, then quickly going through the kitchen to call her husband.

Kama took off his hat and stepped into the living room. He sat down on one of the straight-backed, lacquered chairs at the round table. Directly above his head were three orange and white paper lanterns hanging down from the low ceiling. Next to the two partially opened windows was a miniature Buddhist shrine with pencil-lead incense sending up a steady wisp of pungent smoke. Beside it, on a metal triangle, was a long samurai sword encased in a black sheath, its handle braided in shiny, gold-trimmed silk. Above the sword was a huge flag tacked against the wall, the round Rising Sun glittering crimson.

Kama studied the flag with warm, misty eyes, his throat congested with lumps, an overpowering sensation spurting up his spine.

"Gusuda-san, what's this about Nihon airplanes attacking Pea-ru Har-bah?" Tall, spare Mr. Fukunaga ran excitedly into the living room in an oversized T-shirt and a pair of mud-stained khaki trousers. His gaunt face was dripping with sweat.

"Hail Sensei," Kama reassured, jumping up to his feet, bowing several times. "They have been attacking since early this morning."

Mr. Fukunaga stepped hastily over to the radio near the window and clicked it on.

In a few seconds the radio announcer was repeating the same news Kama had heard back at Lin Wo's. Only this time, the announcer was commanding all fire fighters, doctors, nurses and servicemen of all branches to return to their post of duty at once.

Mr. Fukunaga's jaw dropped. His eyes narrowed into tiny slits. His thick eyebrows bunched together as he kept staring numbly at his wife, then at Kama. Speechless. After reaching into his back pocket for his handkerchief and wiping off the beads of perspiration on his forehead and cheeks, he said in a crisp, conspiratorial voice: "This is serious. Very serious. Pea-ru Har-bah being attacked by Nihon airplanes."

"What's going to happen now?" Kama asked, studying the teacher's tense face catching the reflection of the sunlight pouring into the room from the window.

"I don't know. It's hard to tell. They might send troops ashore and take over the islands."

"All of Hawaii? Maui, too?"

"Yes," Mr. Fukunaga replied, "Maui, too." He walked over to the chair at the table and sat down.

His wife, standing beside him with both hands cupped to her mouth, remained absolutely silent. She kept staring at her husband.

". . . Attacking 'Merica," Mr. Fukunaga mumbled to himself, looking down at the table as though in a spell. "It could mean only one thing: An all out war!" he said, pondering. "It was inevitable from the beginning when 'Merica interfered with the war in China. —But attacking Pea-ru Har-bah!"

"How long do you think it'll be before the troops take over the islands?" Kama asked, holding his battered hat before him, fingers twisting its brim anxiously.

"It'll depend," Mr. Fukunaga said, looking up, dark, intent eyes narrowed again. "If the attack in Honoruru is successful, all of Hawaii will fall in a day," he went on, stolidly.

"One day!" Kama was flabbergasted. "You really think so?"

Mr. Fukunaga turned his head and stared at the Japanese flag on the wall.

Kama watched the teacher's square jaws clamped tight together for a while, then finally, unable to stand the smothering silence, said: "Excuse me, Sensei. I must be going home." He backed towards the door, bowed low several times, tarnished gold fillings in his front teeth reflecting under the ceiling light.

Mr. Fukunaga, standing up, walked over to the door and opened it for Kama. Mrs. Fukunaga joined them.

"Thank you very much for informing us," Mr. Fukunaga said, conspiratorial, bowing back a curt nod, his lanky, angular body framed in the doorway. "I'll let you Okinawans in Kapuna Valley know what's happening as soon as I get more information," he called out as Kama approached the pickup.

There goes that damned teacher distinguishing Okinawans from the Naichis, non-Okinawan Japanese, again, Kama told himself irritably, climbing up into the pickup. "Thank you. Thank you, Sensei. We'd appreciate that," he nevertheless called back, bowing ingratiatingly. Why must the teacher always draw a line between the Okinawans and the Naichis? he wondered dejectedly, starting the pickup and driving up the bumpy dirt road and onto the macadam highway.

The teacher was surprised all right, he congratulated himself, overcoming his irritation. The teacher would know exactly what to do when the heroic Japanese troops came to Maui. He'd probably get all the Japanese together and plan a great welcoming celebration. And Kama, of course, would be only too glad to donate all the pigs they would need for the occasion.

In about ten minutes, he came to the sharp Kapuna bend at the crest of the hill, a quarter of a mile away from his home. He brought the pickup to a gradual stop alongside the stone wall. Everything had happened so fast the past hour he wanted to be alone for a few minutes and catch his breath.

Directly below the stone wall was a two-hundred-foot cliff that dropped sharply to the Kapuna River. He turned his head and followed the river down to the pounding white waves of the ocean a mile away, feeling a rush of cool, salty breeze blowing against his face. Farther west, over towards Kahakauloa—one of the few authentic native villages left in Hawaii—he could barely make out the east end of Molokai. Beyond Molokai was Honolulu.

It just did not seem possible that a battle was taking place that close to Maui. He prayed that Niro was all right in Honolulu.

He wanted to take a piss.

He opened the door and walked around the pickup to the stone wall. Unbuttoning his fly, he watched his urine bubbling on the tiny gravels and pebbles for a second or two, then gazed down at sun-filled Kapuna Valley expanded before him.

He was astounded by the thundering silence that suddenly swept around him once his loud pissing had stopped. The valley seemed so calm, so peaceful and tranquil. It would be terrible if the war should ever destroy the valley, he thought.

Still standing there with the morning sun beating down on the back of his neck, he realized with a start that he had been passing the same spot for years without noticing the panoramic view. It was really beautiful, a settlement all of its own, accessible by only one road, immersed in deep green, tropical plum, guava, mango and koa trees all year. He traced the narrow, winding river up towards the mountains and watched it form a strip of island as it parted into two streams, then merged near his home. Farther up, he could see the silvery-white waterfall cascading hundreds of feet down the sheer cliff.

He was as much a part of the valley, he felt, as the Kanakas that had lived there for generations. And he was proud of his home built with his own two hands. It wasn't exactly a modern home, but it had three bedrooms, a living room with ceiling, running water in the kitchen and an outhouse with flush toilet. It was one of the few homes around that was painted: the corrugated-iron roof red; the rest green to match the natural beauty of the valley. One of these days, when he had time, he planned to paint the outhouse, too.

He knew that in his own way he had been playing an important role in the valley: His home had the only telephone for miles around and everyone came to use it; and during the New Year celebration everyone—regardless of nationality—came over to share the pig he roasted in the ground, and to drink the good sake he brewed for the hearty drinkers.

Now that Japan will be taking over the islands, will all this change? he wondered, not without a sense of loss; having lived in the islands the past thirty-five years he had become accustomed to the easy, carefree ways of the Kanakas.

But it would be for the better, he told himself. Change was the essence of growth and progress for a place like Hawaii. For him, it was decidedly too late. But for the independent Niseis who were forgetting the traditions of the old country, it would be a salvation. They would learn the true ways of Japan and would be educated under a better system. Eventually, everyone in Hawaii would be speaking Japanese.

He grinned to himself, picturing that sassy Porlegee, Domingo Garcia, to whose restaurant he went to pick up pig slops twice a week, trying to speak Japanese. Now, it would be Kama's chance to mimic that fat Porlegee.

Still grinning owlishly, he pushed himself away from the stone wall and walked over to the pickup. He began driving down the hill, hoping Kimiko would be home so she could listen to the latest American news. Honolulu could have fallen by now, he thought wishfully.

Just before turning into the dirt driveway of his home a colossal thought flashed through his mind: The Americans would not be foolish enough to fight the Japanese forces; they would rather give up and avoid unnecessary bloodshed.

2

WHEN THE FIRST series of bombs fell, Kama Gusuda's number two son, Niro, was gazing out the kitchen window of the luxurious Whittingham house on Pacific Heights. He paid no attention to the rumbling sounds. Like most of the residents of Honolulu, he thought it was just another "simulated" attack the Army and Navy were going through. Lush-green Nuuanu Valley below was as quiet and lovely as ever. The crisp mountain breeze from the Pali was rustling the coconut palms bordering upper Nuuanu Avenue. Early-morning golfers in bright shirts and trousers were already out on the private course across the other side of the valley, their caddies following close behind.

Niro was the part-time, servant-chauffeur-houseboy for elderly Mr. and Mrs. Whittingham while attending the university. He had been with the Whittinghams the past year and a half, ever since Mr. Whittingham had a stroke and had retired as executive of one of the Big Five firms. They furnished Niro a room above the garage, plus board and ten dollars a week. He worked at the pineapple cannery during the summer for his tuition fees. The Whittinghams were cranky and demanding (especially Mrs.

Whittingham, who was ill in bed a greater part of the time), but then, most of the haoles in the islands acted that way towards the Japanese anyway.

Niro had just finished the last of the morning dishes when the next round of muffled boom-booming echoes rattled the cups and saucers on the shelf, the floor recoiling under him.

Jesus! they're sure going through a tough maneuver, he thought, placing the wet dish towel on the rack above the shiny porcelain sink.

"Niro!" Mr. Whittingham called from the living room which adjoined the long dining room.

He hurried over to the dining room and opened the door. "Yes, Mr. Whittingham." He smiled graciously at the Old Man sitting on the couch reading the Sunday Morning Advertiser.

"Those sounds seem louder than usual, don't they?" Mr. Whittingham said, looking up momentarily over the paper, frowning, cluster of gray hair dangling over his deeply lined, pale forehead.

"I'm sure it's just another maneuver, Mr. Whittingham," he said politely. "—Is Mrs. Whittingham all right?"

"Yes, she's resting comfortably," Mr. Whittingham's eyes went back to the paper. His long wooden cane was placed beside him as it always was whenever he was sitting down. "I hope all that confounded noise doesn't disturb her."

"Shall I take her some warm milk?"

"That won't be necessary. I'll go in in a few minutes and see how she's feeling. —That damned noise is getting louder, isn't it?" he interjected when another round of reverberating boom-boom-boom vibrated the house. "You sure it's just another one of those maneuvers?"

"I'm sure it is, Mr. Whittingham," Niro said. He tried to hide the anxiety from his own face, holding his head sideways, small dark eyes narrowed with concern. The booming sounds were definitely louder and stronger than any other they had ever experienced.

"Go out in the front yard and see if anything unusual is going on," Mr. Whittingham ordered gruffly.

"Yes, sir." He quickly went past Mr. Whittingham through the spacious living room filled with old furniture.

Opening one of the double glass front doors and stepping out on the wide lanai, he quickly noted that it was a clear, warm morning with hardly any clouds in the blue sky, the breeze from the sea stirring the palms and hibiscus hedges along the driveway. The air smelled of fresh gardenias and roses. Aloha Tower, almost directly below at the waterfront, loomed majestically into the glittering sky.

Niro, short, stocky and comfortably dressed in white T-shirt tucked in his faded levis, stepped down the steps and walked over to the far edge of the big front lawn where Kato-san, the slight, wiry old Japanese gardener, was doing his Sunday morning chore, trimming the hibiscus hedges.

"Good morning," Kato-san greeted toothily, trimming away with his sickle. He was dressed in a patched denim shirt and baggy denim trousers wrapped at the legs with a roll of brown, threadbare Japanese leggings, an old pair of ta-bes meeting the leggings at the ankles. He stopped trimming now and gazed over his shoulder towards Pearl Harbor, then looked back at Niro, puzzled.

"Isn't that a big fire going on over there?" Niro asked, pointing beyond Kamehameha Heights. There was a column of black, ominous-looking smoke mushrooming up into the sky.

"I've been watching it the past five minutes," Kato-san answered in Japanese. "Those sounds seem real, don't they?"

"Aw, it's just another air raid practice," Niro said, trying to shrug it off, intense eyes concentrated on the black smoke, right hand over his forehead.

Kato-san dropped his sickle. He joined Niro watching the scores of tiny airplanes flashing silver in the blue skies over Pearl Harbor. "It sure looks like a real battle."

"Yeah, it looks like the real thing all right," Niro agreed, again feeling the ground trembling under him as another round of booming sounds rumbled through the city. "They're getting better all the time."

"Look!" Kato-san suddenly cried out, pointing excitedly

[19]

over towards the ocean this side of Pearl Harbor. "That plane is on fire! It's falling into the sea! Look!"

Niro, squinting his eyes, quickly looked where Kato-san was pointing. "Jesus Christ!"

The tiny speck in the low sky crashed into the water, splashing up white foam before disappearing.

"There's another one! Over there!" Kato-san exclaimed, pointing slightly to the right this time.

"Whatdahell kind of manuever is that?"

"Niro!" Mr. Whittingham called out from the lanai. "What's going on out there!"

"They're sure putting on a funny kind of manuever, Mr. Whittingham," he answered. "They're shooting down the airplanes. And the bombs!—they're really setting fire to the ships!"

Mr. Whittingham came over, limping-hopping, breathing whizzingly.

"Good heavens!" he cried out, towering over them, stoop shoulders bent forward, right hand capped over his eyes.

Three of them stood there with mouths wide open, not saying another word, only staring, stupefied, towards Pearl Harbor.

Suddenly! an ear-splitting, weird whistling noise charged out of the sky. It was immediately followed by a deathly explosion near the base of the Heights.

"Good God!" Mr. Whittingham muttered, face turning chalk white. "That sounded like a bomb. What's happening! What's going on! —Niro, go into the house and call the police department."

Niro kept standing there.

"Niro!" Mr. Whittingham grabbed hold of his shoulder and gave it a hard shake. "Didn't you hear me? Call the police department."

Before Niro could turn to dash up to the house, a lone, single-engine aircraft, its motor sputtering falteringly, swooped over the Heights above their heads, made an abrupt turn, and headed back towards the ocean.

Kato-san, eyes squinting against the glaring sunlight, suddenly stiffened. He looked over at Niro, then back at the aircraft heading for Pearl Harbor. "Why, that was a Japanese airplane," he uttered, flabbergasted, eyes wide

[20]

open. "Did you see that! It was a Japanese airplane," he repeated to Niro. "They're all Japanese airplanes!" he went on, awed.

Niro, stunned and shocked, exchanged quick, scowling glances with Mr. Whittingham, then looked over at joyful Kato-san.

Before Niro could stop him, Kato-san began yelling: "Japanese airplanes! Japanese airplanes!" waving a yellow, mucous-stained handkerchief at the planes miles away. "Did you see that!" he screamed into Niro's face. "Japanese airplanes bombing all the ships in Pearl Harbor. Banzai! Banzai! Banzai!"

"Why you goddamn little Jap!" Mr. Whittingham roared menacingly at the wiry old gardener. "You no-good Jap spy!" Mr. Whittingham screamed, raising his cane and swinging it down murderously on Kato-san's half-bald head.

Kato-san reeled for a second, hands clutched over his head where the cane had landed, then collapsed helplessly on the grass.

"You sonofabitch! I'm going to kill you!" Mr. Whittingham threatened savagely, stepping over Kato-san's balled-up form, raising the cane high in the air with both hands, ready to strike the gardener again.

"Mr. Whittingham!" Niro cried. "Don't! He didn't know what he was doing."

"I'm gonna kill this little sneaking bastard!"

"Mr. Whittingham!" he cried out again, reaching up for the cane before it could land on Kato-san's head. He began struggling with Mr. Whittingham who suddenly lost his balance and, letting go of the cane, went sprawling backward onto the grass.

He meant to help Mr. Whittingham up, but the Old Man, pushing himself up with both hands, came charging for him.

"Why, you Jap bastard, you!" Mr. Whittingham cursed viciously, reaching up for the cane in Niro's hand.

"Mr. Whittingham! I was only trying to stop you from hurting Kato-san."

"You no-good Jap!"

Niro, realizing he could not appease the Old Man, heaved the cane way over towards the lanai. The Old Man grabbed his arm and began shaking him violently.

He gave the Old Man a desperate shove and watched him stumbling hard on his back.

"I'm gonna get you two!" Mr. Whittingham screamed, pushing himself up. "I'm gonna get my shotgun and blast you two Jap bastards!" He went limping towards the house.

"C'mon, Kato-san. Get up!" Niro said, helping the fanatical old gardener up to his feet. "Let's getdahell outa here."

Kato-san staggered up slowly to his feet. He kept rubbing the large pinkish lump on his half-bald head. "What's happened? Why did that old fool strike me with his cane?" he wanted to know.

"C'mon, let's go. Where's your truck? We gotta get outa here fast."

"It's over there. On the road, outside," Kato-san said, picking up his sickle and running, bowlegged, to Pacific Heights Road just beyond the Whittingham ground.

The truck, a black Model-T, was parked against the curb facing downtown Honolulu. The back was filled with gardening tools and a hand lawnmower. Kato-san, hopping amazingly quickly on the running board and jerking a wire choke on the dash a couple of times, got down again, went up front, and began cranking the hell out of the Model-T.

The tinny sounding engine chugged a couple of times. It missed. Kato-san tried again. It missed once more.

Niro got out and took over. "Get inside. Hurry!"

He cranked desperately. The damned thing kicked once, then missed. Mr. Whittingham, carrying a long-barreled gun in one hand and his cane in the other, was limping-hopping to the main gate.

When Niro gave the junk a flurry of cranks, it caught and the engine coughed, sputtered and heaved, Kato-san pumping the choke.

"C'mon, let's go!"

Kato-san, glancing over his shoulder and seeing Mr. Whittingham charging at them with his shotgun, stepped quickly into gear, and the Model-T leaped forward. Niro jumped to the side, and hopped on the running board.

Looking up the hill through the back window, he could see Old Man Whittingham shaking his fist with red, bloated face.

"That crazy haole. What's wrong with him?" Kato-san said, barely making the first sharp turn. "Why did he strike me?"

"Kato-san, you shouldn't have done that—waving your handkerchief at the airplane and yelling banzai," he lectured. "We might be at war with Japan."

"You really think we're at war with 'Merica?" Kato-san questioned gravely, shoulders hunched forward, eyes darting up into the skies now and then. They were speeding down the hilly road much faster than Niro cared to be going.

"If that was a Japanese airplane we saw we must be at war with Japan."

"Yes, we must be at war with 'Merica," Kato-san said, eyes once more scanning the skies. He suddenly let go of the steering wheel and pointed through the glassless windshield. "There's another one of our airplanes!" he cried out banzai-ously. "There! Over there!"

"Watch out!" Niro screamed, reaching over for the wheel, the car barely missing a telephone pole. "Kato-san! Keep your hands on the wheel!"

Kato-san drove the same reckless speed down the winding Pacific Heights Road with Niro pressing both feet hard on the floor. "Kato-san, take it easy," he pleaded. "Don't worry about Mr. Whittingham chasing us anymore."

"Japanese airplanes," Kato-san mumbled to himself. "Where did they come from? No one can stop them, those powerful Japanese airplanes."

"You better stop saying that, Kato-san. You wanna go jail?" Niro shook his head. "Whatdahell can you do with an old man like this?" he told himself, still pressing his feet down on the floor. "—Watch out!" he cried, grabbing the steering wheel again, maneuvering away from the high bank the other side of the road. "Chrissake! Kato-san. Watch where you're going!"

"Japanese airplanes bombing Pea-ru Har-bah," Kato-san muttered.

"Kato-san, stop the truck," Niro pleaded when they approached the first level spot. "I wanna get out."

"I'll take you wherever you want to go."

"No, 'at's all right. I'll walk the rest of the way."

Kato-san jammed the brakes; the unresponsive Model-T

began to slow. Niro jumped out, saving Kato-san the trouble of a complete stop. "Arigato, Kato-san," he said, wiping his brow.

"You sure you don't want me to drive you all the way down?" Kato-san asked, looking out the truck as it kept rolling on.

"No. Thanks just the same. Sayonara . . ."

"Sayonara!" Kato-san called back, grinding the gears and picking up speed, scanning the skies again.

How the hell does he do it?—driving that old junk up and down the steep hill every day, Niro wondered, amazed, head going from side to side, now grinning to himself. And yelling banzai in front of Mr. Whittingham! Then, waving that dirty handkerchief at the plane. What a crazy old fart!

He looked around. He was at the corner of Fort and Pauoa, a good ten blocks away from where his friends, Ed Oshima and Hank Endo lived. He hurried down Fort, hoping to find Ed and Hank home.

Both of them were also sophomores at UH. Ed, Niro's high school classmate, came from Wailuku, Maui; while Hank came from Hilo, Hawaii. They lived in a small one-bedroom apartment above the School Street Market, on the corner of Fort and School.

He ran across the street, going around the side alley alongside the market and scrambling up the old stairways.

"Hey, Hank! Ed! Open up! Open up, you guys!"

After pounding the door couple of more times, it opened slowly. Tall, thin Ed Oshima looked out sleepy-eyed, long, tousled, black hair all over his oily forehead. "Whatdahell you want so early in the morning?" he grumbled, pushing back his mop of hair.

"Whatdahell I want!" Niro exlaimed. "How can you keep on sleeping with all that bombing noises!"

"Aw, what bombing noise?" Ed turned around and walked back to the bed and flopped on it sleepily.

Niro shut the door behind him and sat down on the edge of the bed. "Where's Hank?"

"Down the saimin stand where he's supposed to meet Roy. They're gonna go down the CYO gym for the weigh-ins."

"Chrissake! Don't go back to sleep, Ed. The Buddhaheads attacking Pearl Harbor. I just saw one of their planes go down."

"Down where?"

"Into the ocean."

"Aw-w, bull shit. Let me alone. Can't you see I'm all pooped out. I came in pretty late from the university dance."

"Ed! I'm not bull shitting. It's for real."

Just then the same ear-splitting, whistling noise Niro had heard up at the Heights came bursting out of the sky.

Ed quickly sat up on the bed, terrified. He kept staring at Niro, wide-eyed, waiting for the eerie, horrifying, screaming sound to stop. Suddenly, a loud, nerve-shattering explosion roared close by; the building trembled like an empty box.

"What was that!" Ed said, wide awake.

"It was a bomb exploding right around the corner. —You see, I wasn't bull shitting."

"Why didn't you tell me there's a war going on," Ed cried out, jumping out of the bed and grabbing hold of his trousers on a nail, pulling them up his legs over his wrinkled pajamas. "We better go down the saimin stand and look for Hank. C'mon!" He took hold of a shirt on the way out and put it on while taking two steps at a time down the stairway.

Outside, there was a crowd milling around the corner, everyone chattering fearfully and looking around to see where the explosion had taken place. Niro and Hank did not bother to stick around. They continued running down Fort Street towards Kukui.

Everywhere, people were standing on the sidewalks with horrified faces. Some were climbing on roof tops gazing over towards Pearl Harbor and giving a round-to-round description of what was happening. "There's 'nother one goin' down!" some fat Kanaka man in shorts standing on the highest roof at the corner of Fort and Kukui yelled out, hand shading his eyes. "The damn planes all over the place! They bombing the hell outa Pearl Harbor!"

Niro and Ed turned the corner and headed for Nuuanu. Another whistling sound echoed out of the sky. They stopped, stared at each other, petrified. As the deathly sound came closer they hit the sidewalk, their hands covering their heads, bellies hugging the sidewalk.

The explosion shook the concrete under them. It shook the whole block. Niro kept lying face down, feeling his belly juggling over the sidewalk. He opened his eyes slowly. Ed was looking over at him, bewildered, mouth half opened.

"What was that!" Ed uttered, refusing to get up.

Niro got up to his feet a little shaky and dusted himself, looking ahead towards Nuuanu. "Jesus Christ! It landed right on the saimin stand! There's guys all over the sidewalk."

Ed scrambled up to his feet. Numb, both of them looked at each other. Not saying anything, they ran over to the shambled saimin stand.

"It's Hank!" Ed cried, looking down at the first victim sprawled on the street, pieces of lumber strewn all over him. "Hank!" Ed called, pulling him up. "You all right, Hank?"

Hank, blood smeared on one corner of his forehead, continued shaking his head as though tossing off cobwebs from a right that had sneaked through his guard. "Yeah, I'm all right," he said, rising up to his feet with Ed's help. "Whatdafuck was that!"

Niro looked around at the other victims lying helplessly on the sidewalk and street. People were already gathering around the corner. Some were helping with the wounded. Others were too stunned to do anything.

"How's Roy?" Hank asked, shaking his head couple of more times.

"Oh, god!" Niro moaned, looking down at Roy Ito behind Hank. Roy's leg was soaked red with blood. Huge pieces of lumber were all over his body. Niro quickly stepped over and began tossing the lumber aside. "Roy! You all right?"

Roy moaned. He opened his eyes painfully.

Ed and Hank were helping Niro now. The three of them cleared the mess off Roy whose left leg below the knee was split wide open. White, fleshy human meat was oozing out warm blood and soaking Roy's pants leg. Niro, looking down at the deep ugly wound of milky-white, shattered bones, almost vomited.

"My leg! My leg!" Roy sobbed, one arm over his eyes in excruciating pain. "Take it easy with my leg," he cried, tears streaming down his taut cheeks, his entire body stretching out stiffly to fight off the pain.

Most of the crowd was now helping with the other wounded. Some were clearing the debris off the street. A couple of men were directing the snarled traffic on Nuuanu as curious onlookers in cars refused to move. Metallic whirring sirens could be heard charging up the corner several blocks away. There was no telling how many had been injured; how many had been killed. The entire place was in one helluva mess. The saimin stand had been completely demolished; pots and pans and noodle bowls were all over the place.

Actually, the only amateur fighter Niro knew among the gang for tomorrow night's fight was Roy Ito. Roy had been the Territorial bantamweight champ last year and was expected to regain the crown.

"How's my leg?" Roy asked, moaning, eyes wincing tight, refusing to look down at his leg, his slightly flattened nose wrinkled up. "My leg's okay, huh?"

No one answered.

"Hank! How's my leg?"

"It's bleeding pretty bad," Hank at last answered. "C'mon, we'll take you over to Doctor Tokunaga."

"Oh-h . . . No. No, I don't t'ink I can make it," Roy gasped out as Hank and Ed attempted to lift him up to his feet.

Crossing their hands under Roy, Hank and Ed lifted him up, then started carrying him to Doctor Tokunaga's home office on Kukui, half a block this side of Fort. Niro followed behind, still sickened by the bodies he had seen back there.

Like everyone else standing on their porches, young, bespectacled Doctor Tokunaga, the Territorial Boxing Commission physician, stood looking curiously at Hank and Ed carrying Roy Ito. He was still dressed in his bathrobe.

"Doc! Roy got hit," Hank called out when they reached the gate.

"Bring him in here," the pot-bellied doctor said impassively, holding the front door open, now studying Roy's bleeding left leg as they stepped up the front steps.

They carried Roy into Doc's emergency dispensary and laid him on a high metal bed. The small, brightly lit room was filled with white wooden cabinets which, in turn, were filled with medical books and instruments. The room smelled strongly of disinfectants and antispectics.

"How's my leg, Doc?" Roy pleaded in deep pain.

Doc, saying nothing, reached for a pair of scissors and cut off Roy's pants leg where it was soaked beet-red.

"Doc . . ." Roy pleaded again.

"You got hit pretty bad, Roy," Doc finally said. "I might have to operate on it."

"Operate! What you mean—operate!"

Doc now reached for a long stretch of tape and made a tight tourniquet around Roy's upper thigh to stop the bleeding. "We'll have to take you over to Queens Hospital," he finally said, looking down soberly at Roy, then quickly gazing up at Hank across the bed.

"You mean you have to cut off my leg!"

"We might be able to save it," Doc said, placing one hand on Roy's powerfully built shoulder.

"Doc, I'm supposed to turn pro next month," Roy sobbed, frantic. "You gotta save my leg." He looked tearfully at Hank. "Tell him, Hank. Tell him I'm gonna turn pro next month."

Hank's eyes suddenly flooded with tears.

"Don't let him do it, Hank," Roy begged.

Niro, looking away from the bed, felt lumps in his throat. Ed's head was bent low, his eyes watery.

The doctor stepped out of the room for several minutes, then came back changed into a pair of dark trousers and a white, opened-collar shirt. He and Hank lifted Roy up and carried him carefully out of the room, down the front steps, finally into Doc's black 1940 Buick.

They drove out of the driveway: Doc up front driving and Hank in the back comforting Roy. "I'll see you guys up the apartment," Hank called out to Niro and Ed as Doc turned the Buick around and took off for Queens Hospital.

Ed looked over at Niro after the car had disappeared around the Emma Street corner a block beyond Fort. "You t'ink Roy gonna lose his leg?" he asked, eyes moist.

"Ca-rist! I hope not. He's the best bantamweight in the Territory."

"Those lousy goddamn bastards!" Ed said, looking up at the sky towards Pearl Harbor. "Those no-good dirty bastards!"

Niro glanced over his shoulder and could see black smoke spiraling high into the blue sky beyond the old wooden two-story buildings on Nuuanu Avenue.

"C'mon," Ed said, "Let's go back to the apartment and wait for Hank. Damnit! I hope they won't have to cut off Roy's leg."

Walking hastily to Fort, then heading up to School, Niro suddenly realized that the bombing noises had stopped altogether. He looked down at his wrist watch. Eight-thirty. The continual bombing at Pearl Harbor had lasted almost half an hour.

"You t'ink it's all over?" Ed asked.

Before Niro could answer another series of sustained bombardment followed. The sidewalk shook and rumbled under them. "Holy cow! It's getting worse!" he muttered, face turning ashen white, mouth pulled tight.

"Let's take off!" he said, running, Ed catching up from behind. "You know something," Niro said, breathless, "the explosion up the Heights and the one at the saimin stand was no bomb. It couldn't have been. There were no planes flying around. They were American anti-aircraft shells that never exploded in the air. Somebody must have goofed."

"Yeah?" Ed said, face screwed up, running faster. "They keep goofing off like that we better go up the mountains till it's all over."

They climbed up the stairway of the apartment, both of them puffing and out of breath. "I'm beat," Ed said, gasping for air. He was pressing his hand against his belly. He opened the door, walked over to the bed, and flopped on it. Niro sat on the edge of the other bed across the narrow space, still breathing exhaustedly.

For about ten minutes, as both of them now sat on the edges of the beds hardly saying a word, only hoping the lull following the last bombardment would continue, they could hear horns, sirens and fire truck bells screaming all over downtown Honolulu.

Another series of explosions! The building shook and rattled. A baby wailed in the next apartment.

"Jee-sus! How long this gonna go on," Ed mumbled.

Niro looked out the window at the deserted street. An ambulance, its siren blasting away, dashed past.

"—Why didn't I t'ink about it before," Ed said, reaching up and turning on the small radio on the shelf above his head.

"Whatdahell is this! How can they play crappy music at a time like this?" he grumbled, listening to a concert number. "Why don't they keep us informed on what's going on?"

It was now eight-forty. Someday, all this is going to make history, Niro told himself dramatically.

The concert music was cut off.

"An air attack has been made on Pearl Harbor and other military installations," the announcer said in a grave tone. "Enemy planes have been shot down. . . . The airplanes have been identified as Japanese aircrafts. I repeat: Enemy aircrafts definitely identified as those of Japan have attacked the island of Oahu."

The music came on again. In a few seconds it was cut off. "This is no maneuver! This is the real McCoy! Enemy aircrafts are attacking the island of Oahu!" the announcer shouted excitedly into the microphone.

"Holy shit!" Ed cried out, exchanging glances with Niro. "Whatdahell the goddamn Buddhaheads trying to do? Kill us all?"

"It's hard to believe they'd do a crazy thing like that," Niro said.

"You t'ink they're gonna bomb the other islands, too? Maui?"

"What's there to bomb on Maui?" He suddenly thought of his family there, hoping nothing had happened to them.

"This is getting more serious by the minute," Ed said.

"You damn right it's getting serious," he said. "What you think they're dropping? Firecrackers?"

"There must be something we can do."

"Like what?" he sneered. "Get a gun and start shooting

the airplanes? Haole soldiers see us guys with even a water pistol and they're gonna think we're Jap spies."

"Aw-w," Ed scoffed.

"What you mean?—aw-w. You nuts or something?"

After he told Ed what had happened earlier up at the Heights, Ed, unable to hold back laughter, said: "Oh, Christ! You mean that old Japanee gardener actually yelled 'Banzai' at the plane in front of Old Man Whittingham?"

"What's so funny?"

Ed couldn't stop laughing.

"We almost got our asses shot. To top it all, that crazy old man, he almost killed us both coming down the Heights. I don't know how the cops allow a junk like that on the streets."

"What about your things up the Whittingham home? How you gonna get them?" Ed asked.

"I don't know," Niro said, pensive. "I guess I can call the Old Man when things cool off, and try to explain exactly what happened. I don't want him keep thinking I'm a goddamn spy."

"To hell with that bastard. You can stay here with us."

"I don't have anything with me. And we're supposed to have mid-term in my Political Science class tomorrow morning."

"How can you worry about exams at a time like this? We're at war! We'll all have to go in the Army. We're in the ROTC—potential Army officers."

"We're lucky they take us in as buck-ass privates. The only kind of officers we'll ever be is some okole officer in some concentration camp."

"Aw-w . . . . The haoles not all crazy like Old Man Whittingham. He did you a favor when he chased you outa the place."

"It's easy for you to say that. How can I continue with school if I don't have a place to live? My folks not supporting me like yours are. You lucky bugga."

"I just told you, man. There's gonna be no school from now on. And to tell you the truth, I'm damned glad. I was getting sick and tired studying every night. It's gonna be the good old Army for us."

"You're crazier than Old Man Whittingham and the

Japanee gardener put together. They're not gonna take us Buddhaheads in the Army."

"Sure! Why not? I got it all figured out. Us Niseis in the islands can form our own combat unit."

"What for? So the haoles can use us for targets?"

"Aw-w bull shit. We'll talk to the President of the University, or the Governor, or even President Roosevelt. We'll tell 'em all we want is a chance to show them which side we're on. What you t'ink about that, huh? We'll make a good showing for all the Buddhaheads in America."

The door opened slowly.

It was Hank Endo. He walked in dejectedly, head low, chin down on his chest. He sat down beside Niro. He remained silent.

"What—what happened?" Ed asked, leaning forward from his bed. "What happened to Roy?"

"They had to amputate," Hank sobbed, covering his face with both hands, head hanging over his thighs.

"You mean he won't be able to fight no more?" Niro uttered, wincing.

Hank shook his head. He kept his face covered.

"Oh, Christ! Jesus Christ . . ." Ed moaned.

3

SAB HAD BEEN lying drowsily on his bed when his father left for Wailuku to deliver the slaughtered pig. He had not been asleep as his father had suspected, but had gotten up earlier when the bright shafts of sunlight had begun shining into his bedroom through the two, half-opened windows facing the mountains.

Feeling the cool morning breeze coming in, he pulled the blanket up to his neck dreamily, careful not to rub it against the wet, smudgy stickiness of his shorts. How he wished he could lapse into another long, pleasant dream again. It had felt so good; so unbelievably wonderful. He could still feel a warm, convulsive numbness shooting through his body.

It was hard to believe it had been only a dream. It had seemed so real he thought, playing with himself ecstatically. So real, he had actually heard her gasping into his ear; had even smelled the sweet, soft scent of her perfume while she was rubbing her naked body against him. He wished he had been able to control his dream to make it last longer. At least, long enough to have made her experience the same sensation he had felt before exploding all over himself. He speculated whether dreams could be powerful enough to be transmitted into the mind of the person dreamt about.

Stretching his legs out in leg-reaching stiffness, rubbing himself little faster now, he felt he could explode over and over just thinking of her. As though she was sleeping right there next to him.

He slowed down. Then, stopped altogether.

A sudden wretched misery swept over him as he realized she was much older than he. Why did he have to be so young? still in high school? Why couldn't he have been her age? What he'd give to be able to take her to a picnic or a hike up to the mountains. Just to be alone with her. Just to be near her.

Miss Blake. Miss Margaret Blake. Margaret . . .

He was breathing faster. Harder . . . Moaning . . . Miss Blake . . . So soft; so beautiful . . .

Oh, hold him. Hold him tight like she had done a while ago in his dream.

She was so pretty—Miss Blake, his eleventh grade English teacher. He dreamt of her almost every night. How he loved everything about her: her soft, light brown hair barely touching her shoulders; her large, sparkling greenish eyes whenever she smiled at him; her lovely, white complexion still untanned by the tropical climate. And when she walked up front in her classroom, how he enjoyed watching her slender, soft-looking body shimmering under her neatly starched dress.

Miss Blake was a new exchange teacher at Baldwin High School this year. This was her first trip to the islands. She was young, friendly and refreshingly attractive. Having graduated from a university in Oregon only two years ago, she couldn't have been more than twenty-four. She was so different from the other old-bag teachers in school. Not only because she was a pretty haole girl, but because she made her classes interesting and something to look forward to.

Sab actually hated school.

School was for the birds. It was nothing more than a slow, monotonous way of getting older through books. He always wished he was already eighteen and out of school so he could live and experience life in a man's world. Not listen to all that crap from the stupid teachers every day.

Except for his English class, he didn't care to study at all. What he really liked about his English class was writing short stories. It came naturally to him. And Miss Blake had as much as told him this that day back in September, about two weeks after school had started.

"You write very fluently," she had said after having asked him to remain in class.

He was standing at her desk in the corner, facing the rows of low windows behind her, actually looking at her pretty face and staring into her green eyes. He had never gotten close to her before, let alone been singled out from the rest of the forty students. She was even prettier up close, he thought, far prettier than any woman he had seen in his entire life.

He quickly gazed out the window, up towards the brown rolling sand hills, when she caught him staring at her. Her cheeks were flushing.

"Do you like to write, Sab—? Excuse me, how do you pronounce your name?" she asked, brushing back a strand of soft brown hair that had fallen over her girlish cheek. "I'm afraid it'll take me a while before I can pronounce all your names. You see, I haven't been in the islands too long."

"It's Sab-u-ro," he said, slowly, articulately, wishing he had an English name like some of the other Japanee kids.

"Oh," she said, probing her soft, full lips with the tip of her tongue, pronouncing his name silently to herself. "There are three syllables. —Sa-buu-row."

"Uh huh," he nodded, gazing into her eyes again. He liked the way she had said it. It sounded cute. Gee, but she was beautiful. Especially when she smiled like that.

"Well, Sa-buu-row, did you always like to write?"

"Yeah, I guess so," he told her, shrugging his shoulders.

"You have a wonderful style," she continued, holding his composition up against her, causing Sab to hold in a deep breath. It was his paper she was holding against her breast!

Glancing over the paper again, she said: "Other than some minor errors, I think your story was extremely well written."

He kept looking at her with a big happy smile. She

[35]

looked so pure and clean. As though she had just stepped out of a shower.

"Is this an original story?" she questioned. "Or did someone help you with it.".

"I wrote it myself," he quickly replied. "No one helped me."

"Then, it was your own idea!" she said, wide eyes gleaming surprisedly, again holding the paper up against her breast. "That's just wonderful, Sa-buu-row," she added, smiling at him. "If you weren't so young I would have been inclined to believe you intended to have the symbolism in your story."

Symbolism? What was that? he thought, puzzled. But he was real happy she liked his story. He had written it just for her.

As Miss Blake leaned a little forward, holding the paper in front of her, re-reading a part of it silently to herself, he caught himself staring at the V of her white cotton blouse. Her chest looked so creamy white. The soft double mounds in her bra glistened enticingly before his eyes. Swallowing down a hard breath he forced himself to look away. But his eyes automatically shifted back to the shadowy valley between the rising softness. He quickly thrust his hands into his front pockets.

She was like a glamorous actress: a combination Betty Grable-Bette Davis. He felt like reaching over across the desk and placing his hands on her face. It looked so smooth and warm. He suddenly wondered whether she had ever been touched by a man. —No. She wasn't that kind of a woman. She was good. Decent.

When she looked up at him, he quickly shifted his eyes away, blushing. She had caught him staring at her again.

"What ever gave you the idea to write a story like this?" she asked. "It's almost incredible that an eleventh grader could write with such deep insight," she added, her head tilted to one side. "It's simply marvelous, to say the least."

"Well," he said, eyes beaming proudly, hands still deep in his pockets, wondering whether she knew why his hands were in there, "you told us to write anything we wanted to write about."

"Yes, of course, I did say that," she said, smiling. "And

as a whole I was very pleased with the papers turned in. I've made some corrections on your paper—mostly grammatical ones. In a few days, I'm going to ask the class to turn in another composition. But in your case, I want you to re-write this and give it back to me. I may ask you to read it before the class."

"Read it in class!" he protested. "What for?"

"Because I'd like the rest of the class to listen to what you've written. It's a remarkable paper."

"Aw-w," he shrugged, looking away, slowly turning around on the balls of his bare feet and heading towards the door. "I don't wanna read it in class," he bleated, folding his composition and jamming it into his black binder, an instinctive rebelliousness bubbling up in him.

"But, Sa-buu-row!" she said. "Why not? I think the class would be delighted listening to your story."

"Aw, no-o," he told her, dogged, unyielding, "I don't think so," now wishing he hadn't written the damned thing.

Just before turning the door knob, he noticed Miss Blake's pretty face registering befuddlement and disappointment, her jade-like eyes narrowed into a frown. He walked out of the second-story classroom and stood leaning against the concrete wall of the corridor, brooding, feeling lousy for having hurt Miss Blake's feelings. He hadn't meant to.

The breeze blowing up from Kahului beach felt nice and cool against his face. The ocean looked calm without a single white wave splashing over the breakers. It sure would have been a good day to be playing hookey, he thought.

Then, as he thought of Miss Blake again, he felt terrible. But he just wasn't going to read his story in class. The kids would laugh at him. Him! writing a stupid thing like that. When he wrote the story he had known all along it would impress Miss Blake. She hadn't been in the islands long enough to know about Hawaiian legends. Symbolism; insight—Ca-rist! He had never heard of such words before, much less understand them. All he did was write a short story about a simple native who lived in an old Hawaiian village.

Hah! he snorted, pushing himself away from the wall and walking down the corridor to his next class. If

Miss Blake thought his story was that good, imagine what she'd think when he took the trouble to write a really good one.

That had been almost two months ago, Sab recalled dreamily now. He and Miss Blake had come to know each other quite well since. She had told him several times that he was gifted; that someday he might become a famous writer.

He began concentrating feverishly until he could envision the scene he had earlier in his dream. He and Miss Blake were in the dark closet back of the classroom embracing each other excitedly, both of them completely naked. They were clinging to each other desperately, squeezing, moaning, feeling all around, rubbing warm thighs against warm thighs, inflamed belly against inflamed belly, her round, firm breasts pressing hard against his chest. Then, he felt her warm, delicate hand reaching down and stroking him.

Miss Blake! Oh, Miss Blake . . .!

Every muscle in his rigid body quivered in a great upheaval as maddening lightnings and thunders clamored all around him. Gradually, a soft relaxing numbness creeped through him, releasing the tension.

"Saburo! You better get up and wash the pig pens before your father returns from Wailuku . . ." he heard his mother's voice from the kitchen.

"Aw-w," he mumbled, still caught in a state of euphoria. He resented his mother for disturbing him at a time like this. He could have gone on thinking of his lovely teacher forever.

After having his breakfast, Sab, wearing no shirt, his levi cuffs tucked into a pair of old greasy rubber boots, ambled over to the pig pens. The pigs were sheltered in two rows of forty dilapidated, concrete-floored pens made from odds-and-ends of discarded lumber. He began washing the stinking pens with a long, brittle brush and a strong hose, kicking the stupid squealing pigs now and then, disgusted with the goddamn pigs for never learning to crap in one corner near the door.

Pigs! Pigs! Pigs!

In another year when he became eighteen and could take off from home he hoped he'd never see another pig as long as he lived. His entire life seemed surrounded by stinking pigs. The only time he really didn't mind pigs was when he watched a grunting boar mounting an in-heat sow with its long drill-shaped pile driver. It always thrilled the hell out of him.

At about nine o'clock, when he had at last washed all the pens, he washed himself with the hose and trod over in his wet, shit-covered boots to the ramp where the pig slops were cooked. He slumped down on the concrete platform above the muddy ground and wiped off the water on his slightly acned face with the back of his hands.

His father should be coming home any minute, he told himself, looking down the driveway. That is, if his father hadn't stopped over some place to have a drink. That was another reason he wanted to take off from home: He was sick and tired of his old man drunk all the time. A drunken old man and pigs! It was enough to drive anyone nuts.

Well, anyway, as soon as his father returned, he'd dump the slop in the boiler and start the fire so he could go to Kahului to see Punahou High (the all-haole school in Honolulu) play against Baldwin. He didn't want to miss the game. He had five bucks on it with one of the players from Baldwin. He had given the guy fourteen points. That rah-rah sentimental bastard!

He now kicked off his boots on the ground, remembering with a smirk what Yosh Nakata, his gambler friend, had once told him about betting on football games. "Never let that school spirit crap get the best of you. Always bet according to the percentage. Even if it meant betting against your own school," Yosh had said in his cold, cunning way.

Punahou should beat the hell outa Baldwin today, Sab thought shrewdly, imagining himself collecting the five bucks from the sucker at school tomorrow. Just because he was big and was a football player he thought he could go around acting tough, Sab thought, feeling a tinge of envy working up in him. Well, when Sab made the guy cough up the dough the guy wasn't going to feel too big. That bastard!

If Sab had been a little bigger instead of weighing only one hundred and eight pounds, and only five feet three inches tall, he knew he would have made a good half-back. Way better than every one of them big guys. Why couldn't he have been bigger? he wondered, self-pityingly. He was the smallest wherever he went. Always having to take some crap from the guys.

But Yosh was no bigger than he. Yet, everyone respected Yosh. Yosh even had a bum heart—he was always complaining about it. Of course, everyone looked up at Yosh because he was a clever gambler. The best as far as Sab was concerned.

Sab had met Yosh Nakata last summer on Molokai when both of them had gone there to work in the pineapple fields with about two hundred other high school boys from Maui. When Yosh had learned that he was Niro Gusuda's younger brother, Yosh had asked him to room with him. Niro and Yosh had been classmates at Baldwin.

Sab soon learned that Yosh was a professional gambler and had gone to Molokai not to work in the fields but to gamble with the school boys. Yosh was a pale-looking, thin guy with a high, receding forehead. He had an odd way of talking through the side of his mouth, gangster-style, and always had a sneering-frowning expression on his face.

From the very first night, Yosh had begun hustling around for crap games among the boys, and except for a few occasions, had hardly lost during the entire summer. After living together for a few weeks, Yosh had taught Sab to pat-roll a pair of dice on a blanket so the percentage would always be on the roller's side. Yosh had also taught him to switch loaded dice without arousing suspicion.

By the end of the summer Sab had made two hundred and fifty dollars of easy, sucker money through gambling, and one hundred fifty dollars of hard, back-breaking money by working in the sweltering pineapple fields. When he had come home and had handed the working money to his mother so she could keep them for his school books and tuition, she had been very pleased and had told him he was a good boy for working hard and saving all his money. Sab, naturally, had not told her about the other money. He had it hidden in a small can among his clothes. Whenever he needed extra spending money, he'd open the can, count his bankroll, fascinated, then take out whatever he needed.

As of yesterday, he still had two hundred bucks left. He was still riding high with the dough, he thought now, rubbing the back of his neck where the morning sun was striking.

He had seen Yosh only twice since returning from Molokai, but knew where to find him just in case. Yosh must have built himself a big bankroll some place, because when he last spoke to Yosh in front of Iao Theatre, Yosh had shown him a brand new wrist watch with diamond-studded numerals.

—Wheredahell was the old man, anyway? he wondered, gazing down the road again. It was almost ten. He sure hoped the old man hadn't stopped someplace for a drink.

At last, while he continued sitting there on the ramp with his bare feet dangling down and watching the driveway one hundred yards down the back yard, his father suddenly drove in with the pickup.

Instead of backing up the pickup to the ramp as he usually did, his father got out and came running excitedly up to the ramp. Oh, Christ! The old man was drunk again.

"Saburo!" his father said breathless, running the sleeve of his shirt over his sweaty forehead. "Where's Kimiko?"

Sab studied the old man's eyes. It was the best way to tell whether his father had been drinking or not. The old man's eyes appeared normal. They weren't glazed-looking at all. "I think she's down the river painting," he answered, still wondering why the old man was so worked up.

"Where's Okaasan Mother?"

"She's in the house."

"Go down the river and call Kimiko. Quickly. Tell her to come home right away," his father ordered, turning around and sauntering off to the house.

"What for?"

"What for!" his father roared back, stopping in his tracks, looking over his shoulder, mouth pursed tight. "Becuase Japan just attacked Pea-ru Har-bah!"

"What!" And he had thought the old man was sober.

When he refused to get off the ramp, his father, facing him, shouted: "Saburo! Don't keep sitting there like a

[41]

monkey. Go down the river and call your sister. Tell her to come home immediately. We should all be together at a time like this. There's no telling what might happen."

"Aw-w, Otoosan Father. Who told you Japan attacked Pearl Harbor?" he said skeptically, teasing the old man. It was the last straw. Ichiro's speech last night must have been too much for the old man.

"The radio—that's who!" his father scolded. "Go over into the house and listen for yourself, you lazy, sonnabagun boy, you!" He stamped his foot hard on the ground.

"Aw-w, all right," Sab muttered, jumping off the ramp and jogging away to the house. Anything to please the old man, he told himself, snickering.

Five minutes later, he was running over to the old wooden bridge near their home, heading for the ocean looking for his sister, Kimi.

The old man was right. The Buddhaheads had really attacked Pearl Harbor. Sab could still hear the frightened voice of the radio announcer ringing in his ears. The guy had said Japanese airplanes were all over the place.

Those damned Buddhaheads! he thought, hopping barefooted from rock to rock, jumping over the trickling water in the semi-dry river. Who do they think they are? attacking the United States.

There went today's football game, he told himself, chagrined. The game was sure to be called off.

Mid-way between the wooden bridge and the ocean, directly below the two hundred foot cliff dropping down from the bend, he stopped for a few seconds alongside the bank of the long, deep Kapuna pond. One bank was situated against the sheer cliff, and this side, where Sab was standing, widened into a narrow bed of black sand. The sun had not yet passed beyond the cliff; the cool, emerald-like water, a picture of tranquility.

Sab looked around, whipped out a crumpled Lucky butt from his pocket and lit it with hands cupped up to his mouth. He took several quick drags, then flicked it into the pond, watching it floating away.

He started hopping to the ocean again, wondering where Kimi could be.

4

HALF AN HOUR before her brother came looking for her down at the mouth of the Kapuna River, Kimi, dressed in a maroon and white T-shirt and a tight pair of old blue jeans, her long black hair tied into a ponytail in the back, sat stiffly on a flat rock doing a watercolor painting. Her boy friend, George Kealoha, was leaning back against a huge boulder nearby, strumming his ukulele and singing soft Hawaiian melodies.

"You almost pau with the painting?" George asked out loud, his voice barely audible over the din of the roaring waves.

"No. Not yet," Kimi answered, small, almond-shaped brown eyes looking up at the scenery.

"You've been saying that all morning," George grumbled. "C'mon, Kimi, let me see what you've done."

"Just a minute," she insisted, busily doing the finishing touches. She raised her head a little further back, studying the painting. It was done on a spread of plain white paper attached to a home-made easel which she held on her lap. She had tried to paint the multi-colored scene before her: The ferocious waves splashing relentlessly against the jagged, gray-white corals and black rocks; the calm, placid, miniature lake near the other bank of the river; the towering belly-shaped Haleakala mountain in the background reaching up into the curdling blue skies.

Something was still missing, she frowned, head held sideways, the tip of the brush playing lightly on the edges of her warm lips. Dipping the brush back into the watercolors, she painted an old man in the river staggering head-on into the monstrous waves, hands held over his head, eyes fixed stoically at the angry sea.

There! she told herself, breathing deeply and feeling invigorating salt air filling her lungs. That made it more meaningful. She wrote "Destiny!" on the lower right hand corner and below it: "December 7, 1941."

"Here, George!" she called, brushing back strands of hair blown over her cheeks by the strong wind, standing up and handing the painting over to him enthusiastically. "I'm finally done."

"Well, it's about time," he said, feigning anger. "He laid his ukulele down on the mat and sat up. Holding the painting before him, he began studying it with dark, keen eyes, while Kimi stood there looking down at him.

George had taken off his aloha shirt and had been basking under the bright morning sun in his light tan gabardine trousers. His soft, wind-blown black hair was all over his forehead, his shoulders already pinkish red from the heat. She couldn't help marvelling at how handsome her boy friend was. He had a flawless, dark brown complexion with a slightly wide forehead, long-lashed dark eyes, aquiline nose, and full, warm mouth that disclosed gleaming white teeth whenever he smiled. Unlike most of the Japanese boys she knew, George, a full-blooded Hawaiian, was tall and broad-shouldered. They had been going steady the past year and a half, ever since their senior year at Baldwin.

"How come you called it 'Destiny'?" George wanted to know.

"Can't you tell?" she asked, disappointed. She sat down beside him on the mat and explained: "The river starting from a tiny spring up in the mountains and now meeting its destiny—the ocean—and the old man coming to face the end of his road, represent the fate of all things in the world."

"Aw, Kimi," George said, placing his left arm around her, still studying the painting, perplexed. "You're being too dramatic. The old man looks out-of-place."

"What do you mean?—out-of-place," she said, pushing his arm aside and looking sharply into his dark eyes. "I had to put him in there to make the painting meaningful. His presence tells a story."

"What story?"

"The story of the fate of all of us. We're all going to die someday. We're no different than the mountain water being swallowed up eventually by the all-consuming sea."

"Aw-w, Kimi. You're always trying to put deep meanings into your paintings. Why can't you just paint something simple? Like the mountains, or the ocean. Just for the beauty of it; not for some meaning or story."

"You just don't want to understand my paintings."

"Sure, I do. They're all nice. But I don't wanna look for deep meanings."

"But paintings are more than just looking at their surface, George. It's something deeper; something finer. The true beauty lies in the meaning."

"Aw—" George said, befuddled. "Why can't you accept life for what it is? Why try to change it all the time? Look at me. I'm satisfied with things as they are. Why keep chasing the rainbows all the time?"

"Who's chasing rainbows?" she demanded, moving away, staring at him cold-eyed. "The trouble with you, George, you don't want to better yourself. All you ever want to do is play that silly ukulele and sing those old sentimental songs."

"What's wrong with playing the uke and singing?" George brooded, laying the painting to one side, avoiding her eyes.

"Nothing! If you're truly happy. But don't you ever want to accomplish something during your lifetime?"

"Like what?"

"Oh, I don't know . . . Something to show that you've made your life meaningful, I guess. Not just playing the uke and singing all the time."

"It was good enough for my Tu-tus grandfather and grandmother. Why can't it be good enough for me?"

Kimi's mouth suddenly pursed tight into a sullen pout,

refusing to speak to George anymore. Folding her arms across her chest, she leaned back against the boulder, looking out at the rolling white waves fifty feet away.

George reached for his ukulele and started strumming it.

Oh-h, George thoroughly infuriated her at times, she thought, determined not to speak to him until he apologized for that nasty remark about her painting. She wasn't even going to listen to him, she told herself adamantly, hearing him begin to sing her favorite song, "Maui Girl," with improvisations:

> I love a pretty Maui girl
> She lives at Kapuna
> With pearly teeth and rosy cheeks
> And lovely dark black hair
> Her waist is oh, so slender
> Her opu to much nui-nui
> And of all the wahines I ever did aloha
> Sweet Kimi she beats them all.

He was now singing the chorus in his beautiful, high falsetto voice, and she was still determined not to listen to him. Keeping her arms folded tight, she continued gazing out at the pounding surf.

Somehow, it seemed that long before she had come down the river with her hand bag, containing her painting paraphernalia, sandwiches and the straw mat they were sitting on, she was feeling terribly depressed. She had kept thinking of her oldest brother, Ichiro. She had almost burst out crying when she first heard him over the radio last night. He had sounded so lonely and homesick, she wished he had not left home. He had always been so understanding and kind to her, the only girl among three brothers. She wondered whether he had changed at all. Whether he had picked up any of the Japanese customs she so intensely disliked. No—she had told herself assuredly, he would always be the same warm-hearted big brother. He would always cherish the American way of life.

Poor Georgie, she now thought, looking up at him and listening to him singing. She gradually rested her head against his arm, realizing she had been picking on him all morning. He had nothing to do with the melancholy way she was feeling. She moved over closer and placed her arm around his tanned, broad shoulders.

George stopped singing. He laid the ukulele down and put his arm around her. His head came lower and he kissed her lightly on her cheek. "Why must we always argue?" he said apologetically, pressing her closer to him. "I love you. I love you too much to be arguing with you all the time."

"We weren't arguing, George," she said, feeling the warmth of his slender body glowing against her. "We were just discussing something."

George said nothing. He pressed her closer to him and spun her around gently so she was facing him, her mouth up to his. He kissed her warmly, tenderly, his strong arms holding her very tight. She wrapped her arms around his neck, feeling his passionate mouth pressing down harder onto hers. "Oh-h, George . . ." her eyes closed dreamily. "I love you," her mouth up to his ear now, her fingers running through the lower fringes of his hairline in the back.

She felt him pushing her down on the mat, his arms firm around her so she could not resist. "George, somebody might see us."

"There's no one around."

"There might be somebody up the road."

"No, no one's around."

"No, George. Please. Don't . . ." she moaned, feeling one of his hands working up her back under her T-shirt. "George . . . Don't . . ." His hand kept rubbing her back. It felt warm, soothing and wonderful. She slid her impassioned mouth alongside his cheek until she felt his warm, full mouth on hers again. "Oh, George . . ."

"Kimi . . . Oh, Kimi . . ." He was lying flat on her, thighs pressing down hard on her, both hands now stroking all over her glowing back. She felt one of his hands coming around slowly to her chest under her bra strap and was beginning to caress her breast in his quivering cupped hand.

"George!" she moaned. "George, don't. George! George, you're not listening to me. Stop it! I said stop it!" She finally managed to fight off his hand and push his head away from her neck.

George reluctantly pulled his hands out from under her shirt and got off her. He sat up slowly, panting short, hard breaths through open mouth, eyes looking away, frustrated.

She sat up quickly, straightening her loose hair and shirt, breathing equally hard. She looked at George, who was gazing out at the sea, refusing to look at her. "George," she pleaded, "don't be angry with me. One of us had to stop." She moved over closer to him and lay her face against his warm arm. "Somebody might see us."

He looked the other way, over towards the miniature lake.

"George . . . George, please. Don't be angry with me."

"I'm not angry with you," he finally relented, still not looking at her, hands stiff at his sides as though fighting off an impulse.

"Then look at me."

He turned his head around slowly. Putting one arm around her, he embraced her hard. "How long this gonna go on, Kimi?" he asked. "How long we gonna keep doing this to ourselves? We can't see each other at nights no more; we can't meet each other when we want to; you won't let me make love here . . . ."

"Don't say things like that, George," she tried to console, both arms tight around his waist, face pressed snuggly onto his warm, bare chest. "We've gone through all that before. Please try to understand."

"Understand what? What's there to understand? You love me; I love you. It's as simple as that. It's your father and mother who need understanding. You're always afraid they might see us together. What's wrong with me? I got leprosy or something?"

She could think of nothing to say. She kept holding on tight to his slender body, rubbing her tears on his chest.

"Why don't you take me to meet your father and mother?" George said daringly.

Shocked, she jerked her head away and stared at him. "You know it won't do any good."

"Then what we supposed to do? Keep sneaking and meeting each other like this forever? Who your father and

[48]

mother think they are? One of the Big Five families? They're no better than my folks. Why they keep thinking I'm not good enough for you?"

"George, oh George, it's not that at all. They don't even know who you are. They're from the old country. Their ways are different from ours. They think it's not right for a Japanese girl to marry outside her race. Please, George . . . Please, let's not go through all that again," she sobbed, again placing her face against his chest. "It'll work itself out somehow," she murmured. "I just know it will. We'll be able to get married someday."

"Someday! How long you expect me to keep waiting? All my life?"

"Please, let's not talk about it anymore. Just hold me tight."

He held her face in his hands and pushed her away gently, looking piercingly into her eyes. "Kimi, let's get married," he begged. "Let's get married right away. Without telling anyone about it. After it's all over there's nothing anyone can do about it. I have a good job. We can make a pretty good living on what I earn at the County Treasurer's office."

She lowered her tear-filled eyes away from his. Swallowing hard, she slowly looked up at him again and said: "You know I can't do that, George. I'd like to. But—but I just can't—"

"Forget about your folks for once," he pleaded, dark brown eyes slightly moist. "Think about us. You and me. We got our own lives to live. We're not kids any more. This is Hawaii—America. Not the old country. You don't have to stick to the old country traditions. To hell with all that."

She continued looking up at him tearfully.

"You understand what I'm trying to say, Kimi? —Just us; you and me. We have to think about ourselves."

"I understand, George, but—"

"But what?"

"I just can't do it. I wish I could, but—"

"You mean you won't. That's it, huh? For once, Kimi, tell me the truth. You don't want to. That's why you keep blaming your parents all the time. You don't love me enough to marry me."

"That's not true! You know that's not true!" she sobbed out as George dropped his hands down from her face and turned the other direction. "If I didn't love you I wouldn't have—I wouldn't have let you—"

"Then, why won't you let me have you now? Why can't we make love like we used to?"

"Because . . . Well, because . . . We just can't do it right here in the open. Someone might see us."

"You're just making an excuse. You don't love me no more."

"Yes, I do. You know I do. If we can see each other at nights like we used to when I was able to tell my folks I was going to stay overnight at my girl friend's place . . . . But I can't anymore. My girl friend's in Honolulu attending UH."

"That's another thing I want to talk to you about," George said, mouth pouted. "You always wanted to go to UH, too, huh? That's another reason you won't marry me, huh?"

She wiped the tears away from her eyes. "Yes," she confessed softly, "yes, I've always wanted to go to UH. But that has nothing to do with us not marrying. Even if I did go there—even if I could ever afford to go there —I'd always love you. Nothing would change as far as we're concerned."

"But if you went to the university we wouldn't get married for—for I don't know how long," he burst out, desperate, turning his head and staring at her. "We'd never get married if you went there. Ever!"

"But, George, we're both so young. We're only eighteen. We can wait."

"You'll meet some guy in Honolulu and forget all about me."

"No, I won't."

"Sure, you will. I know . . ."

"George . . . George, why can't we both go to UH?" she said, suddenly enthused. "We'll save whatever we can and go there next year. We'll find part-time jobs. My brother, Niro, is doing that. Then, when we graduate we can get married. Why don't we, George?" she went on vigorously.

"Me? go to UH?"

"Why, sure, George. You were always bright in school. You made good grades. You shouldn't have any trouble getting admitted."

"Naw. Not me. No university for me. I had enough of school. I'm happy with things as they are. I have a good-paying job. I'm satisfied."

"How can you ever be satisfied with a job like that? You're nothing but a—a machine in that office."

"What's wrong with that? I get paid a hundred twenty-five a month for doing almost nothing."

"And you're going to be satisfied the rest of your life doing exactly what you're doing now?"

"Sure! I'm happy doing what I'm doing."

"But that's just it, George. You're doing nothing. Absolutely nothing! It's almost as bad as my job: a salesgirl in a five and dime store. Gads! If I thought I'd be doing that all my life I'd die. It almost makes me sick just thinking about it."

"Kimi . . . Don't get too ambitious. That's why people get restless and unhappy. They're dissatisfied with their own lives, so what do they do? They go around making others miserable. I don't wanna be like that."

"Oh, George! you have no foresight at all," she said exasperatedly, pushing him away, sitting up against the boulder.

They said nothing for a few minutes, just kept looking out at the wild, angry waves and listening to the strong wind whistling-humming through the driftwoods, dry corals and tiny volcanic rocks on the seashore. Across the wide bay, on the other end of the island, they could see the green cane and pineapple fields of Makawao gleaming under the bright sun. Over towards the west end of Haleakala mountain, mid-way between the ocean and the lip of the crater, Kula Sanitarium shone brightly.

"Kimi . . ." George now murmured, slipping his hand into hers and holding it affectionately, "why can't we be happy with life as it is? Why must we always try to outdo each other? Just like in school, everyone always trying to make better grades than others. What does all this prove?"

She squeezed his hand tenderly. "I don't know, George. I guess the world was made that way—full of competition. If we don't compete we get left behind."

"And you're afraid to be left behind?"

"Yes, I guess so. But it's more than being left behind, George. It's—oh, I don't really know how to explain it. It's—Look, George, look out at the horizon. What do we see? What do we see out there?"

"Just the horizon. What else is there?"

"That's exactly what I'm trying to tell you," she said annoyedly, "you have no imagination. No initiative. Beyond that horizon is another world. A promising world. There just has to be! Life couldn't be just living on a place like Maui and—and just existing. The world is full of intrigue; challenges. You don't want to live and die here."

"What's wrong with that?" George asked, sitting up and turning to face her. "I was born here; I wanna die here. Maui No Ka Oi—Maui is the best. Nothing short of an all-out war can take me away from Maui."

"I'm not saying Maui isn't a good place. It's my home, too. What I'm trying to say is that there must be more to life than—well, than just living like the way we do."

"What's wrong with the way we live? How do people live anyplace else?—Beyond that horizon of yours?"

"That's just it. I don't really know."

"Well, hell, if you don't know, then Maui must be just as good a place as anyplace else in the world."

"Oh, George . . . You're not trying to understand me at all."

He looked at her, puzzled, thin, dark eyebrows arched up over the bridge of his aquiline nose.

"George," she went on, "I've never left the island of Maui in my life. So help me! no matter what happens, I have to see other places. Even if it means taking only a short boat ride to Molokai or Lanai."

"Once, three years ago, I went to Honolulu with my father," George said. "I thought I was gonna like it there. But after one day—just one day—I wanted to come home. The place was so crowded: people hurrying all over; cars going like hell; everyone shouting at each other. Where they all going? I asked myself. Oahu is smaller than Maui. How many times can they go around the island?"

She gazed beyond the furious white waves, pushed back a lock of hair on her forehead, then once more wiped off sticky salt water from her lips.

George reached over for something on his right. He brought up a pyramid-shaped gray sea shell and started digging into it with his finger tips.

"George, you're not going to eat that?"

"Sure. It's Opihi. It's good for you."

"Raw? Just like that?"

"'At's the only way to eat fresh Opihi—raw."

"How do you know it's fresh?"

"What you mean—how I know it's fresh! It's still, alive. See—It's moving."

He scraped the gooey-looking meat clear out of the shell and, sticking it into his mouth, began chewing on it.

"Oh-hh . . . George . . . Does it taste all right?"

"Sure. And it's good for your health, too. Lots of iron in it. Want me to get you some?"

"No. No, I don't think I'd like it raw. I like them boiled."

"Aw, you spoil the taste when you boil them. Us Kanakas can never starve," he said, chewing delectably, exaggeratedly, bringing his mouth up close to Kimi's.

"Oh, George!"

"'At's why my ancestors were able to travel far away on their canoes without starving. They could eat anything raw. Even raw shark meat. Sometimes, even raw dogs and salted human flesh."

"You and your ancestors," she scoffed. "What about my ancestors? They came here all the way from Japan. That's almost five thousand miles away."

"They came on big ships," he shrugged. "My ancestors came on small out-rigger canoes. They were powerful people."

"My ancestors swam all the way here," she said.

"My ancestors were ten feet tall. All strong. They could throw a spear half a mile."

"My ancestors could move mountains."

"My great-great-great grandfather was the greatest of them all—King Kamehameha, the great king of the islands. He conquered all the islands and united them. When

Captain Cook tried to fool around with him, the King kicked his okole back to the ship and chased all the ships away with his big spears."

"One of my noble ancestors was Genghis Khan," Kimi said, straight-faced. "He conquered all of Asia. Then, when he got tired of fighting, he gave the land to his loyal friends who were called: Japan, China, Manchuria and Okinawa."

"Yeah, I heard that one, too," George said, suddenly laughing uproariously, giving Kimi a warm tender hug. "Oh, how I love you, Kuuipo."

She flung her arms around his neck. "I love you so much, too, George. Sing me that song, 'Kuuipo,'" she said, kissing him lovingly on his warm cheek.

He let go of her slowly and, reaching for his ukulele, strummed the introduction, then began singing the tender Hawaiian love song into her ear.

When he was half-way through, she thought she had heard someone calling her over the pounding roar of the surf.

"Just a minute, George," she said, squeezing his arm, straining her ears to listen carefully.

George stopped singing. He stared inquisitively at her. "What's the matter?"

"Sh-hh . . . I thought I heard someone calling me."

"You're hearing things. That was me singing."

"There! Someone's calling me," she said, alarmed, jumping up quickly to her feet and climbing up the high boulder. George stood and watched her.

It was Sab. What in the world was he doing way down here, anyway?

"I'm here, Sab! Over here! Sab!" she called out, waving. "—It's all right, George," she said, looking down. "It's only my brother, Sab. —Sab!" she called out once more, looking up the river. "Over here!" She kept waving one hand high in the air, the other brushing back her wind-blown hair, a few strands slipping between her lips.

Sab came hopping over, terribly excited over something.

"Hi! What are you doing way down here?" she questioned, looking down at Sab, his slightly acned face perspiring profusely, his long black hair fallen across one eye.

[54]

"Father said to come home!" he said, looking up at her, puffing, rubbing his forehead.

"What for?"

"Japan just attacked Pearl Harbor."

"What in the world are you talking about!" She gave her brother an outraged look.

"I'm not lying, Kimi. I heard it over the radio—Station KGMB. The announcer said it's not a practice air raid. It's the real stuff."

"Oh, Sab. April Fool's still a long way off."

"Honest, Kimi. I'm not fooling. You think I'd run all the way down here just to fool you?"

She suddenly felt nauseated. Spurts of cold shivers raced up her spine. She began climbing down the boulder on the other side, where George was standing with his ukulele.

Sab came around to her side. "—Oh, George, have you met my brother, Sab?"

"What d'ya say, Sab?" George greeted, friendly, tossing his head at Sab.

Surprised, Sab stared at George suspiciously, then looked down at the mat and the painting.

"Did you hear that, George?" she said, standing between him and Sab. "Japan attacked Pearl Harbor."

"You're joking . . ."

"Hell, no, I'm not joking," Sab said belligerently. "I just heard it over the radio."

George turned around and exchanged somber looks with Kimi. "C'mon, let's get into my car and listen to the radio."

"No, George. I'll have to be going home with Sab."

"I'll drive you both home."

She shook her head, eyes fixed meaningfully at him.

"Sab, help me carry some of these things," she said, feeling bile working up into her mouth, thinking of Hawaii being ravaged by war. It just couldn't be. Anyplace else, but not Hawaii. It must be some kind of a war game.

After she and Sab had gathered up her belongings, she turned to George and whispered: "I'll meet you here next Sunday."

He looked warmly into her eyes.

"C'mon, Kimi. Let's go," Sab said impatiently, ignoring George.

"All right, I'm coming. —Goodbye, George," she said softly, puckering up her lips.

"Who's the guy?" Sab questioned, mouth twitching, jerking his head back at the boulder where George stood looking at them.

"Just a friend," she answered, looking over her shoulder and waving.

"'At's George Kealoha, the hot-shot basketball player from Baldwin last year, huh?" Sab asked disdainfully.

Kimi nodded, hopping from rock to rock beside her brother.

"Your boy friend?"

She flushed a little.

"You don't have to worry about me telling Father and Mother."

"Oh, Sab . . ." She forced a ring of mirthless laughter. "We weren't doing anything wrong. We're just good friends, that's all."

"Yeah, sure. Just don't let Father find out you're seeing him. You know what the old man thinks about them Kanakas."

"I just told you, Sab. We're just good friends. We were classmates."

"Well, anyway, c'mon. Father wants us to be home right away. He thinks Japan's gonna take over the islands. Maybe by nightfall. I think he's nuts."

Kimi shuddered. The thought of Japanese bo-bura soldiers tramping the streets of Maui almost sickened her. Good God! Her father would probably want her to marry one of them, she thought, cringing, picturing the round, moon-shaped, pale face of Kenyei Shiroma.

Not that she hated Kenyei. After all, he was a good friend of the family. But Kenyei had tried to embrace her in their kitchen once, a couple of years ago, after making sure her father and mother weren't home. Ever since, she couldn't stand being around him.

Japanese soldiers in Hawaii! Oh, no, she prayed silently to herself, watching Sab up front jumping here and there with light, springy legs, left hand flicking short jabs like a boxer.

"Saburo! Wait for me!" she called. "Don't leave me so far back!"

"C'mon, slow poke!" he called back over his shoulder, swinging the hand bag in his right hand. "There's a war going on!"

War!

Her knees weakened. Those crazy, war-mongering fools! There went her plans of attending UH next fall. Most likely, she would be stuck at Kress—at that uninspiring, monotonous, damned job—for God knew how long. Gads! Maybe forever.

5

When Kimi, exhausted and perspiring, at last climbed up the bridge behind Sab and walked home hastily, she noticed her father in the garage busily digging a hole with a long-handled shovel.

They walked over curiously into the damp, semi-dark dirt garage under the house and stood silently behind their father.

"What are you doing, Otoosan?" Sab finally asked.

"Huh!" Her father jumped up suddenly, startled. "Baka! Don't scare me like that. I thought you were the policeman."

"Policeman?" Sab snickered, exchanging glances with Kimi.

Standing beside Sab with the mat under her arm, the painting in her hand, Kimi noted that her father had dug a hole about a foot deep in the ground. Next to the hole was a small cracker box tin can filled with all kinds of Japanese documents, photographs and a folded Rising Sun flag.

"Otoosan," she said, realizing what her father was planning to do, "there's nothing wrong with possessing those things. You don't have to hide them. We don't know for sure whether we're at war with Japan."

"Not sure!" her father scolded, frowning. "Even Saburo heard it over the radio."

" 'At's right, Kimi. I heard it, too," Sab confirmed.

"Well, even if Japan did attack Pearl Harbor, that's no reason for hiding those personal things."

"You want your father to go to jail?" her father said, frowning again, leaning on the long-handled shovel, wiping off beads of perspiration on his forehead.

"Oh, Otoosan, they can't put you in jail just for owning those belongings," she said.

"Some of these things are souvenirs I received from the Shintoku Maru when they were here last year," her father said anxiously.

"Aw, hell," Sab said, shaking his head, grinning, "if they gonna lock you up for owning crap like that, every Japanese family in Hawaii would have to be locked up. Carist! Otoosan. Stop kidding yourself. You're no more a spy than the President of the United States."

"You crazy boy, you. You don't know nothing. Stop talking and help me dig this hole before someone comes around," her father said, shoving the shovel at Sab.

"Aw, for crying out loud," Sab grumbled, taking the shovel after laying the hand bag on the ground. "All right, if it's gonna make you feel any better." Lackadaisically, he started shovelling dirt out of the hole.

Her father squatted down and began going through the different souvenirs and pictures of Japan sent by Ichiro during the past six years.

Kimi knelt down beside her father and watched him inquisitively. She was still positive there was nothing wrong with owning those unimportant, unincriminating Japanese household possessions. Her father was now studying a photograph of Ichiro in a school boy's uniform taken in Kyoto among cherry trees.

"My goodness! Otoosan," she said. "Don't tell me you're going to hide Ichiro's picture, too. That's silly. There's nothing wrong with having a picture of your own son."

"Ichiro looks like he's got a military uniform on," her father advised. "The policeman might think I have a son in the Japanese Army."

"Heavens! That's not a military uniform. Anyone can tell that just by looking at it."

"Kimiko! Don't tell your father what to do," her father chided. "Don't you think your father knows what he's doing?"

"You're carrying this too far, Otoosan. Why would anyone want to put you in jail? You haven't done anything wrong."

"Kimiko! You're talking too much for a girl. Go to your room and see if there's anything you might want to hide in this can before I put it in the hole."

"Me? hide anything?" she said, letting out a ring of disrespectful laughter.

"Yes, you! Who do you think I'm talking to? Didn't Ichiro send you lots of pictures of Japan?"

"They're just pictures of the different places he visited. I'm not going to hide them. If anyone wants to lock me up for having them—well, let him."

"If you won't do as I say, just remember when you get in trouble with the policemen, I told you so," her father said resignedly. Then, in a soft, disgruntled voice, he muttered in Okinawan: "These two . . . There's not a thing you can tell them anymore . . .

"—Saburo!" he screamed, "keep digging that hole before someone comes around."

"Aw-w . . ." Sab moaned, shovelling out more dirt.

"Kimiko," her father now said, standing up slowly, straightening his back, pounding it with his fist, "when you go to work tomorrow try and change all of your paper money for whatever silvers you can get."

"Huh?" She stared at him, puzzled. "Why?"

"Because the paper money won't be worth anything soon."

Sab stopped digging again, looked over at Kimi, then at her father. "What makes you think it's not gonna be worth anything?"

Her father gave Sab an exasperated look. "I thought you were smarter than that."

Kimi exchanged glances with Sab once more.

"Otoosan," she finally said, "why do you want me to change my paper money for silvers?"

"When Japan takes over the Hawaiian islands all the paper money going to be burned up."

"Aw for—!" Sab laughed. "Who told you that, Otoosan?"

"Never mind! You lazy boy, you. You don't know nothing. Keep digging that hole."

"If that's the case, Otoosan, I might really get in trouble for looking forward to Japan winning the war," Kimi said.

"You don't have to make it look obvious," her father suggested. "I'm not asking you to do anything wrong. All you have to do is change the paper money into silvers. What's so wrong about that?"

Kimi, lost for words, looked over at Sab who had again stopped digging.

"Give me that shovel!" her father cried out, furious, pulling the shovel out of Sab's hand. "You—you good-for-nothing boy. You don't even know how to dig a simple hole in the ground. If you won't listen to your father, get away from here. You're nothing but a nuisance anyway."

"Aw, c'mon, Otoosan," Sab said, taking back the shovel. "Okay, I'll dig the hole for you—" giving Kimi a wide-eyed, blank look, head held sideways, shoulders shrugged up in a what-can-you-say gesture. "How deep you want the hole?" he asked, pushing the shovel into the ground with the heel of his bare foot.

"About six inches more will do," his father ordered peremptorily, arms folded across his chest like a general.

"Don't dig too deep, Sab," Kimi teased. "You might dig all the way to Japan." She walked out of the garage quickly before the general could scold her.

"Kimi!" Sab called out just as she stepped out of the garage into the bright sunlight, "you better leave that painting of yours here so we can hide it."

"Hide it! What for?"

"The FBI might think you painted Fujiyama instead of Haleakala."

"Oh, you—" She joined Sab in laughter, hearing her father scolding Sab.

She hurried up into the living room from the front porch and turned on the small Emerson radio, and in a few minutes was shuddering at the impact of the dreadful news. It was not a hoax after all. Japanese planes had really attacked Pearl Harbor.

"Kimiko," her mother said, sitting anxiously on the linoleum floor of the small living room. "Is it true? Japan has attacked 'Merica?"

She looked at her mother, dressed in a plain cotton dress, her long black hair combed back into a loose bun. "Yes, Okaasan," she answered, "it's terrible. But why start a war with America? They haven't even been able to win the China war?"

"You think our Niro might be in danger in Honolulu?" her mother asked, terrified, her lips quivering. "How far is Pea-ru Har-bah from Honolulu?"

"It's not too far. But I'm sure Niro is all right. The radio announcer said nothing about the city of Honolulu being attacked," she tried to console.

A little later, as she and her mother continued sitting close to the radio, Governor Poindexter spoke over Station KGU and proclaimed a state of emergency in Hawaii. Then, at about eleven-forty, the announcer said that the Army had ordered all the commercial radio stations off the air. He suggested, however, that everyone keep tuned for special announcements that were definitely forthcoming.

About three o'clock in the afternoon (the silent radio still on in the living room), fat Mr. Higa, the wealthy merchant from Kahului came to call on her father. He told of daring feats of the Japanese pilots while bombing Pearl Harbor. When Sab, sitting in the kitchen then, questioned Mr. Higa's dramatic news, her father promptly ordered Sab out of the kitchen.

"Well, how can Mr. Higa know about those things when he was on Maui all day?" Sab said defiantly, bolting into the living room to join Kimi and her mother. "Boy! These old folks. They can come up with the craziest stories. You know what that old man just told Father, Kimi?" Sab asked, sitting lazily on the wicker chair, one foot up on the arm rest.

"Sab, leave them alone," Kimi lectured. "Nothing you tell them is ever going to change their minds anyway."

"Aw, whodahell wants to listen to all that crap. That Mr. Higa, he expects us to believe everything he says. He's telling Father that one of the Buddhahead planes actually landed at Hickam Field and shot up a whole hangar, then the brave pilot got off the plane and raised a Japanese flag on the roof before taking off again. —Now, tell me, howdahell can that be possible? Chrissake! A five-year-old boy knows better than to believe crap like that," Sab said glumly. "That old man," he tossed his head towards the porthole separating the kitchen from the living room. "Just because he's got lotsa money he thinks he can go around bossing everyone."

"Saburo," Kimi's mother chided, "it's not right to criticize a guest of the home."

"Aw, Okaasan, don't tell me you believe what Mr. Higa's telling Otoosan," Sab said skeptically.

"If your father wants to believe Mr. Higa that is his business," her mother advised. "You go on believing what you want to and let your father believe whatever he wants."

Sab said nothing.

While Kimi was waiting for the latest news, Kenyei Shiroma, the Japanese-educated bo-bura, came dashing up the front door, his knee-length, taro-patch trousers coated with thick mud, round face perspiring profusely. "Oi! Gusuda-san," he called breathlessly, wiping his bare feet on the steps and heading for the kitchen, ignoring everyone in the living room. "I just heard over the Japan station that our airplanes have annihilated all of Honolulu. Have you folks heard about it?"

"Kenyei, you actually heard it over the Japan station?" Kimi's father asked, his voice packed with emotion. "Oh, we really must be at war with 'Merica."

"Oh, ca-rist! Now we've got the whole gang here," Sab moaned, snickering to himself, shaking his head. "I betcha that bo-bura is gonna come up with a bigger story than Mr. Higa. He'll probably tell Father Japan already conquered the world."

"Sab, leave them alone," Kimi said, unable to hold back laughter.

"Kenyei sure looked excited, didn't he?" her mother said, stretching her legs on the linoleum floor and craning her neck to gaze into the kitchen.

"You mean you folks had already known about the attack?" Kimi heard Kenyei saying in disappointment.

About four-thirty, an announcement was made over the radio that Major General Walter C. Short, Commanding General of the Hawaiian Department, was now the military governor of Hawaii. The announcement was then made in Japanese for the benefit of the non-English speaking Japanese population in the territory.

Then, a few minutes later, after another spell of suspenseful silence, the announcer said that all of Hawaii would be completely blacked out tonight and that the military government would summarily prosecute anyone violating the law. The announcer also made it emphatically clear that a curfew would take effect immediately after sundown and that no one was to be outdoors unless on official duty. Again, the same announcement was repeated in Japanese.

"Did you hear that, Okaasan?" Kimi said anxiously. "We'll have to black out the entire house. It'll be dark soon. We better hurry and cover all the windows."

"We better just do the living room and kitchen windows, and do the rest tomorrow," her mother said, worried, pushing herself up from the floor, rubbing her muscle-strained thighs. "Saburo, don't just sit there," she scolded. "Go downstairs and gather as much cardboards as you can. And bring the hammer and nails from the warehouse."

"Those stupid Buddhaheads!—starting a crazy war," Sab grumbled. He stood up reluctantly from the couch where he had been lying comfortably after being out feeding the pigs and chickens. "Now we'll all be living like rats." He went through the kitchen to the back porch.

In another hour, just before darkness set in, the three of them finished covering the three windows in the living room and the sliding window in the kitchen with thick slabs of cardboard.

Everyone was now in the kitchen: Kimi's father, Mr. Higa, Kenyei and Ishi (Ishi, the old man who lived with Kenyei across the bridge, having arrived a few minutes after Kenyei), sitting around the rectangular table drinking home-brewed sake; Sab standing against the wall listening to them; and Kimi helping her mother prepare a chicken-fry dinner at the stove. The four men were quite intoxicated. They were talking boisterously of daring feats of past Japanese heroes, and were speculating how long the present war was going to last. Even Kenyei, who seldom drank, was loud for a change. He kept staring—leering—at Kimi every chance he had.

"How can 'Merican soldiers be compared with the Japanese soldiers?" Mr. Higa said to Kenyei, his fat red face puffing on a big American-made cigar, paunchy belly bulging out over his tight American-made belt. "Hah!" he snorted, "the Japanese soldiers are too brave for the 'Mericans."

"Of course. Yes, of course," Kenyei agreed.

"Do you remember the heroic suicide mission of the three Japanese soldiers in the Russo-Japan war back in 1904?" Mr. Higa asked, his voice suddenly jumping into a squeaky falsetto like it always did when he was drunk.

"Yes. Yes, of course," Kenyei replied, nodding, mouth revealing chubby, tobacco-stained teeth. "They were called the 'Human Explosives.' If those three had not sacrificed themselves carrying those explosives through the barbed wires the Russians might have won the war. It was the spirit of Yamato-damashi that made those three die for the Emperor."

"That's right," Mr. Higa confirmed, taking another sip of sake, then drawing heftily on his American-made cigar.

"Where did you hear that?" Sab questioned, leaning against the wall near the refrigerator, arms folded across his chest.

"Saburo!" Kimi's father said, furious, "don't keep standing there doing nothing. Go feed the pigs and chickens."

"I did that long time ago," Sab said sullenly, changing positions, arms still folded across his chest.

Kimi gave her brother a scowling look.

"These young Niseis," she heard Mr. Higa's falsetto voice at the table. "They don't know nothing about Japan."

Toothless Ishi, who had been sitting near the window opposite her father hardly saying a word, grunted several times and took a big swig of sake. "Japanese soldiers are the best soldiers in the world."

"Who told you that?" Sab questioned, clucking his tongue, laughing a loud derisive laughter.

"Saburo! Go do your studies," his father ordered, glowering.

Sab changed positions again.

Kimi walked over to him. "I thought I told you to leave them alone. If you can't stand listening to what they're saying, go into the living room. Heaven's sake! Stop needling them."

"Oh, all right. I won't say another word. I'll just stand here and listen to them talk," he promised.

"Now, Sab," she warned, "I meant it. I don't want you to bother them." She pinched his forearm.

"Ouch!"

"I'll pinch harder the next time you bother them. It's bad enough listening to all that nonsense without having you cause an argument," she lectured, stepping back to the sink.

"When I was in the Japanese Army back in Okinawa," Kenyei Shiroma now boasted, "we used to call the Russo-Japan war the war of the Russian balls."

"Why did you call it that?" Mr. Higa wanted to know, his voice again jumping into a falsetto.

"Because the Russians were so big compared to the Japanese soldiers that the Japanese soldiers always ended up sticking their bayonets up the Russian soldiers' balls."

They all laughed hilariously.

Then, Kenyei, apparently having thought of another one, burst out laughing to himself.

"I wonder what the Japanese soldiers are going to call this war?" he said, smirking. "They probably would call it the war of the asses."

"Why would they call it that?" Mr. Higa asked, playing the straight role, rubbing his dewey eyes, preparing himself for another round of laughter.

"Because whenever the 'Merican soldiers come across the Japanese soldiers they're sure to run. And the only place the Japanese soldiers would be able to stab them would be up their asses."

They could not stop laughing. They all agreed that was better than the first one.

"That's a good one, all right," Ishi said, giggling with mouth half-closed to conceal missing front teeth. "The war of asses."

Kimi watched Sab.

"Hah! Hah! Hah!—" Sab gave out a burst of dry

laughter, sneering contemptuously. "Bunch of bull shit!" he told the men, stalking quickly into the living room before she could say anything.

Kimi could hardly keep from laughing to herself. Not at what that bo-bura had just said, but at the way the men were carrying on at the table. They were like innocent children gaping over marbles just won from an ill-fated shooter. Really, they were!

She was somewhat amused, too, at the way the older men were letting Kenyei dominate the conversation. Ordinarily, Kenyei would have sat there not saying a word. The news of the war seemed to have changed him altogether. He had suddenly become a loud, overbearing clown.

Good Lord! If Kenyei was an example of war-mongering Japanese soldiers, just imagine what those other bo-buras must be like!

6

LATER IN THE evening, long after all the guests had gone home and Kimiko and Saburo had gone to bed, Kama, feeling exaltedly drunk, sat alone at the kitchen table while his wife, short and plump in her baggy kimono, was washing the dirty dishes at the sink. The blacked-out window was shut tight and the stuffy, stale air in the kitchen still smelled of Mr. Higa's acrid cigar smoke.

It certainly has been a momentous weekend, Kama told himself, taking another sip of sake, bleary eyes behind the bifocals straining to stay open. Last night, it was Ichiro making his great speech over the radio. Today, all of Hawaii practically in the hands of Japan. What a grand weekend!

"Oi! Jisan Old Man," Tsuyu said in Okinawan over her shoulder from the sink while Kama poured more sake into his cup from the uplifted gallon jug, "you better not drink anymore. Remember what Doctor Honda said about your high blood pressure?"

"Oh, Basan Old Woman, don't worry about me," he slurred, filling the cup to its brim, then capping the jug.

"I have every reason to drink tonight. Why, our number one boy might become governor of Maui soon."

"Drinking as much as you do every night, one night is no different from another for you."

"But what other pleasures are there for me if I don't drink a little every night?" he asked, running his hand over his foaming mouth. "I'm already sixty one; I don't have any urge to make love to you anymore." He gave out a ring of laughter.

"Aw, shud-uppu, you. The children might hear you."

"We've lived a good life together, Basan," he continued, getting up from his chair and heading for his confined, dark bedroom next to the kitchen to change into his kimono.

"Jisan!" Tsuyu called out excitedly. "Whatever you do, don't turn on the light in your room. It's not blacked out."

"How do you expect me to change in the dark?" he grumbled but did not turn on the light. He struggled to take off his sticky, slop-stained shirt and trousers, then put on his sleeping kimono. He was glad he had begun sleeping in that room after his number two boy, Niro, went to Honolulu. It was better sleeping alone than staggering all the way over to Tsuyu's corner bedroom.

"Basan," he said, teetering out, "Doctor Honda might be right about my high blood pressure, but if I were to die tomorrow I would have no regrets. Of course, if I die I'm coming back for you. You're too old for other men; I don't want you to live alone in this world."

"Don't talk like that," she said. "It's not good talking about death all the time."

He slumped down on his chair, one foot lifted up, his sensitive testicles under his home-made, rice-bag BVD's dangling down between his thighs, his loose kimono wide open from the belt down. He did not expect to die yet. Not now when there was so much to look forward to. On the other hand, one shouldn't be afraid to die, he told himself impassively. What was more conclusive than death? Even the rich plantation managers, despite their wealth, have to die someday.

In a few minutes, Tsuyu, at last done with the dishes, came and sat across the table from him.

She remained silent, hands folded before her on the

table. After gazing down at them for a moment, she asked: "What did the school teacher say when you told him about the attack this morning?"

"Oh, he was surprised. Very surprised. He thought Japan would be landing troops in a day or two."

"That means there might be more killing."

"It can't be helped, Basan. War is war. If a war can be won without killing, I'm sure Japan would have been the first to discover it."

"Are you sure our Niro is all right in Honolulu?" Tsuyu asked, soft dark eyes behind her rimless glasses filling with tears.

"Yes, I'm sure he's all right, Basan. Don't worry. Why would the Japanese airplanes want to kill civilians. They're not barbarians."

"It's just horrible when you think about all those people killed today," she said apprehensively. "It's going to be a terrible shock to the mothers of all those young Japanese and 'Merican boys who died. Why must there always be wars?"

"I guess it's hard for a woman to understand, but wars have been a part of mankind from the beginning of time. Victories represented strength and power. Defeat, weakness and disgrace. Many times wars are economic necessities, too. Take Japan, for instance. They have to go out and conquer other countries. The islands of Japan are too small for its large population. That's why it had to take over Manchuria and Korea."

"But can't these things be accomplished without wars? When we came here to Hawaii we came peacefully."

"Oh, Basan" he said, taking a deep drag on his crumbling cigarette, "you don't seem to understand. We came here as immigrant laborers on a quota basis. You don't see Japanese laborers permitted here anymore, do you? It's the same story everywhere. The Japanese population is growing and growing, and the people have nowhere to go. They had to start a war."

"Do you think our Ichiro will have to go into the Japanese Army?" she asked, gravely concerned. "And what about Niro? Will he be called into the 'Merican Army?"

"No," Kama answered, head shaking emphatically, "it'll never happen. The war will be over before Niro gets called into the 'Merican Army. As for Ichiro, he will be needed in the big factories over there in Japan."

"I hope the war ends soon so there won't be anymore killing," Tsuyu said, hands cupped up to her mouth once more, moist eyes looking down on the table.

"It'll be over soon," he reassured.

"—That Shiroma, Kenyei," she said, digressing. "He sure was excited today, wasn't he? It was odd listening to him carrying on as he did. He's so quiet most of the time."

"Yeah," Kama said, grinning impishly, "he was like a young school boy. But he was educated in Okinawa. That's why he was excited about the attack."

"He sure is a funny one sometimes," Tsuyu said, a smile crossing her face for the first time. "When he jumped up and screamed 'Banzai!' after Ichiro's speech last night, I thought he had gone out of his mind. It was a good thing the school teacher joined him. Otherwise, he would have looked silly."

"Yeah, that Kenyei, he is a diehard all right."

"Did you see him almost crash into that car with his bicycle the other day?" she asked. "Goodness! he nearly scared me to death."

Kama gave out an uproarious laugh, head going up and down.

He had been sitting at the back porch that day when he saw that near-sighted Kenyei come racing down the hill on his bicycle, obviously not noticing a car crossing the bridge. Akisamiyo! If the driver had not honked his horn in time that Kenyei would have crashed head-on into the radiator. The funny part was, after cursing the car, Kenyei had kept on peddling furiously across the bridge.

"I hope our Ichiro doesn't turn out to be a fanatic like him," Tsuyu said.

"No. Of course not. Their standards are as far apart as the North and South poles. Our number one boy was educated at the best university in Japan."

After a passing silence, Tsuyu, standing up and stepping over to the refrigerator behind her for a glass of cold water, said: "Do you think the school teacher and his wife enjoyed their dinner here last night?"

"Sure they did. We fed them the best chicken hekka they ever had. And the teacher drank a lot of my good sake. But I didn't like him implying that Ichiro had represented only the Okinawans in Hawaii. That's not true. Ichiro is everything that those proud Naichis would want in a son. I still don't understand why that teacher is always distinguishing the Okinawans from the Naichis."

"The Naichis are always looking down on us," Tsuyu said, sitting down on her chair again. "They're no better than us. Like us, they had come to Hawaii because they were poor back in Japan."

"Basan, I guess it goes way back to when Okinawa became a possession of Japan. The Okinawans failed to better themselves as fast as they should have. Our parents were content to live off the dead soil that grew nothing but sweet potatoes. They were no different than the Kanakas here."

Tsuyu looked up at him, said nothing, then looked down at the glass in her hand.

Kama went on: "When the monsoon and typhoon came each year and destroyed their homes, they said: 'Shikata Ga Nai—it could not be helped; what will be, will be'; and went on building the same kind of grass shacks."

He paused, looked across the table at his wife. When she said nothing, but kept spinning the glass of water meditatively between her fingers, he said: "The only way Okinawans can become first-class Japanese is by education. Most of us here in Hawaii are considered lowly pig raisers by the Naichis. Even last night, as I walked the school teacher and his wife to their car, I noticed them wrinkling their noses at the pig-shit odor coming down from the pig pens. They probably wondered how in the world we can stand such awful stench."

Tsuyu said nothing for a while. Finally, pushing back her chair and standing up, she said: "Yes, I guess you're right. —I think I'll go to bed. Don't you think you better go to sleep, too? It is getting late."

He reached over for his Bull Durham and started rolling another cigarette.

"Be sure to turn off the light," she said, going through the dark living room to get to her bedroom.

He lit his cigarette and puffed drunkenly.

After a while, pressing both hands flat open on the table, the cigarette dangling down between his drooling mouth, he got up wearily from his chair and staggered to the tiny crack in the floor that separated the spare room from the kitchen. He squatted down directly over the crack and, aiming carefully, began urinating through it. He could hear the steady flow of his urine splashing on the sodden ground under the house. This was his private urinal. It saved him the trip outside the yard, or a long walk up to the outhouse.

He stood up waveringly, his legs numb from squatting down too long, and reeled back to his chair.

"Ichiro, my number one boy," he mumbled, "you have made your father proud of you."

He began singing his favorite Okinawan ballad:

> When you go away
> Be sure to come back wealthy
> If you don't come back wealthy
> There was no sense going away.

then clucked his tongue like a twangy samisen string:

> Tang! Tang! Tang! Tang!
> Tang! Tang! Tang! Tang! Tang! Tang!

Life is so much easier for the young ones, he thought, head feeling heavier and drowsier by the minute. But it was only proper that the children did not have to go through the hardships he himself had gone through back in Ginoza Village in Okinawa. Everyone had always been so poor and hungry there. After his father had died of chronic alcoholism, Kama, the oldest among four brothers, had to assume the family responsibilities. He hardly played when he was a boy. Everything he did had practical reasons: When he went to the mountains it hadn't been for a hike or a picnic, but to gather fire wood, mushrooms and bamboo shoots; when he went to the beaches it hadn't been to swim or relax on the sand, but to catch some fish or squid for the family's meal. Times had been so hard for his family even rice had been a luxury.

It must have been God's will when he had to go to Naha City that day to sell molasses candies. His youngest brother, Seitatsu, had been terribly ill and Kama was sent to Naha to purchase incense from the proceeds. The cure-all incense was to be burnt on Seitatsu's back to drive away the high fever.

After travelling two days and a night through high, rugged mountain trails with his donkey, Samurai, Kama had at last reached his destination. "Molasses Candy! Molasses Candy!" he had begun calling out, peddling the crowded, noisy streets of Naha.

In a few minutes, a group of young, barefooted children had begun following, mimicking and laughing at him for wearing old, threadbare, wrinkled shirt and trousers. "Hey! Yambara mountain man. Why don't you go back where you belong! We don't want your candies! They stink as bad as you!" Several of them threw pebbles and small rocks at Samurai, yelling: "The Yambara man and his donkey!"

When he had finally sold all the candies and purchased the incense, he wanted to leave the city and return home right away, but had gotten so hungry smelling the delicious aroma of noodles everywhere he walked into a noodle shop after tying Samurai to a post outside. The small, hot, earth-floored restaurant had been crowded with city people.

Taking off his shapeless, straw hat, he was about to sit down at a table when a wiry, kimono-clad woman had suddenly rushed up to him. "Get out of here!" she had shouted. "You smell up the whole place. And take that dirty, stinking donkey away from there!"

As he put his hat back on, the loud woman pushed him out of the door, the patrons laughing at him.

Walking to the edge of the city, head hung low, Samurai following behind, he came across a large gathering in the middle of the dusty street, listening to a man yelling excitedly:

"Yes! One 'Merican dollar a day! That's right! One dollar a day! Hawaii! We will be leaving in a week!"

One dollar a day! It was unheard of!

Inquiring, Kama had found out that the speaker was hiring men to go to work in a place called Hawaii. Imagine, a dollar a day! It was the answer to poverty, hunger and humiliation. A chance to return to Okinawa wealthy and respectful. Not caring where Hawaii could be, he had followed a long line of men into a wooden shack where, barely able to write his own name, he had affixed it with determination on a dotted space.

When he had reached home with the incense, it was too late. Seitatsu was dead. Blaming himself for not having incense available when needed, Kama, more determined than ever to overcome poverty and hunger, had promised his mother and two remaining younger brothers he would return a wealthy man from Hawaii in two years. The following week, he made another trip to Naha. This time to embark on a long boat ride to some far-away land several thousand miles away from Okinawa.

That was over thirty years ago, he remembered now, eyes staring wearily at his sake cup, head weaving back and forth, still in deep reverie.

The promised dollar-a-day had not been easy to come by when he arrived in Waipahu, Oahu, near Pearl Harbor, in 1905. He had never worked so hard in his life: cutting sugar cane with a heavy bolo knife under the scorching tropical heat and loading them by bulks on train cars; and cultivating young canes with back-breaking hoeing all day when there wasn't harvesting to be done. It had been work, work, work. Six days a week. Sun-up till sun-down.

After living in Waipahu for two years and barely managing to save a little over one hundred dollars—indeed a far cry from what he needed to retire back in Okinawa— he had come to Maui, hoping to find better working conditions. But working in the sweltering Lahaina plantation fields on the west end of the island had been no better.

Finally, convinced he could never return to Okinawa a wealthy man, he paid a local marriage broker three hundred and fifty dollars to have a picture bride sent from Okinawa. He had been thirty-two then, and had wanted a wife badly.

Tsuyu had looked so young and innocent—almost like a child—that day when he and the marriage broker went down to the wharf to greet her. She had on a beautiful orange and white kimono with dainty white ta-bes covering her feet. Her smooth, light complexion with pleasant smelling face powder had glistened prettily under the blazing sun. When he had walked up to her she bowed graciously several times, eyes looking down at her feet, bashful, utterly feminine, so unlike the dark Kanaka wahines he had been going to bed with for a dollar and a half.

About a year after that, he and Tsuyu had packed what meager belongings they owned and moved to Peahi on the east end of the island to grow pineapples for Libby Pineapple Cannery.

Their four children were born in Peahi.

In 1931, when they heard of the huge pineapples that grew in Kahakauloa near Kapuna, he and Tsuyu and the children had moved to Kapuna. They prospered beyond belief the next two years. Their pineapples were the biggest they had ever seen. He had hoped at last to return to Okinawa with his family, but the pineapple depression hit the islands and wiped them out the following year. Knowing no other way to support his family, he had become a pig raiser. It was better than slaving in the cane fields.

His eyes were barely open now. His head sagged down, corners of his mouth drooling with saliva. He began grinding his teeth in grating noises.

"Ichiro," he called out, "do your best at all times."

He suddenly lurched forward as his foot slipped off the chair, his head landing on the table with a dull thud.

He staggered up to his feet, remembering to cap the gallon jug. Then, reeling over to his bedroom door and pulling it open, he felt his way into the darkness with hands extended against the wall. The screen door screeched sharply, closing behind him.

He flopped down on the bed face down, the world twirling and spinning all around him before he finally passed out.

7

AFTER LEAVING THE kitchen, Tsuyu, shuffling to her dark corner bedroom in her Japanese house slippers, was thinking of what her husband had just said about the Naichis and the Okinawans. Her husband was right, she told herself, opening the screen door, but look at what Ichiro—an Okinawan boy—had achieved. He was one of the most educated Niseis in Hawaii and had been honored in Japan.

She remembered not to turn on the light (the two windows were not blacked-out), and felt her way into the room until her eyes became gradually accustomed to the darkness. Outside, the entire valley was in silent darkness as though a sudden catastrophe had wiped out every living soul.

Hearing her husband mumbling drunkenly in the kitchen, she hoped he'd be going to bed soon. He had not been drinking too much since his last illness, but she doubted whether he knew how bad drinking was for his high blood pressure. If that were the only thing wrong with him she wouldn't be too concerned, but Doctor Honda had warned that Kama also had a heart condition.

She took off her slippers and laid them against the wall

then, reaching over for her pack of Kools on the trunk, sat down sighingly on the matted floor alongside the huge, old iron bed that occupied half the space in the small room. She bent low and quickly lit her cigarette with tightly cupped hands, watching the coal glowing red at the tip. How long will the war last? she wondered with deep-rooted fear, reminding herself to black out all the bedroom windows first thing in the morning.

To her, wars were always associated with the death of her oldest brother, killed in the Russo-Japan war. He had volunteered in the Japanese Army, and when news of his death reached Okinawa, her mother, outwardly stoic, wept night after night in the quiet solitude of her bedroom. Will this terrible tragedy happen to one of her own sons? she asked herself with a shudder. She prayed that the war would end before any of her sons was called into the Army. Winning or losing was not important; in the end no one really won anyway, only succeeded in killing and maiming each other. The important thing was, it be a short one with as little annihilation as possible.

Forcing herself to think of more pleasant things, she envisioned her husband sitting in the living room last night, listening to Ichiro's grand speech. Kama had looked so proud and happy, head held high, eyes brimming with tears. It was such a wonderful climax to all the years of hardships and struggles in sending Ichiro to college.

Kimiko should have gone to college, too, she thought, smoking her cigarette and flicking the ashes into an empty sardine can at her knees. Kimiko's grades in school were just as good as Ichiro's and Niro's had been. But a college education was so expensive. They had just barely managed Ichiro's expenses.

Kimiko, in a way, was strange. She hardly associated with the local Japanese girls. Every Sunday morning she would make a basket of lunch and go down to the ocean by herself, not coming home until late in the afternoon. Sometimes she would bring back lots of watercolor paintings of the river and the ocean, then destroy them after showing them to everyone. She was a very pretty girl, yet did not seem interested in boys. Of course, it was quite a relief that she did not go around with Kanaka or Porlegee boys like some of the wild Wailuku Japanese girls did.

Funny, but she used to be such a cheerful girl when she was younger. Her father always had to scold her for being loud and unladylike. Then, about a year ago, she seemed very quiet around the house, hardly discussing anything with her father or mother. Well, anyway, she would one day meet a nice Japanese boy and get married. Since she did not particularly care for Japanese customs there was no sense in having a marriage broker find her a husband.

Right now, Tsuyu was more concerned about Saburo than anyone else. In a way, she had spoiled him, being the youngest. But he was becoming uncontrollable and did not respect his father anymore. Earlier tonight, for instance, when his father had told him to stop insulting the guests, he shouldn't have spoken back. What a bad impression that must have made on Mr. Higa!

It was partly Kama's own fault for having lost Saburo's respect. The boy had hardly seen him sober at nights. Saburo probably regarded his father as a drunkard. —That wasn't right, she told herself, shaking her head dolefully, taking another deep drag. Kama hardly drank in his younger days. Only occasionally at Okinawan parties.

Naturally, she understood her husband more than anyone else. They had been married for almost thirty years. Thirty years! The years certainly have gone by fast. Just imagine! nearly thirty years have passed since she came to Hawaii. It seemed only yesterday.

So many things, so many many things have happened since then, she reminisced. But the most striking thing in all those years had actually taken place only about a month after she and Kama had gotten married.

They had just finished their dinner of fried Aku fish and rice that night, she remembered, and were sitting on the bare floor of their living room talking of the day's activities, when Mrs. Oshiro, their neighbor, brought over an envelope.

"Why, it's from Kentaro, my younger brother!" Tsuyu exclaimed excitedly after Mrs. Oshiro left.

Kama appeared pleased.

She opened the envelope nervously and read the one-page letter which told her that everyone back in Okinawa was fine and that they were all looking forward to her return.

She quickly handed the letter to Kama.

He reached for it slowly, hesitantly; an uncertain, vacant look in his eyes. He held it before him with an unmoved expression. She waited for him to say something.

He remained silent.

She suddenly realized that he was holding the letter upside down. Oh, no! she gasped, hands jumping up to her mouth, head drawing back, shocked. Her husband couldn't read! She should have known: the absence of reading materials in the house. Tears flooded her eyes.

Just then, she caught him gazing over the letter at her helplessly, a mixed expression of hurt and anger in his pleading eyes, his mouth tightening into a half-grin, half-bewildered sullenness.

She forced a strained, brittle smile. "It's a well-written letter, isn't it? Kentaro is only fifteen years old."

Kama kept looking at her, blank-faced.

"Yes," he finally uttered, looking down at the letter in his hand, then handing it back. "Yes, your brother seems to be a smart boy."

She looked away, fighting back sobs, and put the letter back into the envelope. Getting up from the floor, she gathered the dirty dishes on the low table and hurried into the earth-floored kitchen in the back. There, at the galvanized sink, the kitchen pipe opened all the way, she burst out in pitiful cry. Forgive her! Oh, forgive her! She did not know. How awful it must have been for him to make believe he was reading the letter.

Later, somewhat composed while doing the dishes, she kept thinking of ways to teach her husband how to read and write.

It had not been until years after they had moved to Peahi, and Ichiro was in the first grade in both English and Japanese schools, that she had been able to carry out her plan. Each evening after dinner, she and Kama would sit on the living room floor with Ichiro and help Ichiro with his Japanese lessons. Ichiro would point to the different characters and read out loud while his father followed him as though instructing him. Tsuyu, then, would read the same words carefully, pretending to be teaching only Ichiro. In the beginning, Ichiro used to insist that his father read to him, too, but she would always make excuses for Kama and ignore Ichiro's pleas.

As the months rolled by and Kama learned most of the basic characters, he would sometimes turn to the advanced lessons forgetting he was supposed to be teaching his son.

"Otoosan, you're going too fast for me," Ichiro would complain. "I haven't learned those words yet."

"Oh, yes, of course," Kama would say, turning back the pages. "I forgot you were still learning the simple words."

Late one night, she asked her husband: "Now that Ichiro is able to read, don't you think we should subscribe to the Nippu Ji-Ji?"

Kama had pondered for a few seconds. "Yes, that would be a good idea," he said. "I've been thinking about it myself."

While on a shopping trip to Wailuku several weeks before, she had found out that the Nippu Ji-Ji was a semi-weekly Japanese-American newspaper published in Honolulu and distributed throughout the islands. The advanced Japanese characters were quite difficult to follow, but printed alongside them were the basic letters, enabling the less educated Japanese in Hawaii to read the paper.

During the next several years after the first paper had arrived, Kama spent most of his evenings reading the week-old news over and over, practically memorizing every article. Whenever coming across phrases or words he had difficulty understanding, he would discuss them with Tsuyu as though testing her.

Once, while she was sewing, Kama handed her one of his rare letters to his brother in Okinawa and had asked her to read it. She had quickly set aside her sewing to read the short letter.

"Ah-h, Kama," she had said, "some of the beautiful words you use are too hard for me to understand."

"Those are the same words I use in all my letters," he had told her.

"Yes, I've noticed that," she had said, smiling radiantly.

It was just about that time that Kama had at last managed to scribble his name in English, instead of the usual "X" he had been affixing for years on their pineapple contracts.

"Yes," he had told her, "that number one boy of ours is very bright. He even taught me how to write my name in English."

"Ichiro is a smart boy, all right," she had told her husband, "but you're better in Japanese than he."

"Of course!" Kama had declared. "As long as I have a thorough knowledge of the Japanese language why should I waste my time learning English?"

Taking the last few puffs on her cigarette now, Tsuyu suddenly felt her heart leaping up to her throat. Kama had staggered against a chair in the kitchen. Thank goodness! he had not fallen down.

If he'd only stop drinking, she thought wistfully. Actually, though, he had not started drinking heavily until the last few years. It had all begun when he went into debt over Ichiro's education. On the other hand, she felt her husband was justified in drinking. He had worked hard all his life and had hardly known what it was not to be under some kind of financial strain.

Despite Kama's drinking habits he had managed to do many wonderful things for his family, she told herself. In 1930, when the pineapples were sold at a good profit, he had sent fifteen hundred dollars to his mother in Okinawa to erect a family burial shrine. Until then the Gusudas had been disgraced for being one of the few families in the village not owning one.

Kama was proud indeed when Mr. Higa, returning from a visit to Okinawa, brought back a snapshot of the shrine. Mr. Higa had said it was by far the biggest and most beautiful one in all of the neighboring villages, if not in all of Okinawa.

The shrine, according to the photograph, had been built against a high embankment with tall Matsu trees in the background, huge concrete blocks molded together in an oval-shaped, turtle-back form, the stone walls surrounding it a good four feet high. Beautiful flowers bordered the walk to the three steps climbing up the seal, where a body was entombed seven years before taken out in decayed bones to keep in a sacred urn.

Kama's mother who died in 1937 had been the first to

be entombed. Perhaps, three
undoubtedly over by then),
Ginoza Village for a visit and join
in the seventh anniversary of his
thought. He had not been back sin
The trip would do him good.

Although her own family had been t
shrine, she remembered her mother telli
shrines were built in a turtle-back shape
womb. When a body was sealed into it, it s
restoration of its soul which someday would be reincarnated.

She heard Kama's bedroom door screeching shut.

She crushed her cigarette butt on the bottom of the
sardine can, got up from the floor, walked to the kitchen
to turn out the light, then returned to her bedroom. Kama
would probably want to get up early to listen to the
latest war news from Kenyei, she told herself, winding the
alarm clock and setting it for five-thirty. She would get up
before him and have his coffee ready.

Tossing on her creaking old spring bed and shutting her
tired eyes, she could smell the familiar reeking stench of
pig kukui seeping into her dark, serene bedroom.

Ah'samiyo! The pig pen smelled worse than it normally
did, she thought, wrinkling her pert nose, reminding herself to shove some wet newspapers into the window sill
cracks tomorrow. She finally felt friendly drowsiness shrouding her senses.

8

WHEN KIMI WENT to work the following windy morning she felt a smothered, tense excitement as soon as she stepped into the front doors of Kress Store. There was a kind of suspenseful uneasiness among the Japanese sales-girls who spoke to one another in low, hissing whispers. How horrible all those sailors and soldiers dying! What made Japan do such a terrible thing?

The Porlegee and Chinese salesgirls kept to themselves and spoke in hushed, subdued voices. Even Mr. Newman, the young bespectacled manager who had come from California only a few months ago, was noticeably cold towards the Japanese girls when greeting them at the door. He stood there in his light gray tweed suit, hands clasped behind his back while teetering back and forth on the balls of his feet, repeating constrained "good mornings," his usual benign smile absent from his boyish face.

Kimi, dressed in a plain blue cotton skirt and a white blouse, had walked over to the first counter (her counter) and had immediately begun dusting the envelopes, pencils, typing papers and other office supplies. Betsy Watanabe, who occupied the other half of the long counter (and had come in a few minutes late as always), began rearranging the different assortments of children's color books.

"Kimi," Betsy whispered, treading over with a feather duster in one hand, looking around for Mr. Newman. "What's going to happen to us?"

"What do you mean?" she said, watching Mr. Newman entering his private office at the extreme back after saying something to one of the girls at the last counter.

"You think Mr. Newman might fire us?"

"What for!"

"He probably thinks all the Japanese in Hawaii want Japan to win the war," Betsy whispered, taking a step closer.

"Oh, Betsy. I'm sure he knows better than that. Besides, almost all the salesgirls are Japanese," Kimi said, looking at the six rows of counters and the two long flanking side counters.

"Did you notice how unfriendly he was towards us this morning?"

"How did you expect him to feel after what happened?"

"He didn't have to make me feel responsible for it."

"You're letting your imagination get the best of you," Kimi said, walking to the other end of the counter. That Betsy, she sure lets herself get carried away.

Gazing out the two wide glass doors up front, she noticed that Mr. Newman had put the store's large Fourth-of-July American flag out on the sidewalk. The red-white-and-blue was flapping gloriously against the crisp December morning breeze, the long pole wavering back and forth on its tripod stand.

That was one good way of showing everyone that Kress was one hundred percent American, she thought, small eyes twinkling.

Kress, the only five-and-dime store on Maui, was located about half a block west of the Market Street intersection, on Main. Having worked there the past six months, Kimi had come to know almost the exact time different people went by. This morning, however, everyone's schedule seemed disrupted. It was already nine and Mr. Atkinson of Bishop Bank had not yet appeared. Neither had Mr. Canons of the Grand Hotel next door. Even her father, who always parked his pickup in front of Lin Wo's across the street at about eight-thirty, had failed to show up.

She continued dusting, glancing over towards Betsy now and then. Betsy and Haruko Okamoto—the girl at the next counter—were whispering back and forth. Betsy, dark complexioned and rather tall for a Japanese girl, was wearing an extra-tight red sweater and a light gray skirt. She wasn't a beautiful girl, but she had a lovely figure accentuated by up-standing breasts that always fascinated the men that came into the store. It sort of disgusted Kimi whenever Betsy walked along the aisle of the counter with her chest deliberately sticking out.

"Do you know what Haruko just told me?" Betsy said, walking over with a writhing look. "She said her father was picked up by the FBI last night."

"What for!" Kimi exclaimed, horrified, looking over quickly at Haruko, who was crying.

"They think the trip he took to Japan last year had something to do with the attack."

"How could that be possible! Her father is only a Buddhist priest; not a spy."

"The FBI is picking up everyone who went to Japan the past year," Betsy said, wincing, looking around for Mr. Newman.

Kimi was suddenly alarmed at the thought of her own father being picked up over Ichiro's speech the other night.

"All the Japanese school teachers are being investigated, too," Betsy went on. "Before we know it, we're all going to be picked up for one thing or another."

"How could they ever do that! There's more than one hundred and thirty thousand of us here in Hawaii," Kimi scoffed. "Where are they going to put all of us? Kahoolawe?"

"Did you hear about the Japanese man getting shot up in Kula last night for leaving his lights on?" Betsy asked. "The MP's said the man was signalling a submarine in Malaea Bay."

"What submarine?"

"There must be hundreds of Japanese submarines surrounding the islands," Betsy advised.

"Who told you that?"

"The plantation camp people were talking about it."

"Where did they get their information?"

Betsy made a face. "If you don't want to believe me you don't have to. Everyone else knows about it."

"Betsy, you shouldn't go around starting rumors."

"I didn't start it. I just heard about it."

"Well, you shouldn't repeat it."

"What about Haruko's father being picked up? That's not a rumor."

Kimi could say nothing.

"You think Japan might win the war?" Betsy asked testily.

"Betsy! Don't say that!"

"They already destroyed half the United States Navy in Pearl Harbor."

"We must have lots of other ships." Suddenly shocked, Kimi said: "Betsy! Don't tell me you want Japan to win the war."

"Oh, no! That's the last thing I'd hope for. They say the women in Japan are treated like dirt.

"Besides," Betsy went on, "I'm really angry with those bo-buras. I was supposed to have gone on a picnic with Glen Thompson yesterday."

"Did he call you?" Glen Thompson, Kimi discovered about three months ago, was Betsy's latest sailor boy friend from the Puunene Naval Air Station.

Betsy shook her head. "You think he might hate me for being Japanese?"

"Oh, Betsy, if he likes you, he likes you for what you are. Not whether you're Japanese, Chinese or a haole."

"I hope so."

"Are you in love with him?" Kimi asked, knowing very well that Betsy had gone out with lots of other sailors since the naval station had opened.

"Oh, Kimi," Betsy said, eyes shut tight dreamily, hands folded before her. "You should see him. He's such a good-looking guy. Honestly! He's the best-looking sailor I've met. He can be taken for Robert Taylor or—or even Clark Gable."

Kimi burst out laughing.

"What do your father and mother think, you going out with a haole?" she asked curiously.

"I wouldn't dare tell them about it," Betsy said. "They'd throw me out of the house if they ever knew. You know how the old folks are—all they ever want you to do is work and work."

"How do you manage to see Glen Thompson without them ever finding out?"

Betsy looked away with scarlet face, one hand up to her mouth. "You make me feel as though I was doing something terrible."

"You don't have to tell me if you don't want to." Kimi turned her head away and resumed dusting.

"You promise you won't tell anyone?" Betsy stepped closer.

"Of course."

"Well . . . I—I always tell my folks I'm going to spend the night at Haruko's."

"Don't they ever check with Haruko's folks?"

Betsy looked over her shoulder towards Haruko Okamoto for a moment, then back to Kimi again. "Remember, you promised not to tell a soul about it."

"But—but where do you spend the night if you don't really go over to Haruko's?"

"Oh, Kimi . . . With Glen, of course."

"All night?"

Betsy blushed. "Glen and I are in love with each other. We plan to get married as soon as he gets his discharge."

"Discharge!"

"I know . . ." Betsy moaned, her voice almost cracking under the strain, her eyes moistening. "I guess he won't be able to get his discharge for a long time now." She coverered her face with her hands, head going down slowly. "Oh, those awful bo-buras, starting a war at a time like this!" she suddenly cried, dropping her hands to her sides in tight fists. "How I hate them! I hate them!" She stamped her foot down hard on the floor.

"What am I going to do, Kimi?" she said piteously.

Kimi, still dumfounded by Betsy's outburst, said: "I guess you'll just have to wait until the war is over."

"But we can't! We just can't! We have to get married now. We just have to—" Betsy's hands jumped up to her mouth. She was trying desperately to fight back sobs.

"Oh, Betsy! Oh, no!" Kimi quickly put her hands on Betsy's shoulders and held her. "Are you sure?"

Betsy kept nodding, hands still up to her mouth, tear-filled eyes looking down at her feet.

"Does Glen Thompson know about it?"

Betsy shook her head. "I meant to tell him yesterday at our picnic."

"Have you tried to get in touch with him?"

"All day yesterday and early this morning. The naval station telephone operator said they're not taking civilian calls."

Kimi continued holding Betsy's shoulders, her own eyes moistening. "You'll just have to let him know somehow. He'll understand."

"I don't want him to think I was trapping him."

"This is no time to talk like that. He'll have to marry you."

Betsy forced a tight smile. "I was nearly going out of my mind keeping everything to myself. I'm so glad you understand. Please don't think I'm terrible, Kimi. I couldn't help myself. I love him so much."

Kimi gave Betsy a strong embrace again.

Betsy drew her head back a little. "I wish I was like you, Kimi," she said. "You're so intelligent; you have so much will power. You're not the type to get involved in things like this. Why couldn't I be like you?"

Kimi felt her face flushing. She shifted her eyes away from Betsy's, a gnawing guilt feeling racing through her.

"Don't worry about it too much," she consoled. "Everything will work out fine." It was odd thinking of Betsy having problems. Betsy seemed so easy-going and cheerful all the time. "—Here comes the All-American boy," Kimi whispered, noting Mr. Newman coming out of his office, the ceiling light reflecting on his glasses for a second. "We'll talk about it later." She pushed Betsy gently towards the other end of the counter.

No matter how much she sympathized with Betsy's plight, Kimi was, frankly speaking, very grateful that she herself had not gotten in trouble after the times she and George had sex. She would have died had he gotten her pregnant, she thought, wincing frightfully at such a dire prospect.

What would Betsy do if Glen Thompson was suddenly

shipped out of Maui? How awful that would be! Her parents would kick her out of her home for sure, and her friends were bound to ostracize her.

Kimi sighed a great big smug sigh. She sure was lucky that George used to take necessary precautions. She looked over at Betsy, waiting for her to face the front.

Thank heaven! Betsy wasn't "showing" yet. But she had better start wearing looser dresses from now on. Kimi would have to suggest it later.

—George, oh, George . . . She shuddered again, standing there looking out the two front doors. Even yesterday morning, for instance, she would have given in to his demands had he persisted for a few more seconds. Right there! In plain daylight where they might as well have invited everyone on Maui to watch them. It was so difficult resisting him. Yet, they must learn to control themselves.

She felt her face turning feverish. She hadn't meant to do it with him that first time. But she couldn't help herself; she was so happy and carefree that night: George, chosen the outstanding basketball player at the tournament, and the dance at the gymnasium afterwards with all those sweet-smelling ginger and gardenia flowers decorating the walls; the beautiful, soft music of the band; and the lovely ride down to the beach near Waiehu Golf course where they parked under the bright Maui moon. Everything had seemed so perfect; just so wonderful.

A woman customer walked up to her counter, picked up several packs of white envelopes, and handed them over to her.

After receiving fifty cents and handing the envelopes back in a bag, she suddenly remembered she had better write Niro tonight and find out how he was. Her mother was greatly worried about him. Was the mail service to Honolulu disrupted? she wondered. It might take several days for a letter to reach Niro. And what about Ichiro in Japan? There was no way to communicate with him anymore.

Those superstitious fools, starting a war! Wanting to die for the Emperor because he was supposed to be God—a descendant of the Sun. How foolish can people be?

Yet deep inside, Kimi had to admit that even she, up until she was about sixteen, had believed in some of the old Japanese folklore of mumbo-jumbo prayers, ghosts and other silly spiritual tales. Then, when her mother, suffering from chronic headaches, had been calling on an Okinawan curer and prophet in Waikapu (a small plantation settlement two miles south of Wailuku) without signs of improvement, Kimi had accompanied her on one of her frequent visits. She had been curious to know what the so-called curer was really doing for her mother.

It cost her mother ten dollars a visit, and after watching the old, shrivelled-up, white-haired man in black kimono going through a series of weird chanting before an incense-burning shrine in his one-room shack, Kimi had suddenly realized how superstitious her mother was. Warm tears coming into her eyes, she had found herself not resenting her mother's ignorance, but understanding her for the first time with great affection. How could her mother have known better when she was brought up to believe in folklore of the old country.

Next day, when her mother still complained of headaches, Kimi had insisted that they see a doctor, and her father took her to Doctor Honda in Wailuku. At the Doctor's sug gestion, she was, then, taken to an eye, ear and nose specialist. The specialist, after examining her, recommended glasses. In a day or two, her headaches disappeared.

"Kimi," Betsy whispered, sauntering over gravely, "Mr. Newman just fired Haruko."

She looked over quickly at the next counter and noticed that Miss Ho, the short, slight Chinese Head Saleslady had taken Haruko's place. "What did she get fired for?"

"Some loud-mouth told Mr. Newman about her father."

"You think it was Miss Ho?" she questioned, giving the Head Saleslady a contemptuous look.

"It could be. You know how she is—always kissing the boss's okole."

"I feel like telling her what I think of her," Kimi said, furious.

"You better not. She'll tell Mr. Newman on you."

"Let her! This isn't the only job in the world. How can they fire Haruko just because her father was picked up by the FBI for questioning. It had nothing to do with her."

"Sh-h, Kimi. Miss Ho might hear you," Betsy warned, glancing side-eyed towards the Chinese woman.

"I don't give a damn if she hears me," she said angrily,

speaking even louder. "If we don't put a stop to things of this sort, they're gonna end up accusing us of dropping the bombs. —Betsy, watch my side of the counter for a few minutes. I'm going over to speak to Mr. Newman."

"Oh, no, Kimi. You better not. He might fire you, too."

"Let him! See if I care. He'll have to listen to what I have to say first," she said, fuming, turning around and heading towards the other exit. She marched past the back counters with hurried, staccato steps to Mr. Newman's private office next to the water fountain.

She knocked hard three-four times.

"Come in," a stern voice called out.

She opened the door, closed it behind her not too softly and walked up to Mr. Newman's steel-gray metal desk. The desk was cluttered with blue and white invoices. The office was small, narrow and warm, the only window being the one above Mr. Newman's head.

"Yes, Miss Gusuda?" Mr. Newman was leaning back on his varnished swivel chair, brown, crew-cut head resting on the chair-back, a yellow pencil in his right hand. His cold brownish-green eyes kept staring at her through black horn-rimmed glasses. There was a bitter-sour expression on his boyish face with faint lines running down from the base of his prominent nose to the corners of his thin mouth.

"Mr. Newman," she said, taking another step closer to the desk, hands clasped behind her, "I'd like to talk to you about Haruko Okamoto."

"What about Miss Okamoto?" Mr. Newman frowned, raised his head up and leaned forward on the desk, the yellow pencil tapping on the green blotter.

"I understand you fired her a few minutes ago."

"Well, I wouldn't exactly say I fired her, Miss Gusuda," he said, forcing an uneasy smile. "Let's say I had to let her go."

"But why, Mr. Newman? She can't help it if her father was picked up by the FBI."

"I didn't say she could. I had to let her go because someone with her background might be detrimental to the reputation of Kress."

"But she didn't do anything wrong. She's a wonderful person. She's one of the hardest-working girls in the entire store."

[92]

"Miss Gusuda," Mr. Newman said impatiently, the smile on his sharp face replaced by a bitter-sour expression. "Are you trying to tell me how to run the store? I don't have to listen to all this from you."

"Yes, I realize that, Mr. Newman. And you'll probably fire me like you did Haruko after you hear what I have to say."

"Well, say what you have to say and go back to your counter. I'm quite busy as you can well see."

"Mr. Newman, how long have you lived in Hawaii?" she questioned.

"Couple of months altogether. Why? What does that have to do with Miss Okamoto?"

"That means you don't know very much about the people here in the islands; at least, not about the Japanese people."

"I wouldn't say that. I went to UCLA. There were a number of your people in my classes. I didn't get to know any of them too well, but—"

"I don't know anything about the Japanese in the Mainland, Mr. Newman," she interrupted, "but I do know many things about us—the second-generation Japanese—here in Hawaii. Our parents might have come from Japan, but we were born here in Hawaii. We're American citizens; not foreigners. And we're proud to be Americans."

"I'm sure you are. And I'm glad to hear that."

"Mr. Newman, Haruko Okamoto is an American, too. —Yes, her father is a priest and was picked up by the FBI. I don't know why, but they did. It had nothing to do with her. She's an American like you; me; like all of us born here in America. If you fired her just because her father is a Buddhist priest, aren't you going against her constitutional right?"

Mr. Newman's eyes slowly dropped to the blotter. "What makes you think all this has anything to do with my letting Miss Okamoto go?" he said at last, looking up again, studying Kimi with penetrating eyes.

"I can't think of any other reason why you fired her."

"I didn't fire her! Dammit! Can't you understand that? I had to let her go because one of the girls complained that her father was a potentially dangerous man to the country."

"Haruko's father is only a priest. Not a spy or anything like that. He's a kind man. He's done a lot for the people

[93]

on Maui—Japanese, as well as non-Japanese. Besides, nothing has been proven against him. He's just being investigated. My folks, like Haruko's, came from Japan, too. Are you going to accuse them of being spies?"

"I'm saying no such thing, Miss Gusuda! I have to look out for the morale and reputation of the store personnel." Mr. Newman's face was turning lobster-red.

"Do you think it was fair to fire Haruko without giving her a chance to show her loyalty?"

"Miss Gusuda!" Mr. Newman burst out exasperatedly, throwing the pencil down hard on the desk, his nostrils flaring red, "I have a duty to perform. It was my duty to fire—I mean to let Miss Okamoto go."

"Why, Mr. Newman?" Kimi said, placing her hands on the edge of the metal desk, looking straight down at her boss, unruffled. "She hasn't done anything wrong? —Mr. Newman, I don't know what generation American you are, but I do know that at one time or another your grandfather, or great grandfather, or one of your ancestors who first came to America was a foreigner. Just because they came to this country before our parents did, does that make you more of an American than us?"

Mr. Newman said nothing. He made a throaty noise and leaned way forward with his arms folded on the desk. His head kept going from side to side, mouth pulled tight into a grim pout, jaw muscles twitching.

"Mr. Newman, what nationality are you?" she asked, curious.

"My parents came from Germany," he said, looking up square chin pointed at her.

"Germany! Then—"

"If by that tone you're implying they are Nazis, you're wrong," he interrupted abruptly. "My parents were born in Germany, but we're not Germans; we're Jewish."

"Oh-h," she murmured, still looking down at her young boss. "Here in Hawaii, a haole is a haole, Mr. Newman. But I understand in other parts of the world—even in the Mainland—Jews are persecuted by the non-Jews. Especially in places like Germany where Hitler murdered thousands of Jews just because they were Jews. Are you going to start firing us Japanese salesgirls just because we're Japanese?"

"Oh, goddamnit! Miss Gusuda!" Mr. Newman flared up

again, lunging up to his feet and pounding the desk. "All right. I'll call Miss Okamoto and tell her she can come back to work."

Kimi, stunned for a second by the sudden outburst, drew her head back, eyes blinking with astonishment. "You will!" she uttered, a slow smile creeping up her eyes and crossing her lips. "Oh, thank you, Mr. Newman. Thank you very much," she said, restraining herself from hugging the young manager. "I knew you'd understand. I just knew it."

Mr. Newman continued studying her through his thick glasses, his bitter-sour expression turning into a warm, gentle smile. "Anything else, Miss Gusuda?"

"No. Oh, no, Mr. Newman. That's all I wanted to say," she said. "Thank you very much again. I know Haruko will be very grateful to you."

She turned, stepped up to the door and opened it. As she was about to walk out, Mr. Newman said, "Miss Gusuda, in the future if you're going to represent others I'd appreciate it if you'd give me a chance to prepare myself," and grinning a pleasant grin, looked down at the invoices on his desk.

She smiled and walked out, shutting the door very gently this time. The boss wasn't such a big Okole after all, she thought, hurrying back to her counter, eyes beaming.

"What did he say?" Betsy asked, worried, as soon as Kimi stepped into the counter aisle. "Did he fire you, too?"

"Oh, Betsy, why would be fire me?" she answered in a small, squeaky voice. "We have an understanding." She was fighting hard to keep her hands steady. "He's not such a bad guy after all. He only looks mean at times."

"You mean he's not going to fire Haruko?"

"Of course not. Not after our long talk. He understands us pretty well now. —I hope." She crossed her fingers behind her.

"Kimi! You're terrific!" Betsy cried out, taking hold of her hands and embracing her.

"Betsy, we better go back to work," she said, looking over coldly at Miss Ho who was watching them. "I told Mr. Newman we were the hardest-working girls in the store."

Betsy hugged her again, then walked over to her end of

the counter where a man was waiting to purchase something.

Kimi stood there looking at Betsy's figure, then, as she turned to face the front and looked out the doors, her heart suddenly jumped up to her throat and began pounding excitedly.

It was George! He was standing across the street talking to several Hawaiian and haole men. When he glanced over her way, she raised her hand and waved. He waved back. After saying something to the other men, he started crossing the street.

"Hi!" she greeted, smiling warmly. George was dressed in a white shirt with a light blue tie and a pair of gray gabardine trousers. "What are you doing in town?"

"I had to go to a meeting at Grand Hotel," he said, now standing across the counter.

"What kind of meeting?"

"Colonel Williams wanted to talk to several of us who volunteered for the Home Guard."

"Home Guard? What's that?"

"Aw, it's nothing too important, Kimi," he said, shrugging an awkward shrug and looking at her with a funny expression. "It's just a bunch of men who're supposed to guard places like the Maui Telephone Building, the water reservoir up at Iao Valley and the Maui Electric Building."

"Why can't the Army do that?"

"They can't spare the men. That's why the Colonel wanted to talk to us."

"That means you're not going to be working."

"Not for a while anyway. —Gee, things look pretty bad. The Colonel was telling us that the Japanese people on Maui might start an internal battle in case of an invasion."

"How can he say such a thing," she said, scowling. "He's got no right saying such a thing."

"Well, that's what he told us anyway," George said, shrugging. "You know how these haoles are—all talk. Remember Old Man Richfield, the manager of Valley Isle Plantation? That bastard suggested that as soon as Japanese troops start landing the Colonel should round up about two thousand local Japanese and herd them down the beach waving Japanese flags. He figures the Japanese troops won't dare open fire, and the American forces can start shooting any time they want to."

"He said that!" Kimi's eyebrows jumped up with anger. "How dare he! How would he like to be herded down the beach?"

"Don't get angry with me, Kimi. I didn't say it," George said, holding up his hands at her. "Besides, it'll never happen. The Colonel never go for the idea."

"I'd still like to choke that old man just for suggesting such a terrible thing. Who does he think he is anyway?"

"Aw, Kimi," George said, trying to mollify her. "People like the old man wanna act like big shots shooting off their big mouths. —Look, I have to be going. The other guys waiting for me down the corner. I'll see you later, okay?"

"All right, George," she murmured, puckering up her lips. "Be careful now . . ."

9

KIMI'S FATHER DID not stop at Lin Wo's this morning, but went directly to Yamamoto-san's restaurant on Market Street half a block west of the Main intersection.

"Good morning, Gusuda-san," Yamamoto-san greeted with an owlish grin as Kama stepped into the front door of the warm, old, wooden-floored establishment. "It sure looks like a beautiful day, doesn't it?"

"Yes, it looks like a fine day," Kama agreed, carrying a fifty-gallon slop can and heading directly for the kitchen in the back through the small empty restaurant. Pale, gray-haired Yamamoto-san was sitting alone at the service counter drinking coffee. He had on a white T-shirt dotted here and there with tiny holes, trousers with cuffs rolled up to his ankles and a pair of dull brown shoes.

The kitchen was crowded with two oil stoves, a big refrigerator, two galvanized sinks and two rows of shelves above the service counter in the middle. It smelled strongly of Japanese cooking marinated in soyu sauce. Kama dropped the empty slop can near one of the sinks close to the back door, and was about to pull out the half-filled one from under the sink, when Yamamoto-san said: "Gusuda-san, why don't you sit down and have a cup of coffee with me."

"Ah, thank you. Thank you very much," he said, bowing, taking off his shapeless hat and rubbing it against his slop-stained khaki trousers. He placed his hat on the far edge of the counter, then wiped his hands on his denim shirt.

Yamamoto-san pulled out a chair from under the counter, then, reaching up for a cup, poured coffee into it from a shiny electric coffeepot.

"That's fine, thank you," he said, holding out one hand.

"Gusuda-san," Yamamoto-san whispered, craning his neck looking out at the restaurant, "what did you think of those Japanese pilots yesterday?"

"They were brave. Very brave," he whispered back.

"Who in the world would believe they would do such a daring thing, huh?" Yamamoto-san said, grinning a sly grin, leaning his elbow on the counter, his hand cupped over his mouth. "They sure fooled everyone, didn't they?"

Kama leaned closer. "They must have sunk all the ships in Pea-ru Har-bah."

"And bombed all the airplanes on the ground, too."

"Yes, the airplanes, too."

"You know what I heard, Gusuda-san?" Yamamoto-san whispered softer, once more looking around him with small squinting eyes. "Japanese troops have already landed in Honolulu and are about to take over the Governor's mansion."

"Is that right! When did you hear this?"

"All the Japanese people in Wailuku are talking about it. Someone heard it over the Japan station."

"This is the first I've heard about it," he said, staring into Yamamoto-san's narrowed eyes. "When did the troops land?"

"Last night."

"Were many people killed?" he asked, alarmed.

"No. The 'Merican soldiers hardly put up a fight."

"Does this mean we're practically under Nihon?"

"As soon as the Governor signs the surrender papers it'll be official. Imagine! All of Hawaii a part of Japan," Yamamoto-san said, wringing his hands together.

"When do you think the Governor will sign those papers."

"As soon as they can find him. He's hiding somewhere up in Nuuanu Pali."

"That Governor . . . You can tell just by looking at his pictures that he is the type to be hiding at a time like this."

"Ah-h, it's too good to believe," Yamamoto-san murmured, shaking his head, pouring more coffee into both cups. "Won't that be something? Hawaii becoming Japanese territory."

"It should have been that way long ago," Kama said, sticking his chin out stolidly. "There's more of us here than any other nationality."

"You're right, Gusuda-san. It's only proper that Hawaii should become a part of Japan. —Excuse me, Gusuda-san," Yamamoto-san now said, pushing back his chair and standing up. "I'll have to go to the ben-jo again. I've been so excited all morning, I must have pissed at least a dozen times already. Help yourself to the coffee. There's lots more."

"This is fine. Very fine," he said, watching Yamamoto-san walking through the back door.

Can it be true? Honolulu about to fall? he asked himself, taking another sip, lower lip protruding over his upper one. How come that Kenyei didn't say anything about it this morning? Was that boy holding back news from him?

Yamamoto-san came back in buttoning his fly, leaving streaks of smudges on his trousers as he wiped his hands on it. "Gusuda-san," he said, sitting down, "did you hear about the parachuters that landed at Kihei last night?"

"What parachuters?"

"Japanese parachuters, of course. A whole bunch of them landed last night. They must be hiding in the cane fields. No one seems to know where they've gone."

"What are they doing on Maui?"

"The Puunene Naval Air Station," Yamamoto-san said nodding knowingly.

"Oh, yes. The naval station. Have they taken over that, too?"

"Not yet. They will soon, though. But I think they landed for other reasons also."

"Oh-h?"

"I've got it all figured out, Gusuda-san." Yamamoto-san

leaned over closer. "You see, when I was in the eight grade in Japan—"

"Ah so! You went as far as the eight grade, Yamamoto-san?"

"I'm one of the few Japanese on Maui who went that far in school."

"Well, no wonder you've always been the leader among us here."

"Anyway," Yamamoto-san went on, "when I was taking a course in military strategy in school, we learned that whoever controls the water source controls the land. This is the way I got it figured out: The parachuters that landed last night are trying to take over the water supply. They might be heading for Iao Valley right now."

"What about Kapuna Valley?" Kama asked, shocked. We have a big spring up there, too."

"Yes, Kapuna Valley, too. The troops might be close to your home this very minute."

"What do you think they plan to do?"

"One of two things: Demand that 'Merican forces surrender or they'll threaten to poison the water, or shut off the water supply and distribute it only to us Nihon-jins on the island."

"You really think they might poison the water?"

"Aw, Gusuda-san," Yamamoto-san said, patting Kama's arm, "don't worry. I'm sure the 'Merican troops will surrender. I know . . ." He tapped his forehead with the tip of a finger.

"When do you think they'll reach the springs?"

"That's hard to tell. They have to travel at night."

"What about the Governor in Honolulu? When he signs those papers won't Maui automatically be turned over to Japan, too?"

"Yes, but they'll have to find the Governor first. It may take days."

"Everything would be so simple if that sonnabagun Governor would give himself up," Kama murmured, looking down into his cup again. "Who do you think will run the Japanese government here in Hawaii?"

"It'll be some high-ranking general for a while. Then, they'll send someone else from Japan. Probably one of those

English-speaking dignitaries who will set up a new form of government."

"You think they might send a Nihon-educated Nisei to help them?"

"That could be very possible," Yamamoto-san said, nodding, taking another sip of coffee. "—By the way, isn't your oldest son attending school in Japan?"

"He just graduated from Waseda."

"Ah, so? Waseda? Your son graduated from Waseda? That's wonderful. Just wonderful. He might be the one sent here."

"You really think so?" Kama watched Yamamoto-san with eager eyes.

"Gusuda-san, you're a very lucky man. Your son might be a big shot on Maui. A Waseda graduate? Yes, he's bound to have a high position here."

"Ah-h, thank you. Thank you very much," he acknowledged, bowing a couple of times, chin almost hitting the coffee cup on the counter. He felt his eyes turning watery. Yamamoto-san was indeed a man of great foresight.

"When your son comes to Maui, Gusuda-san, you must introduce me to him. After all, you and I have been friends for many years."

"Yes, of course. I'll be glad to do that. I'm sure my son will be very pleased to meet you, Yamamoto-san."

"You're so fortunate to have a son educated in Japan, Gusuda-san. My wife and I never had a son; just a daughter—a daughter who married some stupid Nisei who can hardly speak Nihon-go. I even hate to call him my son-in-law. You know who I'm talking about?"

"You mean that young Nisei policeman, Watanabe? He gave me a ticket about a month ago for going twenty-five miles in a twenty-mile zone."

"That's my son-in-law all right. He'd even give me a ticket for that, that stupid boy. Why, last night, he almost turned me in to the FBI."

"You? The father of his own wife? What happened?"

"Well, he and my daughter came over to have dinner with us. When we were all through eating and were sitting in the living room talking about the attack, my daughter asked me how long I thought the war might last. No sooner had I told her it wouldn't last very long, we were practically in Japanese hands, than that empty-headed boy began shouting something about turning me to the FBI if he ever heard me saying that again. Me! His own father-in-law," Yamamoto-san said, greatly distressed, head going from side to side. "What can you do with a boy like that!"

Kama looked astoundedly at Yamamoto-san for a while.

"Yamamoto-san," he finally said, standing up and reaching over for his hat on the counter. "The Niseis don't know what they're doing anymore."

"That is so. Yes, that is so . . ." Yamamoto-san agreed, head held sideways, also standing up.

"I'll have to be going," Kama said, stepping over to the half-filled garbage can under the sink and sliding it out, then replacing it with the empty one.

"Let me help you, Gusuda-san," Yamamoto-san volunteered, reaching for the other handle.

They carried the can through the still-empty restaurant and out to the pickup parked alongside the curb.

"Sayonara. And thank you again." Kama said, bowing once, touching the brim of his hat. He got up front and drove away, heading for Domingo Garcia's restaurant on the next block. He wasn't going over to Lin Wo's today, or any other day, until Lin and his sassy boy apologized for the humiliating way they had treated him yesterday morning. Those two Pah-kes can eat their slop, for all he cared.

He parked in front of the Valley Place and walked into the horseshoe-shaped restaurant with an empty slop can. There were several people sitting at the counter having breakfast. A dark Kanaka waitress waited on them in the horseshoe. He went past them into the hot kitchen where the Filipino cook was frying something in a big skillet. The kitchen was no bigger than Yamamoto-san's, but instead of smelling of Japanese food it smelled of fried bacon and ham. He hoped that fat Porlegee owner wasn't in to harass him this morning.

Stepping up to the sink, he slid out the nearly filled garbage can from under it.

"Hey, you! Gusuda! Come here!" It was Domingo Garcia's strong voice from the small office at the far corner of the kitchen. That fat bugga was in after all.

He left the can sitting there on the floor and walked up to the screen door beside the tall refrigerator. "Good-u mornin', Domingo-san," he greeted, taking off his hat, bowing once.

"Come in, Gusuda. I wanna talk to you," Domingo Garcia said, speaking through the side of his mouth, a crumpled, unlit cigar jumping up and down between his flabby lips.

The office had hardly enough space for a desk and a chair, let alone space for fat-assed Domingo Garcia sitting on one corner of the desk, his legs dangling down.

He opened the screen door, stepped in, and stood uncomfortably, his hat held before him with fingers fidgeting at its brim. Domingo Garcia, a dark, heavy-jowled man with a big nose, dull brown eyes framed at the top by thick, bushy eyebrows, a tuft of grayish hair on the tip of his semi-bald head, studied him for a second or two.

"You just come from Yamamoto's place?"

"Yes, yes. I just come Yamamoto place," he answered, grinning a toothy grin.

"He say anything to you about the attack yesterday?"

"Him? Yamamoto-san? Oh, no. He no say nothin'."

"Now, don't lie to me, goddamnit!"

"Oh, no. No lie you, Domingo-san."

"You better not, Gusuda." Domingo Garcia pulled out the shredded cigar from between his wet lips and held it with thumb and middle finger of his right hand, waving it back and forth before Kama's eyes. "That no-good Jap-anee! I think he's a spy."

"Yamamoto-san, spy? Oh, no. Him, good-u man."

"Good man, hell! The only thing he's good for is stealing my customers. Every damn time I bring my prices down, he brings his lower. That sonofabitch! You tell him, Gusuda; you tell him I ever catch him making a false move I'm gonna have his ass turned over to the FBI. Understand?"

"You turn ah-ss FBI. No worry, me understand,"

"Another thing. You tell him I know he donated bags of rice to that—that Jap-anee ship that came here last year. That naval training ship—"

"Shintoku Maru."

"Yeah, 'at's the one, Shin— Whatever the hell its name was. Anyway, you tell him I know all about it. And I saw him leading that big ban-zai rally down at the Buddhist

Temple in Kahului the night before that ship sailed. You tell him he fucks around with me I'll really have his tail up the creek. Understand!"

"He no hock ah-round you. You send tail Greek. Me tell 'em."

"What about you, Gusuda? You gave something to that ship?" Domingo Garcia questioned suspiciously.

"Me? Oh, no. Too poor, too poor . . ."

"You have no right giving anything to Japan. You're not a goddamn Jap-anee; you're Okinawan."

"Yes, yes, me Okinawan," He grinned a self-effacing grin. How long was this going to go on? he wondered. Damned fat Porlegee! Not Jap-ance; Okinawan . . . Stupid Okole. He didn't even know that his Kanaka waitress was being paid by Yamamoto-san for sending customers over to Yamamoto-san's restaurant.

"Who you think gonna win the war?" Domingo Garcia interrogated, placing the cigar back into his mouth, eyeing Kama with harsh, cold eyes.

"War, no good. No good. Too many people die."

"Who you think gonna win?"

"Nobody win. Only lotsa men die."

"You think Japan might win?"

"Japan? Oh, I dunno. I dunno who win."

"You think America might win?"

"Yes. Maybe . . ."

"Goddamn you, Gusuda! Tell me, who you want win the war? Japan or America?"

"War no good. No good."

"You damned stupid Okinawan! Why can't you say you want America win the war? You're not Jap-anee; you're Okinawan. How many times I have to tell you that? Sometimes I don't know what to make of you. You're either so goddamn stupid you don't know a fucking thing, or you're smart enough to keep your mouth shut."

"Yes, yes . . . Don' know hockin' t'ing." He kept nodding, grinning.

"Well, anyway, Gusuda, you're lucky you're in Hawaii, not Japan."

"Oh, yes. Lucky come Hawaii!"

"Now, I don't want you going around spying for Japan.

And don't talk to that no-good Yamamoto about the war. You hear anything suspicious about him you let me know right away. Okay?"

"Righ' 'way. Righ' 'way."

"You think Yamamoto might be related to Admiral Yamamoto?"

"Him? Yamamoto-san and Ad-mi-ra-ru Yamamoto? I no t'ink so, Domingo-san. You t'ink so?"

"They have the same name, don't they?"

"Domingo-san," Kama said, lowering his eyes for a second, "you heah behore t'is Filipino boxing champion, Garcia?"

"Ceferino Garcia, middleweight champion of the world? Sure, I've heard about him."

"You, him, rerated?"

Domingo Garcia stared piercingly into Kama's eyes. "Goddamnit! Gusuda! Don't start wising up with me!" The cigar in his mouth jumped up and down, his face blood-red.

Kama kept his eyes down, fighting back a grin, pressing the hat brim tight between his fingers.

After several seconds of tense silence, Domingo Garcia said: "Look, Gusuda, I wanna talk business with you."

"Oh-h?"

"How many chickens you got at your farm? Two-three thousand?"

"Maybe, four thousand."

"That many, eh? Well, that's good. How many incubators you got?"

"I havo two."

"You using them now?"

"No. Don' want no more chickens. No feed."

"That's what I wanted to talk to you about. You see, my brother, Tony—he owns Maui Feed Company—he can sell me all the chicken feed I want. You need it. Right?"

"Oh, yes, yes. No more feed; no more chicken. Pretty soon, boat no come from 'Merica with chicken feed."

"All right then. I'll have Tony sell you all the feed you need if you'll sell me your chickens, eggs and little chicks at a discount."

"What kind of dis-coun-tu?" he questioned, not quite comprehending.

"Twenty-five percent."

"Twenty-five pah-cen-tu! Oh, Domingo-san. No more profit for me."

"No discount; no feed, Gusuda. You want all your chickens to die?"

He eyed Domingo Garcia with tight, grimacing face, then slowly looked down at his soiled hat.

"Aw, Gusuda. . . Sure, you'll make a profit. From now on everything's gonna go sky high. My brother Tony's gonna make money; I'm gonna make money; and you, Gusuda, you're gonna make lotsa money."

"Even with big dis-coun-tu?"

"Why not? The price of food—especially poultry products —gonna go up. I sell 'em high to customers; you sell 'em high to me."

"Ah-h, so?"

"You get what I'm trying to say, Gusuda? It's a deal?" Domingo Garcia said, chewing on his cigar and patting Kama's shoulder meaningfully.

"You lemme t'ink over few days."

"Whatdahell is there to think over? Like I said: 'No feed; no chickens'."

"Me t'ink over first. Okay?" Kama opened the screen door. Domingo Garcia followed him out.

"Well, okay, then. I'll give you few days to think it over," he said softly, stepping over to the slop can where Kama stood. "Only a few days, now. I have to let Tony know right away who he's supposed to sell the feed to."

"A'righ', me let you know soon," Kama promised, bending down to lift the slop can.

"Here, Gusuda. Let me help you. The damn thing's too heavy for you to carry by yourself," Domingo Garcia offered, taking hold of the other side of the can.

They walked out the kitchen, passed through the horseshoe-shaped restaurant, and out to the pickup.

He started the pickup, pulled out of the curb and drove down the slight hill to the iron bridge in lower Wailuku, then up the bend to the highway. It was still a crisp, sunny December morning, but dark clouds were accumulating over towards the West Maui mountains, and the green sugar cane leaves were fluttering against the strong mountain wind.

Who to believe? Who to believe? he thought, scratching his head. Yamamoto-san said Hawaii was as good as in Japanese hands; Domingo Garcia said everyone will make lots of money, implying the war was going to last a long time. He pressed the gas pedal a little further down. He wanted to get home as fast as he could so he could start preparing for all possible catastrophes. Maybe, Shiroma, Kenyei, will have good news tonight. Kenyei seemed more reliable than anyone else. He got his news directly from Japan.

As soon as Kama reached home he backed the pickup up to the ramp, dumped all the slop into the big boiler, then hurried over to the house where his wife was just about to leave for the garden.

"Basan," he said, meeting her at the back porch, "you won't have time to work in the garden today. We have more important things to do."

"What important things?" she questioned, holding her Mother Hubbard straw hat in her hand. She was already dressed in her gardening outfit: a ragged, black blouse and a baggy, soiled black skirt tied at the waist with a stringy cord. She had been ready to put on her ta-bes when Kama approached her.

"Gather all the empty containers you can find—gallon jugs, pots, pans, barrels; anything else we can fill with water."

Tsuyu stood there, looking at him bemusedly. "Jisan," she at last said, studying him, sniffing, "have you been drinking so early in the morning?"

"Baka! Who's been drinking!" he scolded. "The water might be poisoned by Japanese parachuters. And the Governor in Honolulu might not be found for a long time."

"Who told you all this?" She kept sniffing with wrinkled nose.

"Yamamoto-san, that's who."

"How does Yamamoto-san know all these things?"

"Basan! Don't keep standing there like a fat scarecrow asking me these silly questions. How should I know how Yamamoto-san know all these things? He's Yamamoto-san, isn't he? For all I know he might be related to Admiral Yamamoto. Just do as I say before it's too late. I'll have to go over to the pig pens and fill the barrels with water."

She laid her hat on the rail of the small, grimy back porch made of widely spaced one-by-six's, then hurried down the three loose steps and went under the house to gather the jugs he kept there.

In about half an hour, after he had filled all the slop cans and barrels full of water at the pig pens, he went back into the house to help Tsuyu wash the gallon jugs.

"Jisan, you sure the parachuters landed just to poison the water?" she asked, washing the last two remaining gallon jugs at the kitchen sink with a long bristle brush while he stood beside her, watching.

"Why else would they land? Don't you know that whoever controls the water source controls the land? Every military strategist knows that."

She looked up at him, greatly impressed. "Don't you think the parachuters know they're many of us Japanese here on Maui, too?"

"Basan! Stop asking me so many questions. There's nothing like taking precautions," he said, giving her a stern look. "It's not costing us anything to fill these jugs with water. The jugs should have been washed long time ago anyway."

She stopped washing. Gave him a suspicious look. "You're not having me wash these just for your sake, are you?"

"Of course not. I told you. It's for storing drinking water. —Talking about sake, it reminds me I have to brew more today. Remember what Higa-san said about welcoming the Japanese troops with home-brewed sake? I think I'll gather all the wooden crocks I can from the people in the valley and brew as much as I can."

"Aw, Jisan, I'm sure the troops will bring their own sake from Japan."

"But it may not be as good as mine."

Before Tsuyu could say anything more, he stepped out of the kitchen, went down to the pickup to begin driving around Kapuna Valley looking for wooden crocks.

He was back in about an hour with six twenty-gallon crocks, and started right away with the culturing which involved steaming pots full of rice and putting them in the crocks with carefully measured portions of water and uncooked koji rice. He planned to let the mixture stand for at least five days. Then, he planned to add more rice and koji—this time both ingredients uncooked. As the fermentation got stronger he would add greater portions of raw rice and Koji until the crocks would nearly bubble like hot lava. He intended to cut the fermentation period in half. There was no telling when the troops would come to Maui.

"Basan, be sure to have all our slippers lined up carefully on the porch tonight before going to bed," he told Tsuyu when they were, at last, able to take a break from the hustling and bustling since his return from Wailuku. It was noon now and they were sitting on the lowest of the three loose steps of the back porch, their feet resting on the ground.

"Huh?" she said, looking at him, pushing back strands of hair over one eye. "Why do you want me to do that?"

"We have to be prepared for everything at times like this. The troops might come to the valley at night while we're sleeping and won't know this is a Japanese home unless we leave some made-in-Japan goods out on the porch."

"That's a good idea," she agreed. "I'll be sure to do that tonight. —By the way, Jisan, what's that gallon of paint doing there?" she asked curiously, pointing to a can behind him on the top step.

"I left it there a few minutes ago," he answered. "As soon as I hear Japanese airplanes coming I plan to climb up the house and paint our red roof all white, except for one big circle in the middle. When the Japanese pilots fly over they're bound to notice the Rising Sun and will be careful not to bomb close by."

"You think that's a good idea? What if the airplanes turn out to be 'Mericans?"

He gave her a blank-faced look. "Don't you think I know the difference between a Japanese and 'Merican plane?" he said, frowning. "Besides, I can always paint the entire roof white, can't I?"

"Why don't you get some blue paint, too?" she remarked, her small brown eyes behind the rimless glasses twinkling teasingly.

"Baka! This is no time to be joking!" he scolded, his own eyes behind the steel-rimmed bifocals beginning to narrow brightly, a broad smile starting from the corners of his mouth.

They sat there, eyes locked with each other's for a second or two, then suddenly broke out laughing.

After wiping the tears from the corners of his eyes and putting his glasses back on, Kama gazed up the high, cloud-draped mountains. "I think it's going to rain pretty soon."

"Yes, it looks like it," she said, glancing up at the mountains, too.

"You think Kenyei will be coming over tonight?"

"He always does, rain or no rain. Ishi will probably be coming with him."

"That good-for-nothing Ishi! I'm going to have him start digging a bomb shelter for us, and have him make up for drinking my sake all these years."

"Have him dig one over there," Tsuyu said, pointing to the upper bank of the short trail leading up to the out-house. "Saburo can help him dig it."

10

DIGGING A BOMB shelter couldn't have been any further from Sab's thoughts when he went to school and was told there would be no classes until further notice. He had wanted very much to see Miss Blake and find out whether she had changed at all since his dream the other night, but he was so happy about the notice he forgot all about her.

Instead of going straight home like most of the other kids did, he had gotten off the bus in uptown Wailuku and had walked over to the corner of Vineyard and Market, hoping he'd run into his friend, Yosh Nakata. Sure enough, Yosh, dressed in deep-pleated black slacks, a printed silk shirt tucked in smartly, and a pair of shiny black shoes, had walked down Vineyard at about eight-thirty. It was a little windy, and as Sab stood barefooted in front of the corner barber shop with Yosh, the bright morning sun already bearing down from the other side of the street, he could smell the nose-tingling stench of sugar cane coming from the mill a mile down the street. He was clad in his school clothes of tight, peg-legged khaki trousers and a bright red and white aloha shirt dangling out.

"Who you think gonna win the war?" he asked Yosh leaning back against the plate glass window of the unopened barber shop, rubbing his bare feet on the damp concrete walk. (A sign inside the glass door said: Open at Ten.)

"Aw-w, I don't know . . ." Yosh answered, speaking through the side of his mouth. "As long as I don't have to go in the goddamn Army whodahell cares."

"I heard lotsa guys went down the armory to volunteer."

"Bunch of suckers," Yosh said, a grim, sneering-frowning expression pulling the corners of his mouth, his soft black hair fallen over his forehead.

"I bet there gonna be plenty of crap games, eh?" he said, lifting one foot back against the ledge.

"Yeah, they'll be lotta money floating around all right," Yosh agreed in a sardonic tone. He flipped his butt out on the street after taking a long drag.

"Why don't you volunteer? You can take care all the guys."

"Who? Me? Volunteer!" He gave Sab a wry look. "You nuts or somet'ing? Besides, even if I volunteered they wouldn't take me," he added lamely. "I got a bum ticker" sticking his thumb on the left side of his chest.

"Oh, yeah, I forget about t'at," he said, looking away. "I sure wish I was eighteen. I'd go down and volunteer right now."

"Those goddamn Buddhaheads! They sure pulled a fast one, eh?—bombing Pearl Harbor like that. Bunch of sneaky buggas." Yosh was grinning in that sneering way of his again.

"My old man thinks Japan gonna take over the islands in couple of days," Sab said, grinning.

"All them old Japanee people must be praying for Japan to take over," Yosh said. "Damn fools! They don't know when they're well-off."

"What you think gonna happen if Japan ever took over?"

"Who knows? Maybe we have to go back to Japanee school."

"Oh, ca-rist! Not t'at."

"What's the matter with going back to Japanee school?"

"No tell me you used to like it?"

Yosh grinned. "Them mean Japanee school teachers. I used to get beat up all the time. Once, I was playing Yo-Yo in class, and when the teacher caught me, he gave me a solid whack on the head with his book. I took the Yo-Yo in my hand and hit the teacher right in the eye with it."

"No-o kidding. What happened then?"

"You don't think I stuck around. I took off for the door."

"He ever catch you?"

"You kidding? I ran so fast he couldn't catch me even if he was Jesse Owens himself. I neve' went back to Japanee school no more after t'at."

Sab burst out laughing. "What about your old folks? They ever find out?"

"Naw-w . . . I always went home late after English school was over. They thought I was still going to Japanee school every afternoon."

"When I used to get beat up by the teacher, I'd go home and get beat up again by my old man," Sab said. "He always used to tell me I must have done something real wrong, or the teacher wouldn't have hit me. Damn old man! Whatever the Japanee teachers did was okay by him. Ca-rist! I hope the Buddhaheads don't take over the islands. I hate to have a lousy teacher kick my ass every day."

Yosh roared with laughter shaking his head. "Aw, maybe the Buddhaheads neve' planned to take over the islands," he said, looking across the street again as though expecting someone. "If they wanted to, they could've taken over yesterday."

"You think so?"

"Why would Japan want Hawaii? We got not'ing here except a bunch of diehard Buddhaheads and fat hula-hula Ti-tas. What they want, I think, is oil and rubber and things like that in those islands near Australia"

When Sab said nothing, Yosh asked, "you notice anything different about Market Street this morning?" glancing down the street, grinning a sly grin to himself.

"Different?"

"Look at all the American flags in front of the stores."

"Oh, t'at . . ."

"Take a look at what stores have them."

Sab still did not know what Yosh was driving at.

"Goddamn Buddhaheads," Yosh said wryly. "Every one of those stores are owned by some Japanee."

Sab looked across the street again. Yosh was right. In

front of almost every Japanee store was an American flag flapping against the brisk early-morning breeze. That was a good one! Only the other day the same stores had Japanee flags waving in front of them.

"Look at t'at one over there," Yosh said, throwing his head toward the right. "Yesterday, it was Nippon Store. Today, it's Victory Store. You see what I mean when I tell you about them two-faced bastards?" he went on, a thin grin pulling the corners of his mouth. "The minute Japan invade Hawaii, t'at sonofabitch gonna take down t'at Victory sign and put back Nippon again."

They both laughed out loud.

"If the Buddhaheads ever start bombing this town the first thing I'm gonna do is run like hell over to t'at jewelry store—" pointing down towards Pacific Jewelries, a block away.

"What for?"

"They're loaded with diamonds. I wanna get my share before somebody beats me to it."

"You mean loot the place?"

"Whatdahell! Like they say: 'Everything's fair in love and war.' "

Yosh sure was a funny guy sometimes. One minute he was talking about the hypocrisy of others; the very next minute he was talking about looting a place.

"T'at Doc Kong," Yosh grumbled, looking down at his glittering, diamond-studded wrist watch. "He told me he was gonna meet me here at eight-thirty. It's already nine."

"Who's Doc Kong?"

"Some Pah-ke guy I'm supposed to be working a deal with."

"Anything big?"

Yosh turned and looked at Sab with a hard expression, then turned his head up front again and gazed across the street. "It's gonna be a big one if we can pull it right."

"What kind deal you guys working on?"

"Aw, you don't wanna get involved in something like this," Yosh said, avoiding Sab's eyes.

"For crying out loud . . ."

Yosh was now looking across the street at a tall, slim man coming towards them. The man wore thick horn-rimmed glasses and had on a gray felt hat with a colorful pheasant lei woven around it. The hat was tilted jauntily to one side of his head.

" 'At's Doc," Yosh told Sab.

"What d'ya say, Yosh?" the slim man said, approaching them. The man gazed over once at Sab.

"Anything new?" Yosh asked.

"No," the man answered. He glanced over at Sab again. "The damned war screwed up the works. No transportation."

"T'at means we don't know when Ah Hong can bring over the shipment?" Yosh asked, thin lips drawn tight over clenched teeth.

Sab turned around and looked inside the semi-dark barber shop, easily overhearing what they were saying.

"Well, he called me from Honolulu this morning," the man answered Yosh. "He said he was gonna call again as soon as he knew when he can fly over."

"Damn war," Yosh said. "It's fouling up everything."

"Just when we had the set-up going good, too," the man said.

"You talked to Clarence Wo?"

"Yeah. I went over the restaurant and told him about the delay."

"What he say?"

"Aw, that Pah-ke. You know how he is?—always bitching about something. But don't worry about him. I got him sewed-up pretty good."

Sab turned around. After glancing up at the tall, slim man for a second, he looked away towards Main.

"Wait any longer Lin Wo might change his mind," Yosh told the man.

"Naw-w, I don't think so," the man said. "Everything's gonna work out okay. It's just a matter of time."

Sab could feel the man eyeing him with distrust as Yosh said: "Don't worry about Sab. He's all right. He's the kid I was telling you about—we was in Molokai together."

"Oh-h, he's the one," the man said. "—I heard about you," he told Sab. "I heard you and Yosh did pretty good in Molokai."

Sab grinned nonchalantly.

"He can hold his own," Yosh told Doc Kong. "Maybe, we can use him in the deal, huh?"

"Well, I don't know," Doc said, shrugging. "We'll see . . ."

Sab broke open into a gleeful smile. He sure wanted to know more about the deal. He learned from Yosh, though, never to ask too many questions if meeting a gambler for the first time.

"How'd you make out in the crap game Saturday night?" Doc asked Yosh, taking out a silver dollar from his pocket and flipping it back and forth over the back of his fingers.

The guy was terrific! Sab thought, watching Doc's fingers in action. Doc winked at him and continued flipping the coin over and over.

"T'at lousy up-and-up game," Yosh grumbled. "I dropped over five hundred."

"Who was the big winner?"

"Moncado. He must have cleaned up over a grand."

"That lucky Filipino. Heard he's been on a long winning streak."

"Yeah. And the guy's so stupid you wonder howdahell he knows when he makes a pass."

Doc laughed. "Those ignorant Ba-yaus," he said. "They're all the same. Moncado probably gonna blow his bundle on some fat wahine."

"I like to get hold of some of his bankroll," Yosh said.

"Why don't you get him in a piute game? You shouldn't have any trouble taking him. Use your marked deck."

"He's too smart for that. I took him for over a hundred the other week. He won't play me no more."

"What about poker?"

"I don't know . . ." Yosh said, placing one foot back on the ledge, watching Doc's fingers going through the same sleek motions with the silver coin. "If I approached him he's gonna think something fishy going on."

"Where's he now?" Doc asked.

"Up by the pool hall. He must be showing off his bankroll to the rest of them Ba-yaus." Yosh stepped over to the end of the building and looked up Vineyard. "Yeah, he's still there," he said, stepping back.

"You think he might be interested in chopping somebody?" Doc asked, grinning a conniving grin.

"He's a greedy bastard. He's always trying to chop somebody."

"Why don't we use Sab here for bait?" Doc said, suddenly enthused, sticking his coin back into his pocket.

"What you have in mind?"

Doc, huddling with Yosh and Sab against the barber shop window, took about five minutes to explain exactly what he had in mind.

"All right, here's what we do," Doc said now, sticking his hand into his pocket and bringing out a thick wad of greenbacks. "—Yosh, you have any 'C' notes?"

After taking two one-hundred-dollar bills from Yosh and counting off three more from his own roll, Doc stuck several dollar bills between the five "C" notes. "Here, Sab," he said, handing him the thick wad of greenbacks. "Put it in your pocket."

Sab fondled the bankroll, fascinated for a second, then stuck it into his pocket with care, waiting for more instructions.

They went over the plan once more. "You understand what you're supposed to do, Sab?"

"Yeah, sure." He was already experiencing a tense, half-scared, half-exhilarating sensation working up in him.

"Okay, then. We got everything set. Right?" Doc said, walking away to the end of the building and looking back over his shoulder. "I'm gonna go up to your room, Yosh. Give me about five minutes before you send Sab up the pool hall."

Yosh's pale, taut face had taken on new life. His small dark eyes were glittering, thin lips twitching at the corners, forehead furrowed with deep, tense lines.

"You think it's gonna work?" Sab asked anxiously.

"We got a helluva good chance. I sure like to take t'at bastard."

"Which one is Moncado?" he asked, stepping over to the corner and looking up Vineyard.

"T'at one," Yosh pointed. "The one with the striped pants." He stepped back quickly. "You see him?"

"You mean the short one with long, bushy hair?"

"Yeah, 'at's him."

"He sure looks mean."

"You got nothing to worry about."

"How I gonna know when to make my move?"

"Doc'll let you know," Yosh said, grinning mischievously.

"T'at Doc, he sure is a sleek one, huh?"

"He knows all the angles."

"How come they call him 'Doc'?"

"From what I heard he used to be a pre-med student at University of Hawaii. He got kicked out when they caught him running poker and crap games at the dormitory."

Sab eyed Yosh. Yosh wasn't kidding.

Doc, Sab had noted, was about forty. He had small slitted eyes behind thick glasses, and the hairline above his ears was slightly gray. Like Yosh, he had a continuous sour grin on his pale face which would break off into a sneering-frowning grin every so often. He and Yosh talked a great deal alike—that George Raft gangster-style through the side of the mouth.

"You gotta do it right so Moncado will bite hook, line and sinker," Yosh said, briefing him once more.

Sab looked into Yosh's cold, determined eyes, somehow expecting Yosh to slap him on the back and whisper, "This is it!"

He walked up to the pool hall where a bunch of Filipinos were standing outside the doorway looking in at a Japanese boy and a middle-aged Pah-ke bucking each other in six-ball rotation at the first table. It was only a little after nine, but the three tables in the small, dimly lit, Filipino-cigar-smelling pool hall were already occupied. Must be because of the war, he told himself, now standing at the doorway and watching the contest at the first table. The war was a good excuse for not going to work in the cane fields.

The first two tables were set parallel to each other, the third one way inside practically against the far corner wall, hardly any playing room around it. Next to it was a Coke machine and a dingy cigarette counter. Sitting on the grimy, time-worn wooden benches were several elderly Pah-ke and Japanee men who spat heedlessly on the unkept concrete floor even though there were couple of spittoons beside the benches. When the Japanee boy had run through the rest of the balls after sinking the first one on the break, the elderly Japanee men on one side of the pool hall murmured their approval, one of them clapping triumphantly.

An old, hunched, gray-haired Filipino racked up the balls

in his triangle rack while the Pah-ke pool shark quitely handed over a dollar bill to the Japanee boy and waited for the boy to make another break.

Glancing side-eyed, Sab noticed Moncado standing to the right of him just outside the doorway. He was talking in loud Filipino dialect to two compatriots, throwing in a few broken English words in between, sounding like a hen cackling away. He was a stocky, dark-complexioned Filipino with a swath of thick, greasy black hair combed straight back and sticking up at the top. He was bragging how he had broken up a crap game by making a half-dozen straight passes and no one wanting to fade him.

Sab waited a few more minutes, then finally approached Moncado.

"Say, my friend," he addressed the well-dressed Filipino friendlily. "How about changing a hundred-dollar bill for me, huh?"—sticking his hand into his pocket and taking out the wad of greenbacks.

Moncado, smoking a long acrid-smelling Filipino rope cigar, turned away from his compatriots and faced Sab. His dark brown eyes suddenly bulged out, staring at the bills in Sab's tight fist. Quickly, he dug into his own pocket, counted off four twenties and two tens, and handed them over, taking back a "C" note in return.

"Thank you, my friend," Sab said, smiling boyishly. He stuck his bankroll back into his pocket, swaggered across the street to the grocery store where he purchased a pack of Luckies, then returned to the doorway of the pool hall.

While standing there smoking away, he gazed over towards the unopened photography shop on the other side of the narrow alley. Yosh was sitting alone on the elevated edge of the shop's door. He turned his head back and watched the pool game. After a minute or two, he looked down again and noticed Moncado sitting beside Yosh. They were whispering to each other, and just before he turned his head again, caught both of them glancing furtively at his direction.

The third time he gazed over, he saw Doc Kong sitting with Yosh and Moncado.

In a few minutes Moncado came over and stood next to him. Moncado began kibitizing the slender, yellowish-looking Japanee pool shark.

"Whatsamattah, Tommy? You no shoot too good today, huh? No can win?" he teased.

"C'mon, Moncado. Get in the game," the toothless Japanee boy coaxed.

"Oh, no. Not me. You no take my money today, Tommy," Moncado said, looking at the other on-lookers, laughing good-naturedly. They all laughed, one of the elderly Pah-ke men saying: "Go on, Moncado. You play 'em."

"Oh, no," Moncado declined again, puffing on his rope cigar, spitting on the floor at his feet with a loud hawking sound. "No-o, I no play him no more."

There was a sudden collective silence in the pool hall as the Pah-ke pool shark now took a leaning, ass-in-the-air stance at the other end of the table and stroked his long, shiny pool stick expertly through a tight arched bridge of his left hand, aiming it at the white spotless cue ball. A cra-a-cking clean shot sent six colored balls streaking all over the green felt table, one of them dropping into the far corner pocket.

"You, Wailuku boy?" Moncado asked Sab amiably, the cigar bobbing up and down between his dark purplish lips.

"No. Kahului."

"Oh-h . . . 'At's why I neve' see you here bepor'. What 'cha name?"

"Johnny Chang."

"Mine, Moncado." He winked once. He leaned closer. "You wanna play poker?"

Sab drew his head back and gave Moncado a disdainful look. "Poker?"

"We get nice game soon."

"Where?"

"Upstairs."

"What kind of game?"

"Draw. Table stake."

"Who's gonna play?"

"You no worry about t'at. Everybody nice pellows," Moncado answered, pronouncing his "f's" like "p's" as most first-generation Filipinos did. "You wanna play?"

"How many guys?"

"Pour of us. Everybody got lotsa money."

Sab pondered. He kept looking at Moncado half-interestedly.

"You see t'em two pellows?" Moncado said, pointing to Doc and Yosh. "T'ey got lotsa money."

Sab scratched his head. "When they wanna play?"

"Any time," Moncado said. "You stay here. I come back." He went over quickly to Doc and Yosh.

He was back in a minute.

"Yeah, Johnny," he whispered. "T'ose two pellows, t'ey wanna play now. C'mon, we talk to t'em."

Sab followed Moncado. Doc and Yosh standing up, were involved in some private conversation.

"Hey, pellows," Moncado said, "t'is Johnny. He wanna play poker."

"That's good," Doc said enthusiastically, smiling friendlily. "We can start with a four-hand game. Someone else might join in later. Let's go upstairs to my room."

As four of them walked through the narrow alley which separated the pool hall from the photography shop, Yosh, turning to Sab, asked: "Where you from, Johnny?"

"Johnny he come from Kahului," Moncado volunteered.

"Kahului, eh?" Yosh said.

Doc led them up a flight of stairs behind the pool hall to a thin wooden door where he took out a set of keys from his pocket and unlocked it.

Walking into the small room, Sab noticed at once that it was a regular hotel room with a face basin in one corner and a single bed set against the door-side of the wall. Between the bed and the far wall was a round, green felt-covered poker table with slots for seven players. Directly above it was a cone-shaped light bulb hanging from the low ceiling. There were two windows: one looking out at the Iao mountains; the other, just above the bed, facing the alley. Both were wide open, no curtains, a nice cool breeze coming from the mountains.

"You sit there, Johnny," Doc suggested, pointing to a folding metal chair close to the door. Doc sat to the left of Sab, Yosh directly across and Moncado to the right.

"We play table stake, huh?" Moncado said, taking out his fat bankroll and unfolding it arrogantly on the table.

"Yeah, table stake—five dollar ante," Yosh said sullenly, also taking out his bankroll. "Let's make the game interesting, eh?"

Doc and Sab brought out their money and laid them on the table, too. As Sab flattened out the layers of bills before him, he could feel Moncado leaning over close, staring at the money with his large ping-pong-ball eyes. For a flashing second, just as he reached over to cut the deck Doc had shuffled, he caught Moncado winking a sly wink at Yosh.

Doc began dealing out the cards with smooth adeptness. The game was going to be played with two decks. The other deck was already in front of Yosh, ready to be dealt out as soon as the present hand was over. Doc intended to gather the played cards and shuffle them for Moncado; the sequence going around the table so there would be no delay. Pair of jacks or better were openers; jokers only for aces, straights or flushes; nothing else wild. If there were no openers the succeeding openers were pair of queens or better, and so on ...

Sab, picking up his five cards for the first hand, couldn't help feeling he was taking part in some kind of a theatrical play, auditioned, rehearsed and plotted. He gazed over at Yosh who was playing his role better than ham movie gamblers. And Doc kept fumbling with his cards as though his life depended on them. He studied them with great suspense then, quickly folding them, began shuffling them over and over in his hands, squinting eyes behind the thick glasses darting around the table.

Moncado squeezed out his cards one at a time, eyes narrowed sneakingly. He folded them together again, took several snappy puffs on his big cigar and looked over at Yosh.

Sab could hardly believe he was playing in a table stake game. Feeling an exciting, flaming streak kindling in the pit of his stomach, he squeezed out the cards one at a time.

Pair of queens! He waited for the action to start.

"Pass" Yosh grunted through the side of his mouth.

"Open," Moncado said, throwing in a ten among the ante.

Sab studied Moncado's beaming eyes for a second. He called.

"Pass," Doc said, folding his cards and laying them on the table, face down. "How many cards you want, Moncado"

"Tree."

Sab gazed over at Moncado again, asked for two.

Moncado remained breathlessly still, studying his pick-ups. He turned and glared at Sab. "I check."

Damnit! Sab had not picked up anything.

Clearing his throat, he muttered: "I bet ten," throwing a ten-dollar bill into the pot.

Moncado looked down at his cards, up at Sab, hesitated, then turned his cards over to show his openers. A pair of jacks. "Sonnavabitch!" he mourned.

Whew! Sab raked in the pot.

"Hey, kid, you're lucky, huh?" Moncado said, forcing a ring of dry laughter. He patted Sab's shoulder. "When you win first game, 'at's good."

Sab caught Moncado winking again—this time to Doc while Yosh started dealing out the cards.

The game progressed in a tense, smouldering tempo for the next hour with Sab gradually building up his bankroll to eight hundred dollars—thanks to Doc and Yosh who had tried bluffing him several times and forcing Moncado out.

The only oddity up till now had been Yosh's consistent refusal to cut the deck. After a while, rather than bothering Yosh, Moncado had gotten into the habit of dealing out the cards without having them cut at all.

Then, it happened!

While Moncado was dealing out the cards this time, Sab felt a sharp kick on his left leg under the table from Doc's direction, and as he glanced over, caught Doc's small beady eyes behind the glasses winking couple of times.

He sat up straight, his throat constricting, avoiding Doc's eyes, wondering howdahell Doc did it.

Picking up his five cards and looking down at them, he nearly jumped clear up from his chair. He shuffled them slowly, nervously, taking in several deep breaths, watching Moncado side-eyed, fighting to appear as calm as humanly possible.

Moncado picked up his cards and began squeezing each one painstakingly as though having some kind of power over them. After peeking at the first three, he puffed a couple of fast puffs on his rope cigar and shifted it excitedly to the other corner of his mouth. He commenced squeezing, now almost in a trance, eyes wide, intense, smoke coming out steadily from his mouth.

Quickly he shoved the cards together and remained breathless. He looked at the faces before him with a sly grin.

Sab threw in a ten for openers.

Doc stayed in. So did Yosh.

Moncado peeked at his cards once more, then laid them down on the table face down. "Ten and one hundred more," he stammered, laying the money in the middle of the table, the grin on his smug face almost exploding into gleeful laughter.

Sab reshuffled his cards, paused, glanced over at Moncado. "I'll call."

Doc gave his cards another fast study. "That's too high for me."

Yosh studied Moncado, then Sab, with that sneering, contemptuous look of his. "You bastards too lucky for me," he grumbled and slammed his cards down hard on the table.

Moncado mopped the sweat on his dark forehead and looked over at Sab. "How many cards, Johnny?" he asked, snickering, blowing smoke into Sab's face.

Sab wrinkled his nose in disgust. He gave Moncado a sour, grimacing look of indecision, rubbing his beardless chin, watching Moncado's ping-pong-ball eyes glowering at him. "One card."

"One card, huh?"

He slid over the card and picked it up.

Moncado suddenly slammed the rest of the deck on the table. "I no want no cards!" he snarled defiantly.

"What!" Sab cried out.

"I no want no cards!"

Sab studied his hand, looked over at Moncado, back at his hand again. "I check."

"Check, huh?" Moncado gloated. Picking up his entire bankroll and counting it, he said, "I bet eight hundred," and flung the whole works in the pot.

Sab looked at Moncado; back at his cards. "I call," he said, laying eight hundred bucks in the middle of the table.

Moncado grinned, then laughed a hard-bitten, cold laughter. "I got aces pull," he said triumphantly, flipping over his cards. Three aces and a pair of kings! He reached over for the pot.

"That's no good!" Sab threw down his cards, face up. Four deuces and a seven!

Moncado's eyes almost popped out of their sockets. He studied the four deuces, dazed, the cigar barely dangling between his thick purplish lips. He glared over at Sab, back at the deuces again, his dark weathered face twisting into an unbearable, almost unendurable, pain. Slowly, speechlessly, still staring at Sab in that snarling way of a violent, wounded animal, he pulled his hand back away from the pot. Now, almost in tears, he looked over, bewildered, at Doc, who was looking at the four deuces with an amazed, stunned expression.

Sab stood up and reached over for the pot. Just as he was bringing back his hand with all the money clenched tight, Moncado grabbed his arm.

"What! You quit! You quit when you win!" he cried, his voice trailing off into a whimpering-mourning sound.

Sab jerked his arm free, kicked back his chair, turned around with all the money in his fist, and dashed for the door.

"You three lousy crooks!" he screamed. "You lousy bastards! I know what you guys trying to do! You wanna steal my money!"

"Hey! Whatsamattah! Come back! You no can quit now. Come back!"

Sab yanked the plywood door open and slammed it behind him. "You guys better leave me alone! I'm gonna call the cops!" he threatened, running down the long wooden-floored porch, down the flight of stairs, through the alley, heading for Vineyard, still hearing Moncado yelling from the top of the stairway.

"Hey! Johnny! You come back here! Come back!"

After coming to Vineyard, Sab went down to Market, then hurried down towards Iao Theatre a block away where he turned into an alley. Breathing hard and feeling his heart pounding ferociously in the back of his eyeballs, he opened the door of a panel truck in the parking lot behind the theatre and slumped down, exhausted.

He counted the money on his lap. Two thousand bucks! Jee-sus Ca-rist!

About fifteen minutes later, Yosh, looking stealthily over his shoulder, came strolling down the alley.

"Look at all the money, Yosh," Sab said, handing over the bills as soon as Yosh had sat down beside him.

Cool and calm, Yosh counted the money.

How can the guy be so calm at a time like this? he thought, studying Yosh's pale, expressionless face. The guy was insensitive, as though not a damned thing had happened.

"Where's Moncado now?" Sab asked.

"He's with Doc." Yosh was still counting the money.

"You think he smelled anything?"

"Him? Moncado? Naw-w . . .

"—Listen, Sab, we made nine hundred bucks," Yosh now said, looking up. "The rest of the money was Doc's and mine. Here's your cut—three hundred."

"Three hundred!" Sab exclaimed, holding the money tight. "T'anks, Yosh! T'anks a lot!"

"You did all right, Sab. I think Doc went for the way you handled it."

"Aw-w, t'at was not'ing," he scoffed, grinning from ear to ear.

"Maybe now, Doc will cut you in on the deal we're working."

"Yeah, you think so?"

"I'll give you a call when Ah Hong flies over." Opening the truck door, Yosh then said: "I better go back before Moncado starts wondering where I disappeared."

As Yosh walked back up the alley, Sab counted his cut. Three hundred bucks! He stuck them carefully into his front pocket, hardly believing his good luck. He had a little over five hundred now, counting the money he had hidden at home. Hot dog!

He planned to buy Miss Blake an expensive Christmas gift. Well, maybe not too expensive—she might wonder where he got the money from. Anyway, he'd get her something real nice to show her how he felt about her.

He waited for another minute or two, got out of the truck, walked up the alley to Market, then turned towards the bus station on Main.

It was only noon yet and he hated to go home. But he feared he might run into Moncado if he stuck around town. There was no telling what that mean-looking bugga might do.

11

SHORTLY AFTER NOON, gusts of high winds had slashed across the valley and the dark clouds up in the mountains had dropped towards the ocean. Then, lightning had suddenly flashed bright in the low skies and thunder had roared and echoed against the sheer cliffs. Seconds later, the rains had come, not in drops but in a furious deluge like the pouring from a water pipe.

It was still pouring quite heavily at night, and the nerve-shattering noise on the corrugated iron roof sounded as though pebbles were falling from the sky. Kama, now wearing his loose-fitting kimono, was talking to Kenyei Shiroma sitting across the kitchen table beside Tsuyu.

"It's been almost two days since Japan attacked Pea-ru Har-bah," he said to Kenyei in a rather loud voice, gazing up at the roof for a second. "When are they going to capture Hawaii?"

"Saah . . ," Kenyei mused, "it's very hard to tell what Japan might do next." He leaned forward stoop-shouldered, head cocked to one side, the front ends of his long black hair hanging just above his small, ever-squinting eyes.

"Didn't you say they planned to take over Hawaii soon?"

"That's what I heard over the Japan station."

Suddenly, Kama turned his head and glared, annoyed, through the porthole at Ishi and Tengan sitting cross-legged on the linoleum of the muggy, smoke-filled living room, a half-empty sake jug beside them. Those two loud-mouths had been playing cards and arguing noisily since dinner two hours ago. Tengan, a dark, bald-headed Okinawan fisherman had come over earlier this evening after spending the night before in jail. The FBI had confiscated his fishing boat yesterday when, totally ignorant of the Pearl Harbor attack, he had sailed into Kahului Harbor with his catch. They had released him after discovering he could neither read nor write, and was not a dangerous Japanese spy.

Kama directed his attention back to Kenyei. "What else did you hear over the radio?"

"Well," Kenyei said, pondering, reaching over for the sardine can ashtray, "the radio said that Hawaii, in a way, has been captured," laughing ingratiatingly with slitted eyes. "They have the islands surrounded with submarines."

Kama gave Kenyei a thoughtful look. "Of course. You're right," he said, enlightened. "If we're surrounded by Japanese submarines, and 'Merican ships cannot come in, we're as good as in Japanese hands."

One of the many strict laws passed by the Hawaiian Military Government right after the attack was that short-wave radios were prohibited in all Japanese alien homes. It had meant that Kama and the rest of the aliens had to extract the short-wave bands on their radios. But Kenyei, who was an American citizen—a dual citizen actually, having been born in Hawaii and reared in Okinawa—was not affected by the law. It had made him the news center in the valley. Since yesterday, he had more dinner invitations than in all the years he had been living in Kapuna.

The rain on the roof stopped. Now there was only the rhythmic pattering of water dropping down from the eaves onto the muddy ground outside the blacked-out window. The kitchen was becoming progressively humid with a heavy blanket of cigarette smoke hovering overhead; and the wrangling, thick, alcohol voices of Ishi and Tengan in the living room did not help it any.

Across the table, Kenyei and Tsuyu were talking in low, subdued voices.

Glancing over at Kenyei, Kama wondered why in the world didn't the boy wear glasses when he could barely see more than a dozen feet. Only this morning, he had almost run into the boy again. That crazy bugga had come charging up the bend on his bicycle with his head low and his shoulders hunched forward like a racer.

Kama had slammed his brakes! And there was Kenyei, finally looking up and staring at the pickup big as life before him.

Akisamiyo! Another inch and Kenyei would have bashed his thick skull into the radiator. After jumping off his bicycle and dragging it aside, he had looked around innocently as though not a thing had happened. He had not even recognized Kama.

Shaking his head, Kama looked across the table once more with a smirk, concluding that God certainly was kind to the blind; otherwise, how in the world has Kenyei managed to live this long? even though he was just thirty-one years old.

Saburo, wearing only a wrinkled pair of levis, his long jet-black hair fallen over his forehead, ambled into the kitchen from the living room and sat down next to Kama.

"Have you studied your Japanese lessons?" Kama asked, as Saburo reached over for the kettle and poured himself a cup of tea.

"Why should I study crap like that," Saburo said disrespectfully.

"Saburo!" he admonished, eyebrows jumping up. "Stop speaking English when you're talking to me."

"For crying out loud!" Saburo grumbled, sipping noisily on the hot tea. "All I did was come here to drink tea. Not to get lectured again."

"Why can't you be like your oldest brother used to be," Kama said, mouth pursed tight, shaking his head. "He was always the smartest boy in Japanese school. Look at him today. Why, he might even become Governor of Maui."

"What!" Saburo made a face and looked down at Kama's sake cup. "C'mon, Otoosan. It's only seven-thirty yet."

This boy! This youngest child of the Gusuda family.

What has become of him? He had no respect for anyone; not even for his own father anymore. If he were a little younger Kama would have clouted him good and hard. Right there and then!

"What's going to happen to you when Hawaii becomes a part of Japan? You can't even speak proper Nihon-go."

"Why don't you stop listening to all that crap about Japan winning the war," Saburo said, giving Kenyei across the table a scorning look. "Japan don't have a chance."

"Japan has already won the war," Kama scoffed, grinning, exchanging glances with Kenyei. "It's just a matter of time before we'll all be under the Japanese government."

"Who told you that?"

"Never mind who told me. I know," he said, tapping his temple. "I was hoping you would, too, but since you don't, you better start listening to your father."

"Look, Otoosan," Saburo said, "if you think Japan is so great, why haven't they been able to beat China all these years? China don't even have guns to fight back."

Kenyei burst out laughing, head thrown back, mouth showing black, tobacco-stained teeth.

Kama joined Kenyei in laughter.

"What's so funny?" Saburo gave Kenyei a disdaining look.

"I guess you're too young to understand these things," Kama said. "China was conquered long time ago. Back in 1939."

"Then, why are they still fighting Japan?"

"But Saburo," he said, "they're not fighting Japan anymore. It's the 'Mericans and English who's been fighting Japan the past several years. Where do you suppose China has been getting its war equipment and airplanes and pilots from?—'Merica and England, of course. Millions of dollars have been made by foreign interest in the China war."

"Aw-w . . . Japan won't stand a chance against America" Saburo bleated stubbornly. "Someday, when American airplanes start bombing Japan, you're all gonna change your minds." He fixed his eyes coldly on Kenyei.

"Nev-ah hap-on! 'Merican airplanes wouldn't get within a thousand miles of Japan," Kama said, gazing over at Kenyei for confirmation.

Kenyei laughed a haughty burst of laughter and shook his head at Saburo.

"The Americans should have shot down every one of those planes that bombed Pearl Harbor," Saburo said.

"Saburo!" his mother scolded, speaking for the first time. "Don't say that. There were enough Japanese boys killed as it was."

"What about the hundreds of American boys killed?" Saburo said, looking at his mother.

No one said anything for a moment.

Then, Kenyei, sitting up straight, said: "It's war, Saburo. You can't help it if people get killed in time of war."

"War, my eye!" Saburo said. "There was no war declared when Japan attacked. They didn't give the Americans a chance."

"That was part of the strategy," Kenyei went on authoritatively. "The minute Japan planned the attack, the war was on."

Kama could see that his son was baffled by Kenyei's shrewd analysis. That Kenyei may be odd at times, but you had to hand it to him for intelligent reasoning. He was clever. Very clever. After all, he had gone through the sixth grade in Japanese school.

"If America had attacked Japan first and killed hundreds of their soldiers you wouldn't be telling me it was all right," Saburo said to Kenyei, mouth twitching.

"Japanese soldiers are never afraid to die for their country," Kenyei said stolidly, chest expanded. "When those pilots came to bomb Pea-ru Har-bah, they knew it would be a one-way trip for most of them. But every one of them felt greatly honored to be selected for the mission," he continued, voice ringing with overtones of school-boy fanaticism, lips curled over stubby teeth.

"And that's why Japan will win the war," he added. "The spirit of Yamato-damashi is instilled in every Japanese soldier from the day he is born. While soldiers in the rest of the world are taught to enjoy life and become play boys, a Japanese soldier is trained to die for his country and the Emperor. Because he is never afraid to die, he is not afraid to live."

"Aw, bull shit!" Saburo said, pushing back his chair and standing up. He stormed back into the living room.

"Saburo!" Kama hollered. "You watch that dirty mouth of yours!

"—That boy," he mumbled, shaking his head, looking over at his wife, "I don't know what's become of him. He hasn't got an ounce of discipline in him."

"He's still young," Tsuyu said softly, eyes looking down at the table. "He'll change."

"He's going to be seventeen in another month. The other two boys were well-mannered when they were his age. It's because you've spoiled him, Basan," he accused. "What's going to happen when we're ruled by Japan? They would never tolerate such insolence and disobedience. I'm telling you, Basan, it's all your fault. I'm washing my hands of that boy."

"It's the 'Merican way of life," Kenyei expounded. "'Merican children are not taught to have honor and respect for the elders; not even for their own parents. I've even heard some of them calling their parents by their first names."

"You're right, Kenyei," Kama agreed, disconsolate. "The children in 'Merica are not being brought up properly. The sooner we're under Japan the better off our children will be. It's getting so the Niseis don't know they are Japanese anymore. They have funny names like: Hah-ry, Ge-o-gie, Wi-ri-am . . .

"Only the other day, while walking down Market Street in Wailuku, I heard someone calling a Japanese boy, 'Rin-con.' Why that boy looked no more like Ab-ra-ham Rin-con than I look like Ge-o-gie Wa-shin-ton."

Kenyei broke out in raucous laughter, beady eyes shut tight, body shaking convulsively.

Tsuyu, too, laughed out loud with hands covering her mouth.

"What's so funny over there!" Ishi asked, looking over his shoulder into the living room. "What boastful lies is that blind boy telling you folks now?"

Everyone stopped laughing.

Kenyei's face suddenly took on a blood-red, savage look.

"You shud up-pu you!" Tsuyu scolded Ishi in the living room. Turning to Kenyei beside her, she consoled: "Don't listen to that drunkard, Kenyei. He doesn't know any better. Just ignore him."

Kama could hardly contain himself. He reached over for his sake cup and kept pressing its edge hard against his mouth to keep from laughing.

On the table, Kenyei's fists were contracting tighter and tighter, the knuckles turning into hard whiteness.

"Hey, Kenyei!" Ishi slurred. "When did you say Japanese soldiers are coming over here to Kapuna Valley? —You know what that blind boy told me last night?" he now said to Tengan in a loud voice, slapping a sakura card on the linoleum. "He said that when Japan takes over Maui, he was going to be appointed landlord of Kapuna Valley."

"Kenyei? Landlord?" Tengan scorned. "Who's going to watch the land for him? He can't even see where he's going!"

"You two in there!" Tsuyu called sternly. "If you don't shud up-pu in a minute, I'm going to ask you to leave. —Don't listen to them, Kenyei. You have to excuse them. They're drunk." She patted Kenyei's tight-fisted hands.

Kama continued pressing the cup's edge against his mouth, eyes glancing back and forth from the table to the living room.

"Hey, Kama!" Ishi called, "you think Kenyei will let you have some land when Japan takes over?"

He felt a tingle of laughter rising up from his chest, but when he gazed across the table at Kenyei again, a flood of pity welled up inside him. Kenyei was staring blank-eyed at the table, lips quivering, veins of his thick neck swelling in a bluish hue.

"All right, you two. That's enough," he admonished, his voice taking on a harsh tone.

"Aw, Kama," Tengan slurred, "don't tell me you believe Japan is going to make that blind boy landlord of Kapuna."

"Tengan! I said that was enough!" And a sharp current of silence penetrated through the two rooms.

"Who are you to make fun of someone?" Kama scolded, glaring over at Tengan through the porthole. "What have you accomplished in your life? except learning to play cards and getting drunk all the time."

"I'm the best fisherman in all Hawaii," Tengan boasted, pounding his chest. "I used to bring in more fish than anyone. I lost my boat because some stupid country had to start a war."

"You're a Nihon-jin, too," Kama said. "You should have pride in your own country."

"I'm a fisherman. Why should I care for Japan or any other country?" Tengan said. "I was minding my own business—enjoying a peaceful life on my boat when Japan attacked Hawaii. They caused me to lose my boat."

"You're a dog! A dog!—that's what you are!" Kenyei screamed, jumping up to his feet.

"You watch out what you say, you—you blind bat!" Tengan screamed back, charging drunkenly into the kitchen with the half-empty sake jug held high over his head, ready to club Kenyei with it.

"Tengan!" Kama jumped up to his feet and snatched the jug just in time. "You get back into the living room and leave the boy alone!" he commanded, pushing-shoving Tengan away from fuming Kenyei who had forgotten respect for elders.

"You—you drunkard, you!" Kenyei screamed menacingly, tight fists moving up and down at his sides.

"Aw-w, you blind bat, you," Tengan mumbled, wiping drooling foam from the corners of his mouth, walking—staggering—backwards to the living room. "You and your Japan," he scorned. "Who you think you are? a son of a samurai? of noble blood? Hah!" he snorted, mouth twisted hard, giving Kenyei a contemptuous nod. "If you're of noble blood I must be the Emperor himself."

"You're a dog!" Kenyei yelled again, corners of his mouth showering a barrage of saliva, right fist pounding hard on the table.

"Don't you call me a dog!" Tengan cried out, charging at Kenyei again.

"Stopit!" Kama grabbed Tengan's arm and pushed him back to the porthole. "Enough is enough!" he ordered. He gestured Kenyei to sit down.

"Kenyei, please sit down," Tsuyu pleaded, tugging at his sleeve. "Don't let those awful drunkards anger you. They don't know any better."

"C'mon back in here, Tengan," Ishi called from the living room. "Leave that boy alone. Let's continue with the game."

"He called me a dog," Tengan grumbled, sitting down

cross-legged on the linoleum again, looking over Ishi's shoulder into the kitchen. "That boy don't even know who his parents are. And he calls ME a dog. I, at least, knew who my father and mother were."

"Don't let him bother you," Ishi said. "The strain of the war is getting the best of that boy. He's getting grand ideas of how he's going to become a big shot when Japan wins the war."

"Big shot! Him! He'll end up chief toilet digger for some proud Japanese general."

Ishi laughed out loud.

Kama, sitting back down on his chair, could hardly hold back laughter.

Those two jackasses, he thought, glancing over into the living room. They're not only living with Kenyei, but not even paying him rent. Yet, every time they got drunk they insulted and heckled him to no end. If he were Kenyei, he'd throw them out of his home tonight.

But how could Kenyei do that? knowing how helpless they are—two hopeless drunkards not knowing the difference between their ass holes and a hole in the ground. Besides, they were fellow Okinawans from the same mountain village back in the old country.

He reached over for the gallon jug on the table, poured himself another cup of sake, wondering how long the war was going to last. The strain of living only two nights under blacked-out conditions was already affecting everyone. Even Kenyei who normally was a calm and composed person had lost his temper.

Tsuyu and Kenyei were again talking in low, confidential tones.

Saburo swaggered back into the kitchen and sat down beside him.

"What was all that argument about, Otoosan?" he asked with a smirk, avoiding Kenyei's eyes.

"Never mind. It didn't concern you," Kama said. "Have you done your studies?"

"Let's not go through all that again, oh, Otoosan."

"Saburo," Kama said, "someday when you're older and realize the mistake you've made by not listening to me, I want you to remember one thing. I may be dead by then, but I want you to remember that your father had once told you about the importance of learning to speak proper Japanese."

"Aw, Otoosan, c'mon. It's hard enough trying to learn to speak good English."

Sadly, painfully, Kama continued: "I don't know what has become of you. You're so different, so unlike your older brothers. I just can't understand it." His eyes suddenly filled with warm tears. "Your brothers used to always listen to their father and mother. You can't be that different from them. You're all fruits of the same tree."

He kept studying the boy's sullen face, wondering if this boy—his number three son—was so Americanized, so Kanaka-ized, he no longer understood his parents.

No, not a son of his. Never! He refused to believe it and held back an impulse to shake his head at the boy.

Where was the missing link? he questioned himself, still looking at Saburo. It seemed impossible to penetrate the boy anymore. He was like a shallow, empty bucket of nothing. No substance. No sense of reasoning. It was terribly disheartening because the boy used to make such good grades before entering high school. What made him change so much all of a sudden. He couldn't be losing his mind. There were no imbeciles in the Gusuda family tree.

Good God! Don't tell him there are traces of imbecility in Tsuyu's family. Could she have been hiding it from him all these years? he asked himself, stealing a glance across the table at his wife who was still speaking in a low voice to Kenyei. Come to think of it, he hardly knew anything about her side of the family. He'd have to talk to her later.

"Look, Otoosan," Saburo said, grinning, head held low, "don't worry about me. I'll be all right. I'm going to America someday. Not to Japan."

"What's going to happen to you when Japan wins the war? What about your future? Your mother and I can't be guiding you forever."

"Stop saying Japan gonna win the war," Saburo said morosely. He gave Kenyei a hateful look. "If the war lasts a couple of years I'm gonna join the Army."

"Saburo!" Tsuyu cried, hand jumping up to her mouth.

[138]

"Don't say that. I don't want any of my sons joining the Army."

"Why not? Lotsa guys join the Army. I wish I was eighteen right now so I could volunteer."

"Volunteer!" Kama said, horrified, pounding the table. "What's the matter with you, Saburo! Don't you know if you went into the 'Merican Army you might end up fighting your own relatives?"

"Who said anything about fighting relatives? All I said was—"

"A Japanese boy must never fight against Japan," Kama said. "Remember! You have a brother in Japan. Don't tell me you don't care if you killed your own brother!"

He exchanged terrifying looks with his wife, his forehead furrowed with deep, painful lines. The boy was really losing his mind. He had no more love for his own kind than the pigs have for one another.

"If I know Niro, I bet he's already volunteered," Saburo said, justifying his own predicament.

"Niro? Never! He's a good boy. He wouldn't do anything to worry his father and mother. —What did Niro say in his last letter?" He was not sure of his children anymore. Saburo shrugged.

"Kimiko!" he called his daughter who was reading in the living room.

"Yes!" she answered. She was sitting to the left of the porthole, away from his view.

"What did Niro say in his letter to you? Is he all right?"

"I'm sure he is, Otoosan," Kimiko said in English, preoccupied. "His last letter was written a week ago so I don't know what his plans are."

"You see" —Kama said to Saburo, inconclusive. "Niro will think things out before making decisions. Why can't you be like him?"

"Every damn time I come into the kitchen I get nothing but lectures," Saburo said, sulking, pushing back his chair. He swaggered back into the living room.

12

KENYEI SHIROMA NO longer seethed with anger as he watched Saburo swaggering back into the living room.

Only a few minutes ago, he had to fight himself to keep from kicking the living hell out of Ishi and Tengan. But deciding to handle those two drunkards in his own way later, his anger had subsided and he now felt actually glad he had not taken to physical violence before Mr. and Mrs. Gusuda. Had he been insulted elsewhere he did not think he could have contained himself.

Calling him a blind bat . . . And laughing at him before Kimiko. He did not even say a word to those two monkeys all evening. Well, he would teach them a good lesson; a lesson they would never forget the rest of their lives.

Straining his eyes and looking into the living room, he could see Kimiko quite clearly from his angle. She was facing his direction reading a book. She had on a pair of gaudy shorts, her smooth, coppery white legs crossed under the round table. Her young chi-chis beneath her tight white sweater were sticking out proudly like two soft rubber balls, and her velvet-like, gleaming throat looked warm and enticing.

He gulped hard. How he felt like running up to her and kissing her all over!

If she'd only marry him, he thought wistfully, suddenly turning his head Mrs. Gusuda's way and nodding a couple of times at what she was saying, then gazing back into the living room to stare at Kimiko.

How could he crave and yearn so much for that girl, knowing she would have nothing to do with him? She had even called him a Japan bo-bura once. Just because he was raised in Japan and could not speak English. But things would change in a few days. There would be no need to know English. Then, he—Shiroma, Kenyei—would undoubtedly become a community leader.

When he became an important man in the valley he'd ask Mr. and Mrs. Gusuda for the hand of their daughter. They would be proud to have him as their son-in-law, a respected leader in the community. And when Kimiko became his wife he would teach her the proper manners and etiquette of a true Japanese wife.

The girl was sure pretty, he thought, staring at her exquisite-looking thighs. Every time he saw her wearing those tight shorts he'd go home and either dream of her all night, or go and call on that dark Kanaka girl who lived across the taro patches. Right now, he felt like going into the living room and grabbing Kimiko and taking her up to the mountains somewhere where he could make mad love to her; make her want him as much as he wanted her; un-virgin her so she'd know what it was to be loved good and hard.

When in the hell are those Japanese troops going to capture Hawaii!

In a way, Kimiko reminded him a great deal of the girl friend he used to have back in Okinawa eight years ago when he was in the Army.

Those were the days . . . The days of sake, musume and samisen. Shiroma, Kenyei, Corporal in His Majesty's Japanese Imperial Army! He and his squad had been stationed right in the heart of Naha near the harbor. And by golly! he had all the beautiful musumes at his feet.

But only Keiko-chan had been his true sweetheart. She was so lovely and so full of feminine charms—like a sweet-smelling flower. Very talented on the samisen, too. And what a lover under the futon!

Then, in 1933, when he was 23, his eyes went bad for no apparent reason, and he was given a medical discharge from the Army. The world around him had become a permanent blur. He had refused to wear glasses, afraid they would make him look timid. He was no longer Corporal Shiroma; just Shiroma, Kenyei, from the mountains, no job and no money. Keiko-chan stopped loving him. He had thought of committing hara-kiri, but did not even have money to purchase the lethal weapon necessary for the ritual.

Distressed, he had decided to come back to Hawaii, his land of birth, where his separated parents had abandoned him to the care of relatives who had later taken him to Okinawa at age three. His return passage to Hawaii had been paid by his uncle, Ikehara-Oji-san, who was visiting Okinawa.

After coming to the islands—Maui to be exact—he had worked for a year in the fields to honor his debt to his uncle, then had moved to Kapuna Valley, hoping to become an enterprising taro-grower—taro being the basic substance for poi, the Hawaiian food—even though he personally felt poi should be fed only to dogs and pigs.

Still straining his eyes, he stared under the table in the living room and imagined himself lying beside Kimiko under a futon and stroking her smooth, warm thighs.

Sonnabagun! She must have caught him, he thought, chagrined. That sassy girl; always arousing him, then cutting him short. Some teaser!

He turned his head and gazed over at the alarm clock near the window. Eight-forty. Tengan and Ishi would be leaving soon.

"Ah-h, it is getting late," he said, stretching extravagantly. He slid his chair back and stood up. "It's about time I went home and listened to the radio. Those two gamblers better be going home, too. If they're caught outside by the MP's they might end up in jail."

"Yes, it is getting late," Gusuda-san agreed, yawning. "I guess the rain has stopped for a while —Hey! You two in there. You better start for home, or the MP's are going to get you. They're even mistaking people like you for spies these days."

Kenyei joined Mr. and Mrs. Gusuda in laughter.

"This will be our last hand," Ishi called back, slapping a card down on the linoleum "Has that blind boy gone home already?"

"Don't listen to him, Kenyei," Mrs. Gusuda said. "Just ignore that old drunkard."

Kenyei forced a smile and bade Mr. and Mrs. Gusuda sayonara. He opened the kitchen door and stepped out into the dark back porch where he suddenly felt the cool, rain-scented night air embracing him. He put on his raincoat, placed his feet into his getas and walked out into the spattering rain, his getas sinking deep into the slushy mud, the rain drops slanting against his face, some landing tastelessly on his lips. He stood there for about a minute, squinting his eyes until they became accustomed to the dark, rain-drenched surroundings, his sense slowly attuning to the night life around him.

He flicked on his blue cellophane-covered flashlight and headed down the garage under the house. There, he quickly looked for the bags of sawdust Gusuda-san kept to boil the pig slops with and, finding them stacked in front of the pickup, he emptied a bag until it was only half-filled.

Lifting the bag on his shoulder, he hurried outside into the rain and slushy mud once more, and trudged heavily to the island between the two old wooden bridges one hundred yards down the streaming road.

He could hear his getas chugging heavily on the wooden surface of the first bridge and could feel the vibrating, thudding sounds of huge boulders bouncing together in the flooded river. He laid the bag down on the stone wall to the left of the island where he sought shelter from the drizzling rain under kukui tree branches and waited for Ishi and Tengan to come walking across the bridge.

Those two useless drunkards, he thought, wiping off water dripping down his forehead and cheeks. They had been living in Hawaii for so many years they were more Kanakas than Okinawans. Even the Okinawan dialect they spoke was no longer the true language of the old country. They spoke a combination of Hawaiian-Japanese-Okinawan, sometimes throwing in a smattering of mispronounced English. They had also become strong believers in the old Kanaka legends of ghosts and witchcraft. They believed that if a Kahuna wanted someone to become ill or to die he could do it by praying and chanting the litany of the old Kanaka black magic. But the legend that really captivated Kenyei's imagination was the one about a dog howling on a dark, lonely night. According to Ishi, dogs have an uncanny power to detect impending death and would warn people by howling for several nights before its actual occurrence.

The last time Kenyei had scared the daylights out of Ishi he was sure Ishi had reformed. For months afterwards, Ishi had been gentle and kind. But everytime that louse, Tengan, visited them, Ishi would forget all about Kahuna and become his abusive self, taking advantage of Kenyei's hospitality, knowing very well Kenyei would never throw him out of the house.

Ishi was over sixty-five and did not have an ounce of brains, Kenyei now thought, feeling small rain drops falling on his matted hair from the branches above. All he did was play cards, get drunk and insult people. He was a burden to society, collecting welfare money from the Countu of Maui.

Kenyei strained his eyes in the gloomy wet darkness again to see if anyone was coming across the bridge.

No. Not yet. But those two should be coming along soon.

Ishi was so afraid to die that the mere mention of death made him shiver in his pants, Kenyei thought, pulling up the collars of his raincoat against his neck, racing one hand over his face to wipe off water. Blind or not, he (Shiroma, Kenyei), at least, was not a helpless drunkard like Ishi and Tengan.

Will he end up like those two someday? he suddenly wondered, shuddering. Drunkards like them? Without any meaning in life? No. That would never happen to him. He would kill himself before he sunk that low. Self-annihilation, man's inviolable right, should be fearlessly exercised when man became a hindrance to society.

Someone was coming across the bridge!

He stiffened under the branches, motionless, narrowing his eyes and staring hard at the first bridge to his right, not directly, but at a slight angle to focus his eyes in the darkness. He waited breathlessly, still unable to make out who it was. Then, he saw two dark figures staggering towards him, soaking wet.

It was them!

Ishi was weaving from side to side, mumbling something and bumping into Tengan, and Tengan, head tilted back, was singing an Okinawan folk song. Their arms were dangling at their sides, their getas dragging clumsily under them, two shadowy figures looming closer.

Kenyei quickly shucked off his raincoat, lifted the half-filled sawdust bag onto his shoulder, reached down for his raincoat and, covering the bag and himself with it, stood up slowly. He was now a huge black headless monster under the dark rasping kukui tree.

He held the flash in his right hand and as soon as Ishi and Tengan were on the other side of the road, flicked it on and off.

"What was that?" he heard Ishi saying.

"Where?" Tengan said.

"Over there. I thought I saw something."

"I don't see anything. You're drunk."

"There! Over there!" Ishi cried out as Kenyei flicked the flash on for another second.

"What's that!" Tengan uttered.

They both stood there petrified, panic-stricken.

Kenyei, barely able to smother a burst of laughter, suddenly let out an eerie, ear-piercing howl:

"BOWWWwwww . . .! BOWWWwwww . . .! BOW-wwww . . .!"

"It's Akuwa!" Ishi mourned, rushing over close to Tengan, hugging the stone wall on the other side of the island.

"Don't run!" Tengan said, pushing Ishi away. "Show him you're not afraid."

They inched slowly to the next bridge, eyes fixed steadily in Kenyei's direction.

Kenyei flicked on the flash again, this time leaving it on a little longer.

"BOWWWwww . . . ! BOWWWwww . . ! BOWWWW-www . . .!"

"It's Akuwa and Kahuna man!" Ishi whimpered, clinging desperately to Tengan's arm, stumbling down in the mud.

"Walk slowly," Tengan said.

"What are we going to do?" Ishi sobbed, staggering up from the slushy mud.

"BOWWWwwww . . . !"

"Tengan!" Ishi bawled, half-stumbling, half-crawling.

Kenyei was now waving the blue light in a wide arch over his head, fighting back gurgling laughter, chest heaving up and down.

"Tengan! Don't leave me behind."

"Stop grabbing my leg, you fool!"

"Hey you, Akuwa! Go away! Go away!" Ishi pleaded frantically, waving, "Go away, Akuwa!"

"Let go of my leg!"

"BOWWWwwww . . . !"

"Tengan!"

Suddenly! Kenyei bent over double, dropping the bag and grabbing his leg below the kneecap. "Agayoi! Aga! Aga! Aga!" —That lousy Ishi had struck him with a rock. Oh-hhh . . . That sonnabagun, oh-hhh, and still Kenyei could not stop laughing as he watched Ishi and Tengan racing up the muddy hill like two fat, squat-assed women outrunning a charging bull.

At last, he pushed himself up to his feet, limped with the wet bag over to the rail of the next bridge and dumped it into the rushing water.

Five minutes later, soaked and dripping wet, his leg hurting, he stepped into his dimly lighted, blacked-out, one-bedroom shack and was appalled at the sight of Ishi and Tengan sprawled on the bare parlor floor. Looking half-dead and covered with thick layers of caked mud, both of them were so exhausted they could hardly open their eyes.

"What happened to you two?" he questioned.

"Where have you been?" Ishi asked, gasping for breath, still sprawled there on the mud-streaked floor.

"Me? I was checking my taro patches, of course. What happened?"

"What happened!" Tengan said, dragging himself up from the floor and slumping back wearily against the wall. "We saw an ugly beast, that's what happened."

"It was Akuwa, that's what it was," Ishi said, sitting up.

"You sure?"

"Sure, I'm sure. You think I'm blind like—"

"Maybe, you two have been drinking too much. I heard Akuwas can smell liquor on a rainy night."

"Ordinarily, I don't believe in Akuwas," Tengan mumbled, head cocked to one side, "but what I saw tonight was as close to any as I'll ever see."

Stifling a wild urge to burst out laughing, Kenyei looked down blank-faced at the two of them, then reached over for the knob of the torn screen door to his bedroom and walked away.

After taking off his wet clothes, he sat down on the matted floor of his small, furnitureless bedroom and examined the painful bruise on his leg. The lump had grown bigger and there was a large area of black-and-blue a few inches below his knee. He spat on it and rubbed it gingerly.

"Go away, Akuwa . . . Go away . . " He covered his mouth and chortled to himself.

Later, in a somewhat somber mood, he reached over to his table model short-wave Philco radio and clicked it on, hoping to hear favorable news from Japan. How he wished Japan would take over Hawaii soon. He wanted Kimiko so badly he did not think he could wait any longer.

And then an inspiring thought flashed from the depths of his mind. Why sure! Why hadn't he thought of it before? That way, he did not have to wait for Japan to conquer the islands. He could go right ahead and marry Kimiko now.

Tomorrow morning, as soon as he got up, he would ride to Wailuku on his bicycle and call on his uncle, Ikehara-Oji-san, who was the head custodian of the Wailuku Sugar Plantation mill and who also was the President of the Wailuku Okinawan Association. His uncle was well regarded by all the Okinawans on Maui and would make an excellent matchmaker.

The Japanese National Anthem came over the radio and Kenyei's head automatically bowed low with deep reverence. Instead of picturing the Rising Sun, however, he was imagining himself cuddled up close to his lovely Kimiko and making passionate love to her.

Kimiko, Kimiko . . . You beautiful girl, you . . .

13

THE FOLLOWING EVENING after work, Kimi got off the bus at the Kapuna bus depot and decided to walk home around the bend rather than take the short-cut trail through the wet koa trees

The tropical rainstorm that had begun yesterday had continued until late this morning when, at last, the unpredictable sun had suddenly and miraculously turned the skies into a dazzling blue. Everything was so nice and invigorating right after a hard rainstorm, she thought, caught in a state of exotic bliss, smelling of the rich, unadulterated air all around her. She gazed at the wet grass along the road, at the keawe trees on the sand hills, then at the lush-green mountainside, and could not help marvelling what a beautiful time of the day it was. The sun had already disappeared beyond the sharp ridges and the only remnant of daylight was the purplish-orange reflection sweeping across the skies.

She strode up gaily to the sharp bend about a hundred yards from the depot and quickly noted the unbroken border of brown, murky water along the ocean front. The river flowing into the rough surf was not as turbulent as it had been yesterday, but it was still flooded and she wondered rather dejectedly whether her sanctuary down by the beach had been destroyed.

Standing by the stone wall, she looked down dreamily at the quiet valley sprawled before her. Dusk was always accompanied by extreme solitude, she thought, studying dark shadows slowly but inexorably blanketing the lower part of the valley in thundering silence; a kind of silence so serene, so peaceful, she could almost feel herself being engulfed by it.

As loneliness swept through her, she felt she was the only living soul for miles around and had been drawn by destiny to live and die alone in the valley. Then, she thought the narrow bed of land lying in the tranquil dusk was like the valley in "How Green Was My Valley." On the left bank of the down-grade road was a tiny red shingled-roof church where every Sunday morning the resonant voices of the Mormon congregation bounced against the sheer cliffs, blending majestically with the quiet surroundings.

How green was my valley? she thought dramatically, eyes turning misty, once again thinking of the at-once confused and love-filled lunch hour she had spent with her George today. How she wished he could be with her now and share the infinite beauty before her, hold her tight in his strong arms and whisper endearing words that came so easily to him. Oh, God, please help me to express myself when writing to him, she prayed, warm tears now streaming down her cheeks, head tilted back, eyes shut tight.

When George had walked up to her counter in Kress today with a sad, pensive look she had not known what to make of him. He had stood across from her for several seconds, not saying a word, just staring at her, as though not knowing why he was standing there. Finally, after he had asked her to have lunch with him, they had driven up to Wailuku Gardens in his car, a short ride to the corner of Main and High.

Sitting across from each other at one of the small round metal tables in the garden, George still hadn't said much but kept looking at her with a painful expression. She had looked up at him several times, puzzled, then had gazed over his shoulders at the maroon-red giant orchids in full bloom in a huge glass hut not too far away from them. She had always heard of the orchids of Wailuku Gardens, but had never imagined they were so big and so lovely.

The Gardens was one of two exclusive tourist hotels on Maui, and although Kimi had passed by it many times, she had never been in there before. She and George were sitting in the large outdoor patio which was banked all around by high bamboo fences. Sheltering them from the scorching mid-morning sun were canopies of crawling green vines hanging down from the extended eaves of the hotel. Except for themselves and a haole couple sitting at one of the tables on the other side of the small square dance floor, the place was empty. To Kimi's right, close by, was a giant, bubble-spouting glass tank filled with tiny red and white double-tailed gold fish. Pots of ginger plants, roses, gardenias, half-grown palms and green, delicate ferns set around the tables exuded a pleasant, refreshing smell.

Kimi smiled, friendly, at the Japanese waitress that had come to the table, but the waitress, after giving her a sharp, inquisitive look, avoided her eyes. Kimi, of course, knew that local Japanese hardly came to the Gardens. After she and George ordered Cokes and hamburgers, she again tried to win a smile from the waitress, but the waitress merely wrote their orders on her pad with a flat, blank face and walked off to the kitchen in the back.

"Kimi," George said, looking at her with dark brown downcast eyes. "Kimi, I gotta tell you something."

She felt herself bolstering against the back of her metal chair.

"I—I'm going away," he muttered.

"Going away? Where?"

"I volunteered in the Army."

"You did what!"

"I had to do it, Kimi," he said.

She stared at him, shocked. "But you said just the other day you'd never want to leave Maui."

George forced a wry smile. "Things have changed since. Anyway, what's the difference whether I'm in the Army or in the Home Guard?"

"Did you volunteer because you wanted to get away from me?" she asked.

"It had nothing to do with you." He reached over for

[150]

her hand. "I had an argument with my father this morning," he said. "I told him I wasn't gonna set foot in the house again."

"What was it all about?"

George's eyes looked away for a second, then locked with her's again. "I—ah, look, Kimi, I just found out this morning that my father and mother; they're not my real father and mother."

"What are you talking about?"

George pressed his lips hard, jaws set tight. "My parents adopted me."

"Who are your real parents, then?"

George wiped his red-rimmed eyes and rubbed his sniffling nose. "My real mother died when she gave birth to me. Nobody knows where my real father is."

"How did you find out all this so suddenly?"

"When I asked my father for my birth certificate so I could take it to the Home Guard office this morning, he kinda hesitated and didn't want to give it to me. I knew it was kept somewhere in the house, but never saw it before. Anyway, when I told him I had to have it, he told me the whole story about them adopting me from the County Orphanage right after I was born."

"And you had a fight over this?"

"Kimi! You don't understand," he cried. "I'm—I'm illegitimate."

"Oh, George . . ." She choked and held his hand in both of hers.

"My mother was only sixteen when I was born. My real father was working on a merchant ship and never came back to Maui."

Warm tears welled up in Kimi's eyes.

"I'm not even pure Hawaiian," George went on. "According to my birth certificate I'm Japanese-Hawaiian on my mother's side. My parents thought my real father was German-Hawaiian."

"George, it doesn't make any difference what nationality you are," she consoled. "It's what you are now that counts."

The waitress approached their table with the order. Kimi pulled back her hand and avoided the waitress's eyes.

George gave the waitress a dollar and told her to keep the change.

Kimi looked down at her hamburger and suddenly decided she wasn't hungry. She took a sip of her Coke, then placed it aside. George pushed his Coke and hamburger away and gazed over at her.

"Where do you think the Army is going to send you?" she asked, her voice quavering.

"The recruiting officer wasn't sure. He thought we might be sent over to Schofield Barracks for basic training."

"That means you'll be in Oahu all the time."

"For a while anyway."

"You mean they might send you away from Hawaii?"

"Kimi" he said, reaching over for her hand again, "I wish I knew what's gonna happen. You can't tell the Army what to do."

"Oh, this horrible war!" she burst out. "It's made everything so confused. No one knows what's happening anymore. Why couldn't you have waited a little longer before volunteering?"

He squeezed her hand, his eyebrows arched up in befuddlement. "I had to get away. I don't want to spend another night at home."

"Why? You're not the only adopted person in the world. There must be hundreds like you right here in the islands."

"It's not that. It's—well, it's— Look, how you like to be living with your father and mother all your life, then getting up one morning and finding out they're not your real parents?"

"I'm sure they meant to tell you all along, George."

"That's not the point," he said, eyes shut tight for a moment. "What am I? Some kind pet people can go up to the orphanage and pick up? I have feelings."

She squeezed his hand. "Your father and mother must love you, George. Or they never would have adopted you in the first place. I've met them only once but they seemed a nice elderly couple, the kind of Hawaiians we read about in our Hawaiian history books: they have dignity and love and understanding."

"They adopted me because they couldn't have children of their own."

"What difference does that make? They love you. It's more than many parents give their real children."

George rubbed his nose with his free hand, his eyes blinking tearfully.

"Did you know that even children who have real parents often feel like orphans?" she said, choking. "I've felt like that many times."

George was looking at her with a vague, distant look.

"I love my father and mother very much, and I know they love me, too. But I've never been able to reach them. We live in different worlds. You understand what I'm trying to say?"

"Yeah, I think so," he answered, still looking at her with a vague look.

"There were many times—sometimes even now—when I wanted very much to sit down and talk to my mother; ask her things about her own young days; about school lessons; about boys—"

Kimi stopped for a few seconds, feeling herself blushing as she remembered that day many years ago when she had her first menstruation and had run to her mother to sob out the horrifying news. Her mother, incapable of explaining the phenomenon, had turned her head away squeamishly and had scolded her in Japanese: "It will go away by itself. You shouldn't go around talking about those things."

"—There were always so many things unsaid because we couldn't talk to one another like some children did with their mothers. As for my father, he always believed girls shouldn't be heard at all."

Two Army captains, silver bars shining on the stiff shoulder paddings of their brown khaki shirts, walked into the garden and sat two tables away from them. One of them looked over at Kimi and kept eyeing her until she gave him a cold look. He quickly turned his head and spoke to his companion.

"When are you supposed to report to the armory?" she asked, turning back to George.

"One-thirty this afternoon," he answered, looking down at his wrist watch. "I still have an hour left."

"One-thirty!" she exclaimed, astounded. "You mean I won't be able to see you after that?"

He shook his head, gazing away slowly. "They don't

know when they're gonna ship us out. It might be tonight or tomorrow morning."

"But George! I can't even go down the armory with you. My lunch hour will be over in fifteen minutes."

He pressed her hand tight. "I'll write you as soon as we reach Oahu. You'll write back, huh?"

"Of course, I'll write you. What about your father and mother? Are they coming down to the armory?"

"I told you—they're not my father and mother."

She eyed him severely. "George, you didn't . volunteer without letting them know, did you?" she questioned, alarmed.

His eyes dropped on the table again, then looked up hesitantly. "What do they care if I volunteered or not? It's none of their business."

"How can you say that? They're your father and mother, regardless."

"Oh, no, they're not."

"Yes, they are! They love you, and I know you love them, too."

George continued looking at her with red misty eyes, then suddenly pulled back his hands and covered his face, sobbing.

After rubbing his eyes and nose, he reached over for her hand again. "Look," he said, "from now on, it's gonna be only you and me. No one else counts."

"What about your father and mother?"

"Kimi, don't let me down now. I need you. There's no one else but you and me from now on."

"They'll always be your father and mother, George," she said, pulling her hand away.

He looked at her, speechless.

"Look," he said, at last, "look, I don't know when I can get back on a furlough, but I'm gonna leave my car with you. And I'm planning to make out my life insurance policy to you, just in case . . ."

"I'm not going to listen to such nonsense," she scolded. "—George, oh, George, I love you," she then sobbed out. "I love you very much but I'm not going to have you hurt your father and mother. You're all they've got. So help me, if you don't go home and tell them what you've done, I'm not going to have anything to do with you. I won't even answer your letters." She pressed her handkerchief hard against her mouth.

Tears flowed down George's eyes. She reached over for his hand and held it tight.

" . . . Besides," she said, working up a faint smile, "I don't want your car anyway. I can't even drive. And I don't want to be named beneficiary in your insurance either. I—I don't know what I'd do if anything happened to you."

They sat there holding hands across the table for another minute, not saying anything, just looking into each other's wet, cloudy eyes.

"You promise you're going home to see your father and mother before going down to the armory?" she finally said.

"Uh-huh . . ."

"The war can't last forever. We'll be together again before we know it."

"Yeah, sure. —Kimi," he said, his eyes taking on a bright glitter for the first time. "I've been thinking about what you said the other day. About us going to UH. Well, maybe, after the war is all pau we can still make it, huh?"

"Oh, George! That would be wonderful! Sure, we can make it, George," she cried, squeezing his hand. "We'll both save our money now, and when you get out of the Army we'll have enough to see us through."

He smiled a determined smile. "I think I better take you back. It's almost one." The two Army captains turned their heads and leered over at Kimi as they both stood up reluctantly from their chairs and walked out of the garden.

Now, as Kimi gazed absently up at the far-away silvery waterfall, she took out her handkerchief from her purse and wiped her eyes, then finally stepped across the crunching gravel along the stone wall and continued on home.

When she opened the front door she found her father and mother, and Kenyei Shiroma and still another man she had never met before, sitting around the living room table having a chicken hekka party. The frying pan on the glowing Japanese charcoal grill was boiling with a batch of sweet-smelling, soyu-flavored chicken, green onions, long rice and bamboo shoots.

Sab was eating alone in the kitchen. Then she noticed that Kenyei was wearing a tie for a change, and that the stranger sitting beside him, a white-haired Japanese man of about sixty, was dressed in a dark, somber-looking suit.

For a moment, everyone stared at her standing there at the door, then they all looked down at the table in hushed silence.

She closed the door behind her and was about to go into her bedroom to change when her father said: "Kimiko, you better sit down. We have something very important to discuss with you."

"Oh-h . . ." she murmured, looking curiously at her father. That was strange, she thought. He was stone sober and there wasn't even sake on the table. Whatever he had to say must be important, she guessed.

She pulled up a chair between her father and the stranger and sat down. "Yes? What is it?"

"Kimiko, this is Kenyei's uncle, Ikehara-san," her father said, nodding respectfully at the white-haired man sitting to her right.

She bowed politely at Kenyei's uncle. Kenyei, sitting on the other side, was smoking a cigarette, his perpetually squinting eyes occupied by some abstract object on the table.

Without preliminaries, as though transacting a business deal, her father went on: "Ikehara-san came over to ask you to marry Kenyei."

"What!"

Silence!

All eyes converged on her. She stared incredulously at her father, at Kenyei, then at her mother and finally at Kenyei's uncle. Shuddering, she looked over at her father once more. He must be drunk! They all must be drunk!

"Kenyei has a fine Japanese education," Kenyei's uncle took over. "It won't be long before he will become one of the leaders of Maui. Perhaps, in a few days.

"I have known your father and mother for a long time; therefore, I know you come from a very fine family. I am sure marriage between you and Kenyei will work out well."

She still felt as though she had just been doused with a bucket of ice-cold water. She looked over at her mother, then again at her father, horrified, wondering whether they had actually sanctioned the arrangement.

Good heavens! How could they?

"I understand you are already eighteen, Kimiko-san," the man went on, taking full charge of the ritual. "It's about time you married a fine young man, don't you think? I have always been very proud of the marriages I arranged in the past. They all turned out to be happy unions. In this case, because it involves my own nephew, I have given it more thought than I ordinarily would. And my conclusion, after seeing what a fine girl you are, is that you and Kenyei would make a happy couple."

Kimi, avoiding the matchmaker's eyes, glanced over at Kenyei for a split second. That bo-bura!

Imagine! having a go-between arranging this sort of thing this day and age. She almost became sick, remembering that time Kenyei had tried to embrace her in the kitchen. Just wait till she could speak to him alone!

"I know all this is a big surprise for you," the matchmaker said, smiling benigningly, patting her hand. "That's why I told your father and mother to talk it over with you before making a decision. I know you will be wise and will accept the proposal. But I want you to make up your own mind. When I come back again we will talk about the wedding and make necessary arrangements for the grand party to be held here at your home."

The man, at last, stood up from his chair. He turned to Kenyei. "Come, Kenyei, we'll leave Kimiko-san alone with her parents so they can talk it over among themselves."

Kenyei stood up and smiled a slow, shy smile at Kimi, then joined his uncle at the door.

Kimi's father and mother got up and walked over to the door. "We'll see you again in about a week," her father said, bowing to Kenyei's uncle.

"Yes, in about a week," the man acknowledged, bowing back.

If she ever saw those two again, it would be too soon! She was damned if she'd even consider marrying that— that blind oaf.

Her father and mother came back to the table and sat down.

"You can't be serious about this!" Kimi cried.

Before her father or mother could say anything, Sab,

ambling into the living room from the kitchen, said: "Don't tell me you're gonna marry him! That bo-bura."

"Saburo! You mind your own business. This has nothing to do with you," her father scolded.

"If Kimi married that bo-bura, he'd be my brother-in-law."

"What's wrong with that?"

"Ca-rist!" Sab snickered. "Who wants him for a brother-in-law, that fanatic."

"You shut your mouth!" her father scolded again.

"But how can—?"

"Saburo! Do as your father says. Be quiet," his mother said.

"But, Okaasan—"

"Saburo!"

"Aw-w . . ."

"Okaasan," Kimi now said, almost in tears, "you mean you approve of this arrangement? You want me to really marry Kenyei?"

Her mother lowered her eyes.

"What's wrong with Kenyei becoming your husband?" her father questioned. "He's honest; he's a hard worker and has a great future. What more you want in a man?"

"But Otoosan," she protested, struggling desperately for the right words, "I—I can't even stand him. We don't have anything in common."

"Time will take care of that," her father said. "Two people don't really get to know each other until they have lived together."

She looked over at her mother, hoping her mother would say something—anything—to make her father understand. But her mother seemed resigned to whatever her father ordained.

"If you were here earlier when Ikehara-san was telling us about the great future Kenyei has, I'm sure you would understand why I want you to marry Kenyei," her father said, looking earnestly at her. "There's no telling how high that boy might rise once Nihon takes over the islands. Ikehara-san promised him an important position at the sugar mill as soon as we're under Nihon."

"Wha-a-t!" Sab said, making a face. "Who's gonna offer Kenyei a position at the mill?" He laughed out loud.

"You shud up-pu before I slap your face," her father threatened. "You don't know nothing. You think Ikehara-san has been working at the sugar mill all these years for nothing? He knows every inch of the mill: every closet; every bolt; every nut and screw in the refinery machines. When Nihon takes over he might be appointed superintendent of the mill."

"Him? That old man, superintendent?" Sab scoffed. "He'll be cleaning toilets till his dying day."

"Saburo! Get back into the kitchen," her father ordered, pounding the table again. "We don't have to listen to your nasty remarks."

"Aw, c'mon, Otoosan. Let's wise up."

"Saburo!" her mother said, frowning. "Listen to your father."

Sab looked at her for a second, then quickly looked away. "Aw-w . . ." he moaned. He stood up from his chair and stalked back into the kitchen.

"What if Japan doesn't conquer Hawaii?" Kimi said, not able to think of any other argument, feeling foolish for even arguing. "Do you want me to marry Kenyei just because you think Japan is going to win the war? Because his uncle thinks he's going to run the sugar mill someday? What about me? My feelings? Don't I have anything to say about this?" she pleaded, looking over at her father, then at her mother, eyes brimming with tears. The whole thing wasn't as absurd as she first thought it was. Her father and mother were really serious.

Oh-h, she should be able to come up with better arguments, she told herself, eyes shut tight, groping for more logical, more forceful reasons. But she simply couldn't think of anything else to say.

"It's because we're thinking of your welfare that your mother and I want you to marry Kenyei," her father said, solicitous. "Under normal circumstances, I wouldn't be too concerned. But with the war on and everything else, there couldn't be a better prospect for you. As for Japan winning the war, it's inevitable. History shows that Japan will some-day rule the world."

Kimi kept looking down at the table, eyes filling.

"Your mother and I are getting old, Kimiko," her father continued, his voice suddenly soft and warm. "We'd like to have grandchildren before we die. Your two older brothers might not get married for a long time. There isn't much for us to look forward to anymore. Is this too much to ask of you? To get married now and offer us grandchildren?"

Holding one hand up to her mouth, she looked over at her father and mother, then, bursting out in choking sobs, jumped up from her chair and dashed into her bedroom.

Later in the evening, having somewhat overcome her traumatic shock, Kimi sat on the matted floor of her mother's dimly lit bedroom, trying frantically to convince her mother that she just wasn't going to marry that—that, oh! she still couldn't find the words to describe that bobura—Kenyei.

The two windows in her mother's room were blacked-out with tarred papers, but the shaded light bulb was lowered almost down to the floor because the tiny cracks all along the wall couldn't be patched.

—And that was final as far as Kimi was concerned. She wasn't going through with the arrangement. She wasn't even going to discuss it further with that—that janitor, that self-appointed sugar mill superintendent or—or whatever he called himself. And if she ever saw that Kenyei again, so help her! she'd really tell him a thing or two. Just wait!

"You'll tell him no such thing!" her mother said sharply, the tiny light bulb casting a glint on her glasses.

"But, Okaasan!" she pleaded, taken aback by her mother's unexpected tirade, "you couldn't possibly expect me to marry Kenyei. How could you?"

"What's so wrong about Kenyei that you hate him so much?"

"I don't hate him. Its just that—"

"If you don't hate him, then you must like him."

"Oh-h . . . Okaasan, I don't hate Kenyei, but I don't like him either," she tried to explain, hands gesturing up and down.

Her mother frowned. She straightened her back and changed sitting position from her left to her right haunch, then squashed her Kool in the sardine-can ashtray at her knees. "How can you say that?" she asked. "You either like him, or you don't."

"Okaasan, please try to understand," she begged, the reasoning tumblers in her head twisting and churning for the right answer. "Have you ever seen Kenyei and me sit down and talk to one another? Have you ever heard us discuss anything?—No, you haven't. And it's because we just don't have anything in common. We're practically strangers to each other. Do you want me to marry someone I can hardly talk to?"

"It's because you haven't tried to understand him," her mother said, unyielding. "If there's anything peculiar about him, you have to blame the pitiful way he was brought up. His parents left him when he was still a baby. Until this day, he doesn't know what it is to have a normal family life. You could help him!"

"Why me? There must be lots of other Okinawan girls on Maui who would be interested in someone like him."

"Kenyei must feel very close to our family," her mother said, looking away, eyes blinking. "He has been coming to our home almost every night since moving to Kapuna. I'm sure he finds much comfort at our home, comfort he never found elsewhere in his life."

"Well, that's good. Wonderful. He can still come here every night. He doesn't have to marry me."

"Kimiko, that boy must think a lot of you," her mother said solemnly. "You shouldn't say bad things about him."

"I'm not saying anything bad about him, Okaasan. All I'm saying—"

"When I left Okinawa many years ago to come to Hawaii to marry your father," her mother interrupted, "I didn't even know who he was or what he looked like. But he was highly recommended by the matchmaker in Katena Village, and that was all that mattered. You, at least, know who Kenyei is. You've known him since a young girl."

"The days of matchmakers are something of the past, Okaasan. It's gone. It's something that happened many years ago. Things have changed. We're living in a different world."

"It's changed only here in Hawaii. In Japan, it's happening every day," her mother said.

"But we're not in Japan. We're here—Hawaii—America."

"Didn't you hear what your father said about Japan taking over Hawaii soon?"

"Oh-h . . . I don't want to discuss the war, or who's going to win it. Time will take care of that."

[161]

Neither of them said anything for a while. Kimi could hear her father mumbling to himself in the kitchen, and could also hear Sab snoring in his bedroom.

"Marriages arranged by a matchmaker never result in divorces," her mother now lectured, looking at her across the cone of the low, shaded light bulb. "Here in Hawaii, we always hear of divorces. It's because young couples get married without sharing the common background necessary for a sound marriage. They speak of liking each other, of loving each other, as though this was the only important thing. Marriage is more than that, Kimiko," her mother went on. "The couple must share a goal. Something they can look forward to; work for; be willing to sacrifice much for it. Without this, the so-called love they speak of will crumble and dwindle away with the first signs of hardship."

Kimi, listening to her mother with moistened eyes, suddenly realized that it was the first time she had ever heard her mother expressing herself in such a warm, endearing manner. She kept rubbing her finger at a dark spot on the mat.

"Your father and I didn't know each other when we got married, but we had something wonderful to look forward to," her mother continued tenderly. "We wanted to offer our children a better life than what our own parents were able to offer us. There were many times, Kimiko, when we worked for months in the hot fields, twelve hours a day, seven days a week, until the bones in our hands did not know what it was not to feel throbbing pains. But we were glad to do it. We dreamt of returning to Okinawa wealthy so our children would be treated with the dignity and respect your father and I never knew back there."

Warm tears streamed down Kimi's cheeks. She kept looking down at the mat, her eyes following the dark, symmetrical pattern of the woven straws.

"Unfortunately, we were never able to accumulate enough money to go back," her mother went on. "But that doesn't matter too much anymore. We were fortunate in other respects. All of you have been healthy. You have all had a good life, a good education, a good home—far more than what your father and I ever had when we were young."

There was a moment of silence in the semi-dark, quiet room.

Kimi wiped her eyes.

"Someday, Kimiko, when you have children of your own, you'll know what I'm trying to say," her mother said, her voice still soft, still warm and tender. "This thing called love that you think you must feel first before marrying Kenyei will be unimportant then. You will learn to like him and understand him. Your main concern will be your children."

Kimi looked up at her mother with filled eyes, wanting to throw her arms around her mother and hug her, but restrained herself. She had never known before that her mother, who was always so quiet and gentle and sweet, had been repressing herself all these years.

"When you were born, Kimiko," her mother said, "I knew that your father was disappointed—you not having been born a boy. But when he saw how happy I was, he quickly reconciled himself. Ever since, he has always been very proud of you. He may not be a man to say much when sober, but you know as well as I that whatever he says he speaks from his heart."

Her mother rubbed the corners of her eyes under the glasses.

Kimi had been tempted to tell her mother about George all along, but had hesitated, afraid of the repercussion it might cause. Now, she felt there was a chance her mother would understand.

"Okaasan," she said tremulously, looking up slowly from the mat, "I've already met a boy I'd like to marry someday."

Her mother studied her across the stream of dim light. A tense second or two went by. "What boy?" her mother inquired. "Do we know him?"

"No."

"Who is the boy, then?"

"He's someone I've known for about a year now."

"Oh-h?"

"His name is George Kealoha."

"Kea— Why, that's not a Nihon-jin name."

"He's not a Nihon-jin, Okaasan. He's a Hawaiian."

"A Kanaka boy!"

Kimi felt herself recoiling, fortifying herself.

"How did you meet this boy?" her mother demanded, her tone cold and harsh.

"We went to school together."

"And—and you want to marry him!"

Kimi nodded timidly.

"And you think your father and I would ever approve of such a marriage.".

"But Okaasan, he's a nice boy."

"How can you know anything about him; you only went to school with him."

"He's my boy friend."

"You mean—you mean you have been seeing this—this Kanaka boy behind our backs!" her mother burst out, taking hold of Kimi's forearm and giving it a painful pinch.

Kimi jerked her arm back and sobbed, rubbing the spot her mother had pinched. Her mother's pinches had always been the severest kind of punishment inflicted on the children.

"How could you! How could you have done such a thing when you were brought up to be a decent Japanese girl!"

"We did nothing wrong," she pleaded, head hung low.

"There must be something wrong with this—this Kanaka boy," her mother said contemptuously. "He must not be acceptable among his own kind."

"He's not like that. He's a very smart boy."

"Then, why doesn't he stay among his own kind? If he's as good as you say he is, he would be accepted by his own people."

"I don't know, I don't know why," she sobbed. "All I know is I love him very much, and he loves me. Is that so wrong?"

"It's not right," her mother said, implacable. "And you better not let your father ever find out about this. He'd kill you first before he'd let you marry a Kanaka boy."

"But why?" she pleaded. "He's a much better man than Kenyei. He's something Kenyei will never be."

"Baka! Kenyei is a Japanese; the Kanaka boy isn't. That's reason enough."

"But I don't love Kenyei."

"You don't know what love is until you have lived with

your husband—until you have become a part of his pains and sorrows, his heartaches and failures. Your life has been too easy, that's why you have these silly notions about love."

Hesitantly, Kimi reached over for her mother's hard, much-labored hand and held it tight in both of hers. "Okaasan, I know my life hasn't been as hard as yours have been, but is this my fault? My doing? You just said that you and Otoosan wanted us children to have a better life than what you had to go through." She kept looking into her mother's piercing eyes, her own eyes filled with warm tears, rubbing her mother's gnarled hand.

"Marrying someone other than a Nihon-jin isn't what I want," her mother said, her voice taking on a softer tone. "And I know your father would feel the same way if he ever found out."

"George is not all Kanaka, Okaasan. He's part Japanese."

"Oh? How is that?"

"His mother was half-Hawaiian, half Japanese."

"What is his father?"

"Half-Hawaiian, half-German."

"German? But that still makes him more Kanaka."

"I wish he was all Japanese so he would be accepted by you and Otoosan, but because he is not, you want me to say he is not a good boy?"

"I did not say that. All I'm saying is that nothing good ever comes from a mixed marriage."

"But why?"

"What about the children? What will they look like? They won't look like Nihon-jins, nor will they look like Kanakas. They will be mongrels, not knowing what race they belong to. And when they grow older it'll become worse. They won't be accepted by either races."

"Yes, they will, Okaasan," she said desperately. "They might be a little different, but in looks only. They will be like any other children, young, pure, innocent. And they will be brought up properly like you and Otoosan have brought us up. They will be proud of their Japanese, Hawaiian and German blood."

"What about the boy's father and mother? Will they accept you? A Nihon-jin? Consider you one of them?"

[165]

Another round of tense silence hovered over the dimly lit room. Outside, a jeep passed the house and was rumbling over the wooden bridge.

"George doesn't have real parents," Kimi finally answered. "They died when he was a boy and his foster parents adopted him."

Her mother looked at her, eyes turning warm and soft. She removed her glasses, wiped her eyes with the sleeves of her kimono and put the glasses back on again. "Where is the boy now?"

"He volunteered in the Army, but we plan to write to each other all the time. When the war is over both of us want to go to University of Hawaii."

"Is he smart enough to go to the University?"

"Oh, yes. He made one of the highest grades in our class."

"It must be the Nihon-jin in him."

"I know you and Otoosan will like him. He wants to meet both of you when he gets back on a furlough."

"I don't know . . ." her mother murmured, indecisive. "I don't think your father will approve."

"How can he judge someone he hasn't met?"

"You know how your father is. When his mind is made up it's hard to change it."

"What about you, Okaasan? Will you meet him?"

"What good will that do, Kimiko? Your father is the one who makes all the decisions."

"You can talk to Otoosan and make him understand."

"We'll have to wait and see," her mother said, deliberating, head bent low.

"What about Kenyei?" Kimi asked. "No matter what happens, I don't intend to marry him."

"I guess I can talk it over with your father before Ikehara-san comes back," her mother said fatalistically. "I'll tell him that you are not ready to marry yet—that you still have your mind set on becoming a school teacher."

"Oh, yes, Okaasan. I want to become a school teacher so badly," she cried, taking hold of her mother's wrinkled hand once more and squeezing it with deep affection. "I know Otoosan will understand after you explain to him," she sighed, bringing her mother's hand up to her face and rubbing it against her warm, wet cheeks.

"Remember, I'm not promising anything," her mother said, pulling back her hand gently. "It'll be up to your father —as always."

"Yes, I understand," she said, gratefully relieved, rubbing away her tears.

"It is getting late, Kimiko," her mother said, pushing herself up from the matted floor, straightening up, pounding the small of her back with one hand and stretching. "We better go to bed."

Kimi got up from the floor, too, stretching her legs, sighing deeply. She didn't have to conceal anything about George from her mother anymore. It was such a wonderful feeling.

She went back to her own bedroom, changed into her pajamas, and climbed up on her bed.

Oh, George, she thought, closing her eyes dreamily, tossing around sleeplessly. She could hardly believe she had been talking to her mother about him.

Please, God, she prayed silently, please watch over him.

14

AT ABOUT THREE the following hot and humid afternoon, Sab, wearing his sweat pants and shirt, was in the warehouse next to the garage punching a heavy bag. He was dejected to learn that he'd have to be going back to school the next day, and the more he thought of it the harder he hit the bag. On the other hand though, he'd get to see Miss Blake, he tried to console himself.

Right now, he decided to forget about school and Miss Blake, and concentrate on his timing. He shuffled back gracefully on his soles, then, stepping forward again, hit the bag with a mean combination: One-two BOOM! He could feel the muscles of his sinewy arms vibrating under the terrific impact.

He sure hoped the war would be over by next October so nothing would interfere with the next boxing tournament. He would have turned out for the last one, but having been a minor and his father and mother refusing to give their consent, the officials had rejected his entry blank. He was determined to fight in next October's matches even if he had to forge his parents' signatures.

He just couldn't understand why the old folks didn't want

him to box. He was a helluva flyweight, lightning fast, could hit hard and could also take a good punch. Whenever he boxed with the boys in his Phys Ed class, he'd always have to take it easy, or they wouldn't box him. He had seen last year's flyweight champ in action and was sure he could have taken the guy, probably could have knocked the guy out with one of his mean rights.

But his mother had not wanted him to box; had not even wanted to talk about it. She had said boxing was barbaric—two men thrown into a ring to pummel each other senselessly while the delighted, blood-thirsty fans yelled and screamed over the brutal beating—and no son of hers was ever going to become a boxer.

Actually, the only boxing match his mother had ever seen was the one held in Wailuku several years back when the Japanese champ, Piston Horiguchi, had come to box the local Filipino pride, Young Gildo. Sab had gone to see the fight with his mother and recalled that whenever the Filipino landed hard blows on the Japanese Piston, his mother would cover her face, then whenever the Piston landed the blows she'd stand up excitedly with the rest of the partisan Japanese fans and yell out: "Hit him! Hit him back, Pis-ton-san!"

When the fight was declared a draw the angry Filipino fans had thrown rocks and bottles into the ring while the Japanese fans had shaken their heads in passive protest. Sab's mother, glad the fight was over, had mourned over the bloody mess of Piston Horiguchi's face. Naturally, she had no idea that Sab had been captivated by the tumultuous yelling and screaming of the fight fans and had vowed that one day the same people would be cheering for him, too.

Sab knew that his greatest asset was his jabs and left hooks. He had been developing them ever since setting up the bag in the warehouse two years ago. He could throw three-four lightning fast jabs in one continuous flurry and follow them up with a devastating left hook without throwing a single right. His right, of course, was pretty explosive, too. He could knock a guy on his ass with it. But, like Dado Marino, the flyweight king of Hawaii, the left was his real weapon. He had read once that Dado, a converted southpaw, could cold-cock a guy with just one good left to the button. He wanted to become that good someday. What he needed was a little more training to perfect his hooks.

He was already working up a pretty good sweat. He kept jabbing and hooking on the heavy bag, following up with solid rights: three straight jabs, a hefty hook, then a thumping right; or a jab, a right, then a quick baffling left hook: One-two Boom!

The warehouse wasn't an ideal place for the up-and-coming champ of the Territory to be training at. It was pretty dark in there, the only light being a stream of sunlight flowing in through the open doorway. It was also confining with chicken-feed bags piled all over the place. The heavy bag hung in the middle of the small space from a four-by-four wooden beam, and whenever Sab wanted to practice on his fancy footwork he'd always have to pile the chicken-feed bags in one corner and shove the feed mixer against the far wall. If he jumped too much while doing his footwork the fine powdered dust on the floor would filter up into his nose and cause him to sneeze. The only time he could breathe freely was when he'd stick his sweat-stained head outside the doorway and take in deep breaths.

His schedule for today was to hit the bag for a couple of three-minute rounds, interrupting them with a minute of fresh-air breathing, then do some shadowboxing to improve his combinations. After that, he'd jog down the river to Kapuna Pond where he planned to take a dive into the cool water, then come back to start the fire for the pig slops.

After taking a breather, he was back punching the bag, sweat pouring down his forehead and cheeks, armpits and back under his sweat shirt dripping with worked-up perspiration. He felt he could go three fast rounds with any flyweight, including Dado Marino—maybe. He threw couple of quick combinations, then snapped back with loaded hooks, picturing his opponent toppling backward on the canvas.

Boy! he sure was glad he wasn't on the receiving end of his blows. Pow! One-two BOOM! One-two BOOM!

What made him really feel like a champ today was the new pair of boxing shoes and punching-bag gloves he was wearing. He had bought them yesterday with some of the money he had won in last Monday's poker game. The shoes and gloves felt smooth and soft, and the clean, fresh smell of new leather made him feel like a real pro. He could envision himself the Territory Flyweight Champ: Hands clasped high over his head; face beaming with a big smile; flash bulbs popping all around him.

All he had to do to make the grade was to hit the bag every day, develop his punches, learn to throw effective combinations and be able to duck, feint, parry and slip jabs, then counter with fast lefts to the gut, then step back and wham! a solid right smack on the button.

Pow!

One-two BOOM! One-two BOOM! (mouth puckered up like a chicken's ass), exhaling loud, whizzing noises from his nostrils, jab, jab, then WHAM! a good, hefty left hook (stepping back real fast), then BOOM! a straight right cross (mouth not too puckered up, but still a chicken's ass,) then a flurry of quick, jarring blows, again stepping back and coming up with a snappy, nerve-chilling left hook to the button.

He sure was glad he wasn't punching anyone. The poor guy would never get up.

Finished with the bag, he took another minute's breather outside, then was back shadowboxing, the bags of chicken feed his spectators. He flicked short jabs in the air, followed them up with left hooks, then suddenly with flurries of body blows to the gut, dancing around lightly on his toes, weaving, ducking, bobbing, countering (grinning at his foe, waving brazenly at him to c'mon, start fighting like a man.)

He was in such a good shape he felt he could shadowbox for a whole hour, but thought he had better stop before he got stale. It was a long wait until next October. What he planned to do now was to get out in the fresh air and do some road-work to develop his legs and lungs. He wanted to have a springy quality in his legs so he could be an ever moving fighter, fast, elusive, weaving in and out, side to side, never tiring, always working the hell out of his opponent. Without strong legs a fighter might as well hang up his gloves; road-work, he once read in a boxing magazine, was the best thing for a fighter. They said the main reason Joe Louis had lost his fight to the German guy was because he had neglected road-work, then when he had concentrated on it for the return bout, he had nearly pulverized the poor German.

Yeah, a fighter's legs were very important, Sab told himself, stepping out gingerly from the sneeze-evoking dark warehouse, eyes squinting at the sudden glare of sunlight, feeling the hot afternoon sun slanting on his sweat-glistening face, every muscle in his body steamed up with youth's vim and vigor. He jogged down to the dirt road, knees bouncing high to his chest, arms held close to his sides, nose whizzing loud like a race horse's, a swirl of fine, reddish dirt trailing behind.

Just as he was about to climb down the first old wooden bridge, he noticed a gray open Navy jeep parked on the other side of the river, along Kenyei Shiroma's taro patch. It must be for some sailor looking for his Kanaka girl friend, he thought, jumping down to a big rock under the bridge. He hopped from rock to rock, flicking short jabs and right crosses in the air.

Bordering the banks of the cool river were lush-green tropical guava, plum, koa and mango trees. Every so often, he could see bright red cardinals and black, chattering myna birds fluttering before him. He would have thrown rocks at them but couldn't be bothered right now. He had to concentrate on his training and forget about such kid stuff.

After ten minutes of intense hopping and jumping—sweating like hell under his pants and shirt—he was only a stone's throw away from the west end of the long pond below the cliff. He suddenly stopped. He thought he had heard voices. He listened carefully; could hear nothing he continued on. Then, he noticed two heads bobbing up and down in the deep cliff-side of the pond.

Aw, for crying out loud! Must be some Kanaka kids from the other side of river. And here he had been planning to swim bare-balls.

He walked slowly on the left bank, away from the rocks and water, brushing past lantana bushes and hono-hono grass, wiping off the warm perspiration on his forehead and cheeks, wondering who the kids were. When he got closer, he discovered that they weren't Kanaka kids at all, but a haole couple: A pale-looking guy with sandy crew-cut hair and a brown-haired girl.

"Frank, stopit!" the girl squealed as her companion splashed water on her face. "You're going to drown me."

"Oh, a little water won't hurt you." The guy laughed and kept splashing more water.

Sab quickly ducked down among the tall bushes, hoping the couple had not seen him. He lay on his belly, head down, and began inching from bush to bush until he was on the upper bank of the pond, opposite the cliff. He still couldn't see their faces clearly, only the back of their heads in the blue-green water.

He crawled little closer towards a big rock partly concealed by hono-hono grass, his knees and belly scraping on pebbles and sand, hands noiselessly pushing aside small koa branches. He finally brought his head up and peeked from the edge of the rock. The couple were only about fifteen feet away from him, still splashing water.

"Oh, Fra a nk! That's not fair!" the girl moaned, turning her head away and brushing off water on her face. "I'm no competition for you. You're getting all that water into my mouth."

"Well, drink it," the guy teased. "It's pure mountain water. It won't hurt you."

Pure water, shit! Sab snickered. The water, of course, was filtered by the time it reached the pond, but if those two knew that people washed their clothes up the river they wouldn't be swimming in it.

His mouth suddenly fell wide open. Oh, no! Not her! It couldn't be! He kept staring at the girl, eyes bulging out, shocked. But it was her—Miss Blake—his English teacher.

The jeep up the river!

He continued looking up front between the blades of green grass. Miss Blake! swimming with some serviceman. As Sab's eyes swept the entire length of the long pond and back towards him, he noticed a blue flower-printed cotton dress and a white sailor's uniform on a red and black Indian blanket under the guava trees to the left.

Miss Blake!—Margaret Blake—swimming with some lousy sailor! He refused to believe it. Not his wonderful English teacher, his beautiful, sweet Miss Blake for whom he had been writing short stories all these months.

"C'mon, Margaret!" Sab heard the sailor calling out from the base of the cliff, "I'll race you to the other end."

It was her! How could she do this to him—Sab!—when he had been led to believe she liked him, too.

"Oh, Frank! I can't swim as fast as you."

Sab forced himself to watch them crawl-stroking towards the shallow end. He could no longer hear what they were saying, but could easily see them from his vantage point. They were lying on their backs in the foot-deep water, the sailor reaching over for Miss Blake's arm and pulling her over to him. Miss Blake, Sab thought, had tried to resist, then had given in. She was now lying on the sailor—on top of the damned sailor!—her body pressing down on him, her arms clung tight around his neck. She was kissing him!

Sab closed his eyes tight, a painful moan grinding out from the depths of his chest. When he opened them again, Miss Blake still had her arms around the sailor; still kissing him as though unable to control herself.

That pig! That dirty goddamn pig!

The more he thought of the long, intimate discussions he had with her at school the more he found himself burning with animal rage and hatred. He had to fight himself to keep from jumping up to his feet and scream at her. Tell her that she was nothing but a no-good slut; that he didn't want to have anything to do with her from now on. She can screw the whole United States Navy. See if he gave a damn! Not one bit!

He dropped his head on the crook of his forearm and wished that the river would suddenly flow over and sweep Miss Blake and her sailor boy friend into the ocean.

Miss Blake, how could she do this to him? Him—Sa-buu-row—when he had planned to give her a Christmas gift and turn in his latest story tomorrow. To hell with her! She was going to get nothing from now on. Not a goddamn thing! He wasn't even going to talk to her anymore.

The story he had written this time was by far his best work, and he knew she would have liked it. It had taken him painful hours to write it. The main point he had wanted to put across—in a subtle and indirect way—was

[174]

that he loved Miss Blake very much and would do anything for her. He had hoped that after she got through reading the story she'd realize that the boy in it was really him—Sa-buu-row—who loved his teacher more than anyone else in the world.

He lifted his head and peeked up front again, tears in his eyes. Miss Blake and the sailor were swimming back towards him. He got up to his knees quickly; decided to run for it. But they got out of the water, and walked to their clothes under the trees. Miss Blake was wearing a skin-tight, one-piece black bathing suit which contrasted sharply with her slender white body. The sailor, a guy about twenty-two or three, had on baggy, colorless swim trunks. He was powerfully built: big arms, big shoulders, heavy chested; he was big all around.

Sab watched every move they made, feeling warm blood surging up his ears and cheeks, wondering what they planned to do on the blanket.

"It's such a secluded spot," Miss Blake said, sitting down, knees bent up, hair dripping wet. She reached for a big white towel and began wiping her hair.

"Yeah, it sure is," the sailor agreed, sitting close to Miss Blake, looking up at the cliff. "Must have taken nature years and years to build this here place." He put his arm around Miss Blake.

"No, Frank. Let me wipe my hair," Miss Blake protested, pushing Frank away. "It's terribly wet. —How in the world did you ever discover this pond?" she asked, rubbing her head with the towel vigorously.

"Oh, couple of us fellows from the base was roaming around this end of the island one day when we came across it." The sailor had a strong, low voice with a drawling accent.

"It's just lovely," Miss Blake said, tying the towel into a big knot on her head and letting it rest there. "It's almost like something out of an adventure book," she continued, tossing her head back and gazing up at the two-hundred-foot drop. "It's a wonder some of those big rocks don't come tumbling down on us."

"They been up there like that for years," Frank said, putting his arm around Miss Blake again.

"No, Frank. Please don't. Someone might come."

"Oh, c'mon . . . No one ever comes around here."

"What about the native children? Don't they come here for a swim?"

"Naw-w . . . Not these kids. They rather go down the ocean. 'At's why they're so damn black like the Niggers back in Alabama."

"Have you ever done any surfing, Frank? I heard it's lots of fun."

"Who? Me, surf? Hell, no. I leave that to the gooks."

"Oh, now, Frank. That's not a nice thing to call the inhabitants of the islands."

"What you want me to call 'em? They're all gooks, ain't they?"

"No. Of course not," Miss Blake said. "The islands are made up of many different racial groups: Chinese, Filipinos, Polynesians, Japanese—"

"Well, they better ship them back to wherever they came from. Especially them Japs. Why, hell, I betcha they're more Japs here than there are in all of Nip land."

"But they're all Americans like you and me, Frank."

"Now, teacher," Frank said, shaking a finger at her, "you've been reading too many of them story books. If you're a Jap; you're a Jap. No if's or but's about it."

"That's not fair," Miss Blake said, pushing Frank's arm away again. "Some of the best students in my classes are of Japanese extraction. In fact, there's one boy who might turn out to be a great writer someday. He's shown great promise. I'm terribly interested in his progress."

Sab felt himself glowing proudly deep inside. If she'd tell the sailor to take her home right now he might forgive her for what she had done up till now, he thought magnanimously. Yet, while he lay there on his belly behind the boulder, he found himself waiting impatiently to see what they were going to do next. He could feel his groin pressing down deep into the crawling grass under him.

"Come here," Frank said, both arms locked tight around Miss Blake, pulling her down on top of him.

"Frank! Don't . . ." Miss Blake struggled to get up, then helplessly gave in. She returned Frank's hungry kisses, her arms around him, holding him tight, soft-looking body press-

[176]

ing down on him. Frank rolled over to one side of the blanket until Miss Blake was pinned beneath him, his free hand stroking her round behind and thighs, his legs sliding up and down all over her.

"Frank, stopit! I said stop it!"

Frank began unzipping the back of her bathing suit.

"Frank! You're not listening to me. Frank!"

Frank pulled down her shoulder strap, but Miss Blake, somehow, suddenly shoved him off her and quickly zipped up her bathing suit. She sat up furiously with her uplifted knees tucked under her chin, hands locked tight around her legs.

"Aw, now, Margaret, c'mon . . . What's the matter?" Frank sat up beside her, panting hard, arm around her again.

"Don't!" She pushed him away. "I meant it! I'm not just another jewel in your crown. I'm not cut out for things of that sort."

"Aw-w . . ." Frank pulled her over to him, undismayed, actually getting bolder. "What makes you think I'm that kind of a guy, Baby. You know how I feel about you."

"Don't call me that! What do you take me for? a—a tramp?"

Frank stared at her, indecisive.

Sab, experiencing a greatly aroused excitement, was no longer regarding Miss Blake as the school teacher he loved very much. He was now afraid Miss Blake might fight off the sailor's advances.

"Don't be like that," Frank murmured into Miss Blake's ear, refusing to let go of her this time. With both arms wrapped around her lithe body, he pulled her down on the blanket, kissing her hard, passionately, then rolled on top of her, fighting to hold her down.

"Let me up! Frank! Let me up!" Miss Blake pushed-shoved Frank, but could not struggle free. "Frank! Did you hear me! I said let me up."

Frank had her pinned down and kept forcing his weight on her, holding one of her hands to her side.

"Frank! You're not listening to me. Frank! Frank!"

Frank's legs were maneuvering all over Miss Blake's white, naked thighs, his free hand unzipping her bathing suit. He took hold of her shoulder strap and pulled it off her arms, then began tearing the entire upper portion of her bathing suit.

"Frank . . . Stopit!"

Jee-sus Ca-rist! Sab, open-mouth, kept staring hypnotically at Miss Blake's shimmering, pearly buttocks. They looked so soft and warm. He could see her firm, up-thrust breasts contorting against Frank's bare chest, round, supple and inflamed-looking.

"You're hurting me, Frank. Frank, please . . . Don't . . ."

Frank, breathing like a wild animal, eyes ogling down at her, refused to let go. He tore everything off Miss Blake and pulled down whatever she still had on to her legs, exposing all of her—her—

"Frank! No. Don't. Please . . . I don't want you to . . ." Miss Blake sobbed and pleaded, her free hand flailing Frank's arm and shoulder, trying frantically to pull up her bathing suit at the same time.

Frank gave the bathing suit a quick shove with his foot. Miss Blake was stark naked now. Miss Blake! Without a single stitch of clothes on! Sab felt as though he was dreaming of her again. He could see her soft, willowy body no more than ten feet away from him. He swallowed dazedly. The long indentation of her back curved down to her trim waist line, every inch of her exquisitely proportioned, not a single ounce of wasted flesh.

"Frank! No-o . . ."

Frank shucked off his swim trunks.

"Fra-a-nk! You're hurting me. Fra-a-nk! . . ." Miss Blake kept pounding Frank's shoulder and arm, trying to roll over to her side, kicking, scratching, struggling to get free, Finally, out of breath and exhausted, she just lay there under Frank. "Please, I don't want you to . . . Please don't . . ." she sobbed.

"I love you, Baby. I love you . . ."

Then, it was all over. Sab could see Frank's body and legs throbbing and quivering convulsively. After a while, Frank, sighing deeply, rolled off Miss Blake and lay on his back, limp, shucked up.

But Miss Blake now refused to let go of him. She rolled over on him, her soft, creamy buttocks rolling all over as though some uncontrollable mechanism in her kept clamoring for more. Frank wrapped his feeble arms around her and lay there utterly relaxed, not stimulated anymore, merely holding on to her.

Sab, lying there pressing his throbbing groin onto the crawling grass throughout the wild scene, suddenly felt tears streaming down his face. And he didn't know why, only felt the warm tears rolling down his cheeks and settling at the corners of his nose and mouth. As he watched Miss Blake maneuvering all over her sailor boy friend his fascination faded into an ugly, sickening repulsiveness.

That bitch! That whore!

Covering his face, he crawled back on his elbow and knees until he was beyond their vision. He jumped to his feet and ran up the river, crying, stumbling and slipping on the slimy rocks into the water, wanting to get away as far as he could from the revolting scene, hating Miss Blake, hating the whole world.

At last, he climbed up the bridge and ran home into his bedroom, grabbed his five-page short story and the Christmas gift, then scurried over to the pig pens. There, he heaved a wheelbarrow load of dry keawe wood into the fireplace of the pig slop cookery and started an angry fire with a pint of kerosene. He ripped the pages of his story and tossed them furiously into the flames.

He tore off the wrappings of the Christmas gift and flung them into the fire, then hesitating for a moment, clenched a fistful of pages from the gift itself and ripped them brutally apart from the binder.

That pig!

The book, "Island Paradise," was an anthology of short stories by Jack London, Somerset Maugham, Robert L. Stevenson, Mark Twain and other great writers who had visited Hawaii. It had cost Sab all of eight bucks and he was looking forward to discussing some of the stories with Miss Blake after she had read them.

That slut!

He tossed the torn pages into the red flames, then threw the rest of the book into it, and remained squatted there before the fireplace sobbing chest-heaving sobs, unashamed, bewildered, feeling that his wonderful, lovely world with

Miss Blake had suddenly crumpled. He stared at the fire, sniffling miserably, not understanding why the rest of the human race and the entire goddamn world were treating him with such wretched indifference.

15

WHILE SAB WAS squatted dazedly by the fireplace, Kenyei
Shiroma was standing rigidly in the tiny bedroom of his
iron-roofed shack across the river, experiencing a great
measure of personal triumph.

Not only because he was again savoring the prospect of
Kimiko, Sab's sister, becoming his wife soon, but also because he had just heard over the short-wave station that
the Imperial Army was advancing towards the British
Colony of Hong Kong, and the troops in the Philippines
were marching towards Manila. Those invincible Japanese
soldiers! Kenyei thought with spine-tingling pride, jaw
bones tightening, eyes moistening with strong emotion. At
the rate they were going they were sure to have all the
Asiatic countries and the Pacific Islands conquered within
a month.

He had just come back from his taro patches and was
still in his mud-stained, knee-length trousers, standing before his small radio listening to the trumpet-blaring Imperial Army Victory March. He walked over to his old
grimy straw suitcase in the corner of the bedroom and
brought out the beribboned blouse of his Japanese Army

Uniform. He flapped off the pungent smell of mothballs and old age, then shouldered himself into the blouse, his small beady eyes beaming nostalgically.

Once again, he was Corporal Shiroma, Kenyei, of His Majesty's Imperial Army. He buttoned up the blouse proudly, wiped off the film of dust on the corporal's insignia, straightened the shoulder padding, then stood at attention while the victory march went on.

After a while, he stepped over to the tiny mirror on his radio and studied the blouse with a stoic, solemn expression. He avoided the sight of his threadbare, mud-stained trousers.

Still captivated by the awe-inspiring music, he began marching around the small bedroom, head thrown way back, chest expanded out, dark eyes staring straight forward. His bare knees bounced up and down:

> Hep! Two! Three! Four!
> Hep! Two! Three! Four!

Suddenly, he stopped in mid-stride, his impassive Japanese soldier's demeanor turning into a meek grin.

That toothless old bastard, Ishi, was standing at the screen door, watching him with a shitty grin.

"What are you doing?" Ishi asked.

"—Huh! Oh, nothing, nothing." He looked away from Ishi's mocking eyes, brushing off lint on his blouse.

"You think Japanese soldiers will be coming to Kapuna today?" Ishi shook his head slowly, and before Kenyei could say anything, giggled out loud and slammed the door shut behind him.

That sonnabagun! Kenyei thought furiously, gradually feeling like a stupid jackass. That nosy old drunk probably ran over to tell his fisherman friend, Tengan, all about it.

Reaching down and turning off the radio, he shucked off the blouse and put it back carefully into the suitcase. He planned to wear it again the day Japanese soldiers marched into the valley. Then, he'd like to see who would have the last laugh.

"Go away, Akuwa! Go away!" he hissed between clenched teeth, staring at the door.

He now lit a cigarette and stepped over to the low

window beside his bed. He stood gazing over towards his taro patches two hundred yards down the road. The late afternoon sun had already disappeared behind the high mountains and the valley was slowly becoming a dome of shadowy, depressing silence. He had difficulty distinguishing distant objects, but could discern the general area of his five acres—a maze of blurred green patches.

He knew that his taros this year were going to be bigger than any other crop he had harvested. After years of painstaking experiments with different kinds of fertilizer, he had at last come up with a powerful mixture. He was quite certain he'd never get caught by the board of health inspector. He had purchased severals bags of commercial fertilizer and had mixed them with human and chicken kukui. The result was amazing! The only reason he had to use chicken kukui, too, was because it was very difficult to locate former outhouses in the valley.

The people were already saying his taro roots were going to be the biggest on the island. Whenever they tried to probe him for his secret he would reply mysteriously that he was using the latest kind of fertilizer: the mixed kind.

Taking another drag and feeling the smoke sinking down luxuriously into his lungs, he began calculating the profit he was going to make. With the prices of everything going sky high he could probably sell his taros for double their former price. Most of the lazy Kanakas were making all kinds of money working at the different defense jobs, and were sure to eat more poi; which meant greater demand; which, in turn, meant higher prices. And if the poi factories were going to make lots of money the taro growers should make a little, too.

With a start, he realized that no matter how much he made he still would have to share it fifty-fifty with the Kanaka who owned the land. They had agreed long ago that he would raise the taros, and they would share the profit right down the middle. Well, damnit! the arrangement was becoming less appealing as he thought about it now. He took all the financial risk and did all the work while that fat Kanaka sat on his lazy okole.

Something definitely must be done about it. As soon as Japan took over, he would see to it that the landlords turned over their holdings to those who did the actual work.

That sure was something. Him! the biggest landlord of Kapuna Valley. Then, he'd have Mr. Napipi, his present landlord, come over and work in the taro patches while he—Shiroma, Kenyei—sat on his okole for a change. And they would share the profit. Right down the middle.

He now gazed towards the Gusuda home across the river, barely noting white smoke billowing up into the sky from the pig slop cookery. They must be preparing to feed the pigs, he thought. Straining his eyes, he wondered what his future bride was doing. What he'd give to have her in his home now! He certainly wouldn't be standing there looking out the window.

Kenyei sure had to hand it to that old geezer uncle of his for handling the proposal so well. If he had thought of his uncle long before he could be going to bed with Kimiko this very minute. On the other hand, he never had any use for his uncle. When he had to borrow money to return to Hawaii, there had been no mention of interest. Yet, he had to pay one hundred dollars more than he had borrowed.

Standing there with his arms resting on the window ledge, he wondered whether Kimiko had put up a fuss after he and his uncle had left her home. But her father had committed himself; there was no way for her to back out, he reassured himself.

Oh, how he loved that girl! He loved her so much that whenever he thought of her while working in the taro patches, or while listening to soft Japanese music on the radio, tears would come to his eyes and his throat would choke with lumps.

Kimiko, Kimiko, Kimiko, if you only knew. If you only knew how much I loved you; how much I wanted to make tender love to you; hold you in my arms and whisper soft, poetic words in the darkness of a quiet night.

Unconsciously, Kenyei was forgetting the age-old Japanese custom of regarding a wife as nothing more than a mere servant to her honorable husband. What, in fact, he was thinking was he would always treat Kimiko as tenderly as one would treat the silky, exquisite feathers of a quivering dove; regard her with the delicacy with which one would regard the infinite beauty of a multi-colored butterfly; worship her with the devotion with which one would worship the sacred words of the great Buddha.

Oh, Kimiko, Kimiko, he thought, eyes brimming with warm tears, sniffling, straining his eyes again to get a better view of the hazy Gusuda home a quarter of a mile away. If you only knew . . . If you only knew . . .

His life was getting increasingly lonely these past few years, he thought self-tormentingly. What he'd give to have a family of his own! To be able to come home from the taro patches at night and find his wife and children waiting faithfully for him at the door. To be able to feel his child's trusting arms around him and hear himself being called Otoosan. How wonderful it would be to have these simple things, he thought, rubbing his eyes with his soiled hand, realizing that there never had been a time in his life when he was surrounded with love or affection.

After all these years in Hawaii, he was still living in an old shack—one tiny bedroom with a combination living-room-kitchen where those two drunks now lived—at times existing for days on canned sardines cooked with potato leaves and rice, and more often than not visiting the Gusudas pretending he 'had something important to tell them when he knew that they knew all along he was there to be invited to dinner. He had been doing this for so long that the fierce pride and self respect he used to have were no longer a part of him.

What a degrading way to live, he thought, depressed. But things would change soon, he told himself. He would soon have a wife to cook for him, care for him, love him, bear him the children he wanted so badly. He would have a wife to share with him the glorious celebration and joy when the Japanese troops moved into the valley.

Yes, everything was going to change soon. Perhaps, in a few weeks. Maybe in a few days.

16

KAMA, ALSO, AT that very moment was hoping that things would change soon.

He was sitting in the outhouse behind the kitchen, elbows placed comfortably on his exposed thighs, holding a week-old Japanese newspaper up close to his face. Will he forever be reading about the Nomura-Roosevelt peace negotiations?

He shuffled his feet a little back on the wooden floor of the tiny, unlighted outhouse, then turned the pages of the Nippu Ji-Ji to the advertising section. Prices of eggs and pork were the same, chicken feed was still expensive and the Japanese radio programs promised the same schedule. He raised one side of his butt up for a second, resettled it, then did the same to the other side. Finding it rather difficult to read the fine printed characters in the semi-darkness, he pushed the clapped-board door wide open then, reaching behind him, flushed the toilet.

The refilling water in the tank kept on flushing. Irritated, he reached back for the handle again, shook it couple of times and heard the water rising. Now, he heard water tap-tap-tapping on the sodden floor. Damned toilet, no matter how many times he stuck tar into the cracks it still leaked. He would have to get another second-hand toilet, he told himself, dismayed. As long as he was going to do that he might as well paint the outhouse like he had been planning to do years ago.

It was while reading the sports section that he first heard the loud BOOM! rattling the loose corrugated iron over his head. He dropped the newspaper and turned his head up. BOOM! BOOM! BOOM! The iron roof shook dangerously again and the floor trembled under him.

Akisamiyo! What was that! His dark eyes behind the bifocals widened, terrified.

When the next booming sounds came, he picked up the newspaper quickly, tore a couple of pages in half, ruffled them together and wiped his behind as fast as he could. Then, pulling up his trousers, he ran down the short trail to the back porch.

"Basan! Did you hear that!" he called out, buttoning his trousers. Not waiting for his wife to come out from the house, he ran over to the edge of the dirt road leading up to the pig pens. "Saburo! What was all that noise about?"

Saburo ran down, mouth gaped open. "Geez! It sure sounded loud."

They stood there, eyes locked with each other's, their feet shuddering by another series of booming sounds.

"It must be bombs!" Kama said, lips trembling.

BOOM! BOOM! BOOM! This time the ground shook as though struck by an earthquake.

Saburo looked at him with a pale, blood-drawn face. "It must be the real thing!"

Before the next thundering noise came, Kama, pushing Saburo ahead of him, ran back to the house. "Go into the house and stay with your mother."

"What are you gonna do, Otoosan?"

"Never mind what I'm going to do. Do as I say—go and keep your mother company."

Tsuyu was standing alarmedly on the back porch, hands covering her mouth. "What was all that?" she asked, voice quavering.

"Japanese planes must be bombing the island!" Kama told her.

The sounds continued relentlessly.

"Saburo! You and Okaasan get into the house and stay there. Hurry!"

"What good will that do?"

"You stubborn boy! If you don't want to go into the house, go down into the garage and dig out the can I hid the other day."

Saburo looked at him with a quizzical look, then, at last turned and trotted down to the garage.

"Jisan! You sure it's Japanese planes?"

"I can tell by the sound of the bombs."

Kama felt the next series of turbulent vibration creeping up his leg to the rest of his body. Then, he heard the distant burst of machinegun tat-tat-tating against the bombing noise.

"The airplanes are shooting at each other," he told his wife. "Parachuters must be landing."

"You think I should go up the bus depot and meet Kimiko?"

"No. She'll be all right. —Hand me that can of paint. Hurry!"

While Tsuyu stood there, refusing to go into the house, Kama, carrying the paint can and a brush, hurried over to the ladder leaning against the lower section of the house and scrambled up the tinny, red iron roof. He quickly pried open the can and drew a big circle. Then, leaving the red in the middle untouched, he began painting the rest of the roof white. As the bombing and machinegun sounds became louder and closer, he painted faster.

Empty silence suddenly took over!

What made the planes stop dropping the bombs, he wondered, breathing hard. He straightened his back and examined the roof. The quick paint job was no work of an artist, but the Rising Sun was unmistakable. Leaving the paint and the brush there, he trotted back to the ladder and climbed down.

He went to the back yard where Saburo, holding the cracker-box tin can, was standing with his mother at the garage entrance. He took the can from his son, opened the lid, and brought out the silk flag given him by the officers of the Shintoku Maru.

"What you gonna do with that Japanese flag?" Saburo

[188]

asked, studying him with a mixed look of alarm and curiosity.

He picked up the long-handled shovel at Saburo's feet and tied two corners of the flag around the handle.

"What you think you doing, Otoosan!" Saburo said, reaching for the flag.

"What's the matter with you, Saburo!" he scolded, pulling the flag away from his son.

"Jisan, you think it's safe?" Tsuyu asked.

"Japanese troops might have already landed," he said, giving both of them a harsh look.

"Otoosan, somebody gonna see you with that damn flag and haul your ass off to jail," Saburo said, again reaching over for the shovel handle.

"Saburo! Don't you think your father knows what he's doing?"

"Look, Okaasan," Saburo now said to his mother, "you better talk to him. Being drunk is no excuse for waving that flag."

"Jisan! Maybe Saburo is right. It's still too early to tell whether Japan has invaded Maui."

"You two don't know nothing!" Kama admonished, stamping his foot hard on the ground. "Didn't you hear those bombs!"

"Aw, Jee-sus!" Saburo moaned, slapping his forehead, "Just remember, Otoosan . . . When the MP's take you to jail, I warned you." He threw down his hands to his sides and shook his head.

While he and his son were arguing over the shovel-handled flag, elderly Mr. and Mrs. Kentaro Kaneshiro from up the road came trotting over excitedly. Kentaro Kaneshiro, in taro-patch trousers and an undershirt, was carrying a rifle; his wife, in a baggy kimono, was carrying a menacing-looking, four-fingered pitchfork.

"Kama, what was all that shooting about!" Kentaro Kaneshiro asked, wrinkled old face pulled tight, breath reeking with sake. "Is this it? Japanese troops have landed at last?" He kept staring at the flag in Kama's hand.

Kama studied the rifle, then glanced over awkwardly at the pitchfork Mrs. Kaneshiro was carrying.

"Where you think we should make our stand?" Kentaro

Kaneshiro asked, hoisting the rifle on his right shoulder, weaving from side to side on unsteady legs.

"Kaneshiro-oji-san! You better put that BB gun away," Saburo warned, closing his eyes and mumbling something to himself.

Tsuyu and Mrs. Kaneshiro were now talking to each other in rapid Okinawan, neither of them listening. Mrs. Kaneshiro, suddenly turning to her husband, said: "Oi! Kentaro. Shame on you. Button your pants."

Kentaro Kaneshiro glowered at his wife, looked down at his pants, then buttoned his fly with an impish grin.

In a few minutes, Mr. and Mrs. Seichi Oshiro from across the river, near Kenyei Shiroma's home, came running across the bridge.

"Oi! Did you folks hear all that bombing!" gray-haired, pot-bellied, Seichi Oshiro called out. "Where have they landed?" He had a printed Japanese towel around his close-cropped head and was carrying a gallon jug. His wife, a frail, white-haired woman, following right behind was carrying a big pot of okazu dinner. "When will they reach the valley?" she asked.

"Oh, Jee-sus!" Kama heard his son mumbling. "See what you've started, Otoosan? Pretty soon, you're gonna have all the crazy Okinawans here."

Kama looked at his son, not having the faintest idea what he had started.

Before long, Mr. and Mrs. Tokushi Inafuku, also carrying a pot and a gallon jug, came scrambling over the bridge. Behind them, not too far back, Ishi and Tengan came staggering over. After a while, a dozen of the Okinawans from the valley were there, everyone talking out loud.

"Holy cow!" Saburo said. "Why don't you be the President of the Kapuna Valley Revolution, Otoosan?"

Kama appreciated his son's confidence, but thought a younger man like Shiroma, Kenyei, was more suitable for the position. He placed the flag in the middle of the gathering.

"Oh-h, that's a nice flag. A nice flag," the crowd murmured their approval.

While everyone was talking excitedly, a dark brown Army jeep suddenly screeched into the driveway.

A hushed silence swept over the crowd.

Kama quickly untied the flag from around the shovel handle and stuck it into his back pocket. The driver was about to turn the jeep around and head back up the road, but noticing them standing there, he stopped and parked. He said something to the other soldier sitting beside him, then came stalking over. He was a big, tall hulk of a figure, the steel helmet on his head almost covering his cold blue eyes, the pistol holster hanging at an angle on his right hip. He had a band on his arm: MP.

"What y'all doin' heah?" he questioned in a low voice, looking down icily at the faces before him.

Everyone kept staring at the MP.

The big MP glanced over his shoulder at his companion in the jeep and jerked his head. The other MP hopped out and strode over in long, powerful strides. Both of them were about the same size—big, strong and cold looking.

"Didn't y'all heah me? I asked what y'all doin' heah," the first MP drawled again.

Kama looked over at his son and their eyes locked.

"We doin' nothing," Saburo said.

"What'cha mean—nothin'?" the second MP said, looking down at Saburo. The MP's right hand went down to his pistol and stayed there. "Don't you know Jap aliens can't be out after sundown?"

"It's still lighted," Saburo said, glancing up at the purplish-orange glow in the skies.

The MP's gazed at each other, then back down at Saburo.

"What'cha name?" the second MP questioned.

"Sab. Sab Gusuda."

"Sab what? —Neve' mind. You live here?"

"Yeah, I live here."

"All these people live here, too?"

"Hell no. Just me, my father and mother and my sister."

"Where's your sister?" the first MP asked, glancing around.

"She's not home from work yet."

"Y'all havin' some kind of Jap conference?"

"These people came to visit my folks. Nothin' wrong with t'at huh?"

"Listen, kid. Don't y'all get wise with me. I'm askin' the questions."

Kama stepped over to his son. "Saburo, what do they want?" he asked.

"Who's he?" the second MP questioned Saburo suspicious-ly, indicating Kama with a jerk of a thumb.

"He's my father." Saburo turned to Kama and said in Japanese: "Otoosan, be quiet. Let me handle this."

"What they all carryin' those things for?" the first MP asked, pointing to the jugs and pots the men and women were carrying.

"Just some stuff they always carry around with them," Saburo answered.

"Y'mean that old man there, he carries a BB gun with him all the time?" the MP questioned, pointing at the rifle on Kentaro Kaneshiro's shoulder. "And that old lady, she always carries a pitchfork with her?"

Saburo looked over at Mr. and Mrs. Kaneshiro and scratched his head. "Yeah, 'at's right. The old man likes to shoot mongoose."

The MP frowned. "And I suppose the old lady likes to chase them with the pitchfork."

Saburo scratched his head again. "Yeah, she does t'at all the time. The old man and the old lady, they're the best mongoose catchers in the valley. And they know how to cook 'em real good, too."

The MP's made a screwed-up face at Saburo, who flinched and swallowed hard.

"Yeah, yeah," Kentaro Kaneshiro said, stepping forward with his BB gun. "Me shoot 'em, mongoose. Bang! Bang!"

The MP's looked at each other. The first one took off his steel helmet and rubbed the sweat off his forehead with the sleeve of his khaki shirt.

"What he got in that there jug?" he asked, pointing to Seichi Oshiro.

"That? It's sake," Saburo answered.

Seichi Oshiro stepped forward. "Good. Bery good," he said, offering the jug to the first MP. "You try. Bery good sake."

"Bery good! Bery good!" a chorus of voices burst forth from the crowd.

The first MP looked over at his companion, hesitant. When he refused to accept the jug, Seichi Oshiro lifted it up to his mouth and, tilting it over, gulped a hefty mouth-ful. He smacked his lips loudly. "Ah-h . . . Bery good."

The second MP reached down timidly and took the jug.

He rubbed the neck-top and took a small sip. He rolled the sake on his tongue, paused, considered, then took a bigger sip, his deep-set blue eyes glittering. "Hey, Daniels, this thing's pretty potent stuff," he whispered, handing over the jug.

The first MP sipped a small drink, then followed it up with a big, thirsty gulp. "Say, it sure is good," he said, eyebrows arched up. He took another swallow.

"No. You keep. You keep," Seichi Oshiro said, when the MP tried to hand back the jug.

"Y'mean he wants us to keep it?" the MP asked Saburo. "What's he gonna have for himself?"

"Aw, don't worry about him. He's got more where it came from."

"Why, hell, man! 'At's mighty nice of him," the MP said, reaching down and shaking Seichi Oshiro's hand vigorously.

"You keep, you keep," Seichi Oshiro repeated, bowing and grinning.

"You thank him—thank 'em all for us," the second MP said, placing his big hand on Saburo's shoulder.

Before walking back to the jeep, the second MP looked over at Kama and formed a circle with thumb and forefinger. "Okay, very okay," he said, winking.

Kama winked back and bowed respectfully.

As the jeep pulled out of the driveway, the same MP hoisted the gallon jug over his head with one hand and waved at the crowd with the other. "Yeah, yeah. Okay, okay," he called out.

Everyone laughed out loud and waved back. "Good-u MP! Good-u MP!"

"Whew!" Saburo sighed, turning to Kama. "You see what I mean, Otoosan! You just missed going to jail. Jee-sus Ca-rist!" He kept shaking his head, then stalked up to the house.

Kama, sighing a deep breath, thought that had been pretty close, too. He took out the silk flag from his back pocket and mopped his brow with it. Everyone was again talking in loud, rapid Okinawan.

Holding up his hands, Kama declared to his fellow Okinawans: "We might as well have a party. It's not too often we can get together like this nowadays. —Basan! Go up to the house and bring mats and sake cups so we can have a Hawaiian-style Japanese party here. C'mon, everybody! Let's go over and sit down on the grass and enjoy ourselves."

Kimi, getting off the bus and heading home through the narrow trail among the koa trees, suddenly halted, and blinked her eyes several times. She still couldn't believe what she was seeing. There was a big Rising Sun flag on the roof of her home. Ohmygosh! she uttered, hand jumping up to her mouth.

She ran down the trail, wondering, horrified who had put the flag there.

"Sab!" she called, opening the front door and finding her brother standing at the kitchen window looking down the back yard. "Sab, who in the world put that Japanese flag on our roof?"

Sab turned around. "What flag?"

"That flag on our roof. You can see it from way up the hill."

Sab pondered for a second. "Oh, no!" he cried out. He ran out the kitchen to the back porch, Kimi following right behind.

"For crying out loud!" Sab exclaimed when he had climbed up the roof. "Father must have painted it."

"Painted it!"

"He was up here during the bombing a few minutes ago. The paint is still fresh."

"What bombing?" she questioned, shocked, looking up at Sab.

"All that noise a while ago—it sounded like bombs."

"Those weren't bombs. It was a target practice."

"Who told you that?"

"That's what most of the people on the bus thought it was."

Sab snickered. "You better not tell that to the old folks sitting down there with Father and Mother."

"You mean that's why they're here? They thought— Oh, no!" She broke out in laughter. "And I thought they had come to visit Father and Mother."

After they both stopped laughing, Kimi said: "Sab, you better repaint the roof before someone sees it. There were couple of MP's parked at the bend a while ago."

"Don't worry about those two. They're good friends of the old folks."

Puzzled, Kimi had wanted to ask Sab what he meant, but he turned around and rambled off to the other side of the roof.

He was back at the edge in a few minutes and climbed down the ladder. "I painted the red circle all white," he said, grinning. "Now, we've got a two-tone roof—one section red and the other white. It's the only kind on Maui."

"Well, that's a lot better than having a Rising Sun over our heads," she said, relieved. "That father of ours . . . What other ideas has he got?"

They walked back into the kitchen and stood looking down at the party going on at the back yard near the clothes lines. Dusk had settled rapidly and now there was only a faint glow of orange light over the mountains.

"I hope the old folks know they can't stay out much longer," Kimi said, concerned, watching bald-headed Tengan and toothless Ishi dancing an Okinawan jig while the women folks sang and clapped their hands.

"Leave them alone. They're having a nice time. They won't get in trouble with the MP's."

"Looks like the whole gang is here," she said, laughing, as Ishi fell on the mat. Mr. Kaneshiro, sitting cross-legged beside her father, had a rifle on his lap and was telling something funny. Every time he cried out "Bang!" everyone around him burst out laughing.

"The only one missing is that Bo-bura, Kenyei," Sab said.

"Oh, don't even mention his name to me," she said, making a face.

"I thought you was gonna marry him."

She slapped Sab's arm. "Don't you dare say that again!"

"He isn't such a bad guy. I think he'll make you a good husband. After all, his uncle gonna run the sugar mill and offer him a good job." Sab broke up in laughter, backed away before she had a chance to slap him.

"Oh, you . . ."

Kenyei Shiroma could not make it for the party because his uncle had told him not to visit the Gusudas until definite plans had been made for the marriage.

He had just turned his back to the window when the loud booming sounds rattled the roof of his home and shook the floor under him. When the sounds continued, he knew it could mean only one thing: Japanese planes bombing the Puunene Naval Air Station, preparing for an all-out invasion.

He rushed over to his straw suitcase, and this time took out not only the blouse but also the trousers and cap of His Majesty's Army uniform. He dressed quickly and turned on the radio to Radio Tokyo, hoping to hear news of the invasion. But the announcer mentioned nothing about Maui; did not even mention Hawaii.

After the booming and machinegun sounds had ceased completely, he went back to the window ledge and stood waiting to hear the next series of bombs falling. When darkness came, he was still waiting.

17

RATHER THAN GOING to school the next morning, Sab got off the bus in town and walked over to the corner of Market and Vineyard where he had met Yosh Nakata last Monday.

It was a bright and cool morning, and as he stood barefooted against the plate glass window of the unopened barber shop with his hands deep in his pockets, he kept wondering about Miss Blake. Would she still be the same prim, virtuous-looking school teacher? Or would she look like a cheap whore, ragged-looking and full of guilt? He could still feel pangs of pain throbbing inside of him as he thought of her, but it was no longer as painful as it had been yesterday afternoon when he had first discovered what a no-good pig she was.

In a way, he wished he had gone to school. It would have been fun watching Miss Blake and imagining her being stark naked like he had seen her down at the pond. But Yosh had called him at home just before he left for the bus station and had asked whether he still wanted to get into the deal they had talked about. Sure, he wanted to get into it, he had told Yosh. Well, be sure to be at the same corner at nine. And oh, by the way, don't forget to bring your bankroll, because they would be needing every penny they could scrape up to pull the deal, Yosh had said before hanging up.

Yosh should be showing up pretty soon, he thought now. He glanced across the street at the different store windows, a snicker creeping up the corners of his mouth. The same Japanese stores he and Yosh had talked about the last time still had big American flags fluttering in front of them. One of them which used to carry nothing but made-in-Japan goods was now a super-patriotic American store with red-white-and-blue, God Bless America banners for sale.

Fingering the roll of bills in his pocket, he wondered what the deal was going to be about. He had overheard Doc Kong saying something about a shipment coming in from Honolulu but knew nothing else about it. He was confident, however, that they would make all kinds of dough again.

"What d'ya say, Sab?" he suddenly heard Yosh calling from the corner of the building.

"Oh, hi! Yosh," he greeted.

"Been waiting long?" Yosh fingered out a cigarette from his shirt pocket and placed it between his thin lips.

"Naw. Just came from the bus depot," he said. Yosh sure looked flashy in a neatly pressed, opened-collar blue dress shirt and dark gray, deeply pleated gabardine trousers with small peg-legged cuffs wrapped around a pair of shiny black and white shoes.

"It's still early," Yosh said, looking down at his diamond-studded wrist watch. He lit his cigarette and, leaning back, rested his butt on the ledge of the barber shop window, his legs stretched out lazily, one hand propped on his knee. "We supposed to meet Doc and Ah Hong nine-thirty at Lin Wo's."

"Ah Hong? He's the guy gonna fly in from Honolulu?"

"He's gonna bring in the stuff."

"What stuff?"

"Diamonds."

"What you guys gonna do with 'em?"

"Buy 'em from Ah Hong. —Look, you got your bankroll with you?" Yosh asked, a mischievous gleam in his small eyes.

"Yeah, suah." He reached into his pocket and brought out the sheaves of bills, then handed them over to Yosh. "I got five hundred bucks."

"Put 'em back into your pocket," Yosh said, pushing Sab's hand away. "We don't need 'em until we get to the restaurant. Between you, me and Doc, we got twenty-five hundred. But we need more. 'At's why we gotta talk Clarence Wo and his old man into the deal."

"How much we need altogether?"

"At least ten grand."

"T'at much?"

"I told you. This gonna be a big one," Yosh said, talking through the side of his mouth in that sneering-frowning way of his. "We got a chance to double our money when we sell the diamonds."

"Yeah, it sure sounds like a big one," Sab said eagerly. "—By the way, Yosh, what happened to Moncado after we took him last Monday?"

Yosh grinned devilishly. "T'at poor bastard. Doc scared the hell outa him, he went over to Lahaina. We neve' seen him since."

"No kidding?"

"You should have seen Moncado's face. He turned pale. I thought he was gonna crap in his pants."

"When you t'ink he might come back?"

"Aw, whodahell knows . . . Why? No tell me you scared of the guy?"

"I hate to meet up with him again. He might have wised up."

"Him? Moncado, wised up? You must be kidding. I betcha he'd be glad to give you fifty bucks if you promised you won't turn him in to the cops."

"Naw, I don't wanna do t'at."

"What! You feelin' sorry for him?"

"Not exactly, but—"

"Hell, he was the one t'at wanted to take you for a ride, remember? 'Hey, my priend, you wanna play poker?' " Yosh went on, mocking Moncado's Filipino accent. " 'T'at boy over dere, Yosh, he got plenty money. Maybe, we take him por a ride, eh?' "

They both laughed uproariously.

Looking down at his wrist watch now, Yosh said: "C'mon, we better start for Lin Wo's. Doc and Ah Hong might be there already."

Walking alongside Yosh with both hands stuck in his

pockets, Sab could feel the cool morning breeze brushing against his face, his bare feet rubbing on the damp concrete sidewalk.

"You folks in Kapuna hear the shelling last night?" Yosh asked, looking over.

"What shelling?"

"You mean you neve' hear all that noise last night? Some Buddhahead submarine shelled the hell outa Kahului."

"T'at was a submarine shelling the island!" Sab said, flabbergasted. "We thought some Buddhahead airplane dropped bombs."

"You crazy or something? One bomb on Maui and the island would sink."

"Anybody get killed?"

"Naw." Then, looking over slyly, Yosh said: "Come to t'ink of it, somebody got bumped off."

"Yeah? Who?"

Yosh looked away, smirking. "Somebody's chickens got blasted."

"Aw-w, c'mon . . ."

" 'At's no bull shit," Yosh said, somewhat serious. "Most of the shells landed on Maui Pineapple Cannery's smoke stack. But one shell actually landed on some Japanee family's chicken coop and killed all their chickens."

"You mean 'at's all the goddamn Buddhaheads did—kill somebody's chickens and shell the cannery's smoke stack?"

" 'At's what I heard."

"Why they wanna do that for?"

"Whodahell knows what the Buddhaheads trying to do. Maybe, they wanted to have chicken sukiyaki."

"Aw-w . . . What about the smoke stack? Why they shell t'at for?"

"They probably think the less pineapples Americans have to eat the sooner we gonna give up fighting."

Sab burst out laughing.

"I bet all the old folks on Maui thought the Buddhaheads was gonna land at last, huh?" Yosh said.

"You should've seen the Kapuna old folks. I thought they went crazy."

Yosh threw his head back and laughed out loud after Sab told him about the MP incident.

"Bunch of diehards," Yosh sneered.

"If we was born in Japan I betcha we'd be eating nothing but sweet potatoes," Sab said.

"And me, I get constipated every time I eat the damn things," Yosh said, frowning.

They were in front of the Valley Drug Store, across the street from Iao Theatre. Yosh stopped to talk privately to a big, fat, Porlegee guy while Sab waited several steps ahead. The posters at the theatre showed a John Wayne movie. Sab strained his eyes to read the words; if he didn't have anything to do this afternoon he'd take in the show and kill some time before going home. John Wayne, his favorite actor, always played in movies with plenty of action.

Yosh, through talking with the guy, now joined Sab, and they continued walking down Market.

"You know t'at guy?" Yosh asked, jerking his head back towards the drug store.

"Who's he?"

" 'At's Rodrigues, the detective."

"Oh, yeah?" Sab glanced back at the big Porlegee guy.

"He wanted to know where some wahine was so he can take her down his house and screw her," Yosh said.

"Oh-h . . ."

Sab, swaggering alongside Yosh, felt kinda big shot, too. Everyone in town knew Yosh: the store owners, the waitresses, the barbers, the cops, just everybody. And they all called him by his first name, or nodded respectfully at him as though he was some kind of important political figure on Maui County.

"T'at detective owns a big, thirty-thousand-dollar house down the beach," Yosh said, walking languidly, one hand in his pocket. "Makes you wonder how a cop can afford something like that, huh?"

"He must be loaded."

"The guy's one of the biggest gamblers on Maui. He's getting paid off by some of the up-and-up games, too."

"Stuff like t'at actually goes on here on Maui?"

"Howdahell you t'ink Rodrigues can afford a big home? He only makes three-fifty a month. His house is better than lotsa haole houses."

"How come he's a good friend of yours?" Sab asked, after Yosh had said hello to someone passing.

"We worked on couple of deals together."

[201]

"You and him?"

"We took Tony Medeiros for over a grand once," Yosh said. "You know, Tony, the Porlegee old man t'at runs the taxi stand next to People's Market."

"How you guys work the deal?"

"Sheez! Sab. You sure nosy."

Sab walked on in silence.

They were now at the corner of Main and Market, half a block down from Lin Wo's, and were passing in front of the Japanese fish market where a couple of bucketfuls of strong-smelling fish were displayed on the sidewalk. They turned right on Main and the warm morning sun and cool tropical breeze blew against their backs.

As they approached Lin Wo's, Sab, knowing that Kimi worked at the first counter at Kress across the street, walked close on the inside of Yosh. If Kimi ever found out he had played hooky again he'd never hear the end of it. The last time she had caught him she had promised not to tell the old folks about it provided he promised he'd never do it again. That had been over a year ago and naturally he had played hooky lots of times after that, but had never gotten caught.

Yosh pushed open the faded screen door of Lin Wo's and walked into the long Pah-ke restaurant, Sab following right behind. The place was empty, and there was the delicious smell of Pah-ke food coming from the kitchen in the back. Sab, of course, had been to Lin Wo's many times with his father to pick up pig slops, and he now wished the deal was going to involve someone who did not know his father.

Yosh, after glancing around the dozen half-enclosed booths on both sides, pulled up the inside chair of the first booth next to the cashier's counter and sat down. The booth was separated from the next one by a green, chest-high partition, and there were two metal folding chairs on each side of the dark, varnished table. Sab sat facing Yosh and quickly noticed old cigarette burnt marks all over the table surface.

"I guess we kinda early," Yosh said, craning his neck to peer out the front door facing him. "It's not nine-thirty yet."

"When was Ah Hong gonna come in from Honolulu?" Sab asked.

"Doc supposed to pick him up at the airport at nine, then meet us here."

"Ah Hong bringin' all t'at diamond by himself?"

"T'at Pah-ke, he's a real smooth operator. I met him in Honolulu once. You can tell right away he's a top dog with the syndicate."

"When you went to Honolulu?"

"I thought I told you . . . After coming back from Molokai I stuck around town for couple of weeks then took a trip with Doc."

"I heard it's big and fast over there."

"Oh, yeah. Not like Wailuku. They have street lights, street cars and big busses all over the place. And the sidewalks always packed with people."

"I sure like to go there someday. You get lost?"

"Naw," Yosh said, still looking out the front door. "I was there before."

"I heard they have lotsa whore joints."

"The place is wide open. Especially down towards River Street and Aala Park."

"You mean you just walk up to one of those places and get a piece of ass?" Sab questioned. He had heard about the whores in Honolulu from one of the older boys in school, but wanted Yosh to tell him more about them.

"All you have to do is get in line. When the whore is ready you pay two-and-a-half bucks to some fat Kanaka wahine t'at runs the place. Then, she gives you a towel, and you go into a small room with the whore."

"What kind they have?"

"All kinds—fat, skinny, beautiful, ugly—"

"I mean what nationality?"

"Mostly haoles from the States. But they have some Titas, too. Somebody once told me there was some Japanee whores, but they won't take Japanee guys."

"Why?"

"She might run into her own brother, or somebody who knows her family."

"How's the haole girls? They real beautiful?"

"For Christ sake! Sab. You neve' been to a whore joint?

They have some right here on Maui—down near Kalama Park in Kihei."

He looked away, flushing. "I don't have chance to go way down there."

"I'll take you there one of these days so you can get laid," Yosh said, grinning.

Sab smiled eagerly. Maybe, he would get a chance to screw some nice blond like they have in the movies.

Clarence Wo, the dark complexioned, lanky, half-Pah-ke, half-Kanaka son of old man Lin Wo, walked over to the booth from the kitchen. "What d'ya say, Yosh?"

"Hi! Clarence," Yosh greeted.

Clarence Wo folded his dark arms across the red and white flower printed aloha shirt he was wearing outside his khaki trousers, glanced down at Sab for a moment then, ignoring him, leaned forward and propped his hands on the table. "Where's Doc?" he asked Yosh.

"He'll be here any minute," Yosh answered, looking at his wrist watch. "—By the way, meet my friend, Sab."

Clarence Wo nodded a haughty nod at Sab then abruptly turned his head towards Yosh.

Sab, not saying anything, knew damned well that Clarence Wo knew who he was. That bastard, treating him like he was a nobody because Sab's father was their pig-slop man. That Pah-ke can kiss my okole, he told himself, enraged, feeling very slighted, eyes occupied on one of the burnt marks on the table. One of these days guys like Clarence Wo was going to look up at Sab Gusuda, he promised himself, determined, refusing to listen to what Clarence and Yosh were saying. Bunch of Pah-kes! They all think they're big shots because their fathers ran restaurants on Maui.

It suddenly occured to Sab that it had been Clarence who had kicked his father out of the kitchen the day the Bud-dhaheads attacked Pearl Harbor. Nobody—but nobody—was ever going to treat his old man like that and get away with it, he had told himself when he heard of the incident. Looking up at lanky, bean-pole Clarence again, he noted that the guy was bigger than he thought. To hell with size. That bastard just better not lay a hand on the old man again, he warned silently, eyeing Clarence through the corners of his narrowed eyes. So help him! he'd kill that Pah-ke—or any bastard—that laid a hand on his old man.

Sitting there still being ignored by Clarence, Sab now noticed Yosh's eyes brightening. Sab turned slightly to his left and, looking back over his shoulder, saw Doc Kong and a short, chubby, cigar-smoking man walking into the restaurant. The chubby man, walking behind Doc, was carrying a shiny, reddish leather brief case which he held tight against his chest.

Doc promptly introduced the man to Clarence, then to Sab, and finally to Yosh who said: "Don't you remember me, Ah Hong? I met you in Honolulu back in September when I was there with Doc."

"Suah, I lemember you, Yosh," Ah Hong greeted, pumping Yosh's hand stiffly. "How's evelet'ing with you?" he asked with a Pah-ke accent.

Ah Hong, Sab observed, was about fifty and looked very distinguished in his double-breasted blue gabardine suit. He had a round face with a black streak of thin mustache over a fat lip, and his thick black hair was parted in the middle with a heavy application of pomade, some of which had melted on his forehead. If it weren't for the big cigar with an ivory holder in his mouth he could have been easily taken for a minister.

"Sit down," Clarence said, pulling back the two outside chairs beside Yosh and Sab.

Doc sat down next to Sab across from Ah Hong while Clarence remained standing.

"You guys want some coffee or anything to eat?" Clarence asked, playing the big-shot role to the hilt. "How about you, Ah Hong? You want anything to drink or eat?"

"No. No t'anks," Ah Hong declined, waving his hand back and forth, sitting rigidly with the brief case on his lap. "—Look, I no have much time. I gotta catch the noon plane back to Honolulu. Got lotsa important business back there," he said, suddenly all business-like, the amiable smile gone. Glancing up at Clarence, then at the three of them at the table, he went on: "Doc tells me you people wanna buy the stuff. How about it? You guys can put up dough?" His small, beady eyes darted around the empty restaurant, his fingers tapping the side of the brief case, anxious.

Sab looked over at Yosh, then at Doc, finally up at Clarence, who was rubbing his bony dark hands together, his purplish lips undulating nervously.

"How many diamonds you got there?" Clarence asked.

Ah Hong gave Clarence a grim look, then suddenly turned to Doc, furious. "Goddamnit! Doc. I t'ought you said you had evelyt'ing a'langed. When I agleed to fly all the way here to make deal, you plomised you get money leady. I got no time foolin' alound. The syndicate takin' big loss sellin' stones so damned cheap."

"Oh, well, Ah Hong," Doc said timidly, "we got the money all right. Clarence just wanna make sure you got all the stones you said you was gonna bring with you."

"Suah! I bring all stones," Ah Hong burst out, angry, his round face turning red, the long cigar holder in his mouth jumping up and down. "When I say I bling stones, I mean it. I no fool alound. Who you guys t'ink you dealin' with? —bunch of plicks? I leplesent big syndicate in Honolulu. No small two-bit outfit."

"Oh, c'mon, Ah Hong, hold your horses," Doc again attempted to calm the syndicate man. "We know we're dealing with a big outfit. Otherwise, I wouldn't think of getting my friends in the deal."

"Okay, okay," Ah Hong said grimly, "let's get down to business. I got no time talkin' small talk. You guys either got the dough, or you don't."

"Don't worry about that, Ah Hong," Clarence said. "We've got the dough."

"Well, c'mon, c'mon, then," Ah Hong said impatiently. "Where's all the money you guys say you got?"

Clarence wiped his mouth. "Lemme see the diamonds first."

"Yeah, Ah Hong," Doc said, putting his glasses back on after wiping the thick lenses with his handkerchief, "let's see the diamonds. I think that's only fair."

"What! You guys no tlust me?" Ah Hong cried out, slamming the table, froth oozing from the corners of his mouth. "Chlist sake! When I say I got diamonds I got 'em! No bull shit." He gave all of them a contemptuous look, then slowly unbuckled the two straps around the brief case. He stuck a small key into the lock and opened it.

All eyes converged on Ah Hong suspensefully.

Ah Hong, at last, stuck his pudgy hand into the case and brought out a small green felt bag tied firmly at the top with a long leather string. Dropping the brief case on the floor at his feet and laying the felt bag on the table delicately, he looked around the restaurant once more, then began untying the string.

A handful of sparkling diamonds, each the size of a small finger tip glittered magically before their eyes.

"Oh-h . . ." Doc murmured, eyes ogling down at the precious stones as Ah Hong spread them carefully on the open felt.

"Jesus!" Yosh uttered, speechless, his usual sardonic expression replaced by a soothing look, stretching his neck to get a better view.

Clarence, standing there, eyes practically popping out of their sockets, could say nothing. He kept staring at the stones, transfixed, mouth gaped wide open.

"Yeah-h-h . . ." Sab said, eyes bulging out. "They sure nice looking." He swallowed hard, then for lack of better description, said: "They must be worth lotsa money."

"You damn light they worth lotsa money," Ah Hong said, the cigar holder in his mouth twitching from side to side, both hands guarding the level of sizzling diamonds. "Nice, huh?" he said to Doc. "Forty locks here; evely one of them sonofabitches can be sold for at least five hundred dollars at light time. If the damn war neve' come the syndicate no sell so cheap. We got no choice now. The war sclew up evelyt'ing. We need money light 'way."

"You're asking two-fifty a piece," Doc interrupted, eyeing the glittering diamonds. "That's a lot of money."

"What!" Ah Hong exploded once more, quickly folding the felt and tying its corners. "Chlist sake! Two-fifty for somet'ing you can sell for five hundred a clack, lotsa money!" he snarled at Doc. "Goddamn you, Doc! I should've lealized you always cheap bugga. If you guys no can dig up money whatdahell you wanna bother syndicate for? Bunch of small time opelators." He was breathing hard, gusty breaths.

Doc, no longer the sharp gambler Sab had earlier regarded, said nothing. He exchanged helpless, self-tormented glances with Yosh, then with Clarence. He finally stuck his hand into his pocket. "I got a thousand bucks here," he said, bringing out a thick wad of twenties and fifties and laying it on the table.

"T'ousand bucks!" Ah Hong scoffed, his face turning into a sour, unbearable expression. "What you tlying to do? Lob me?—steal diamonds flom me, Doc?"

"I got another grand," Yosh said, taking out his roll of bills. "—Sab, how much you got with you?" he asked.

Sab reached into his front pocket. "I got five hundred," he said, laying the wrinkled bills on the middle of the table.

"All ligh', all ligh'. 'At's twenty-five hundred," Ah Hong said, leaning back arrogantly on his chair, grinning that disdainful grin of his. "Where lest of money? You guys still seventy-five hundred short. I told you, Doc. All or not'ing. Ten gland for whole works, or no deal."

Doc, now a hickish big shot just put in his place by a big-time syndicate man, looked up meekly at Clarence. "How much can you and your father put up, Clarence?"

"I—I don't know. I gotta talk to my father first," Clarence answered, hesitant.

"Oh, for—" Ah Hong said, making a face. "If I knew I had to go all t'is tlouble I no come all the way to Maui. Bunch of two-bit opelators," he scorned, leering contemptuously at Doc again. "Well, c'mon, c'mon," he told Clarence, waving him away, not bothering to look up. "Go talk to your father, then. I no have all day."

As Clarence turned to walk to the kitchen, Doc, standing up, said: "Wait a minute, Clarence. I better go talk to your father, too."

"Now whatdahell," Ah Hong groaned, taking a deep puff on his cigar and blowing the smoke over Sab's way. "'At's why I hate do business with 'nother Pah-ke," he told Yosh. "Me—I'm Chinaman, too, but when I do business I make up mind light 'way. No stallin'; light 'way. T'ese Pah-kes, all the time tlyin' to cock-a-roach you. You know what I mean?—always tlyin' to take you for lide"—sticking his middle finger up for emphasis. "Me—I want evelyt'ing up-and-up. T'at way, nobody can squawk afterwards. You know what I mean?"

"I t'ink we getting a pretty good shake," Yosh said.

"Why sure you guys gettin' good shake. Any dumb plick know t'at," Ah Hong said, puffing and forcing Sab to wrinkle up his nose to keep from sneezing.

Doc and Clarence were back in a few minutes.

"Well, you guys make up mind?" Ah Hong questioned, standing up from his chair and giving an ultimatum.

"We're going through with the deal," Doc said, gaping down at all the green, neatly packed fifty-dollar bills in Clarence's hands.

" 'At's more like it," Ah Hong said, wide eyes staring at the stacks of bills. He quickly reopened the felt bag and spread the sparkling diamonds on it.

Yosh and Sab stood up.

"All ligh', Doc," Ah Hong said, "you count 'em. Make sure exactly forty locks here." He stepped aside, and for the first time allowed someone else to handle the diamonds.

Doc, bending over the table, started counting each gem carefully.

Clarence laid eight tightly packed fifty-dollar stacks on the table. "Go ahead, count 'em," he told Ah Hong, defiant. "There's seven one-thousand-dollar stacks, and the small one"—pointing to a half-stack—"has five hundred dollars in it."

Ah Hong, eyes bulging out, began counting each stack somewhat heedlessly, puffing rapidly on his cigar.

After he and Doc were through counting, they stepped back and looked at each other.

"There's forty stones here, all right," Doc confirmed, wrapping up the felt and holding it tight in both hands. He looked over at Clarence, then at Yosh, finally at Sab standing at the middle of the table.

"All money here," Ah Hong said, speaking to no one in particular, still glaring down at the greenbacks. He finally reached down under the table and, bringing up his brief case, dropped all the money into it. "Well, evelybody happy now?" he asked.

"Yeah, sure, Ah Hong," Doc said, reaching over for Ah Hong's hand and pumping it.

"Good, good," Ah Hong said, smiling an overbearing smile. He, then, shook hands with Yosh and Sab, then with Clarence. "No worly, youn' fellow. You guys gettin' good deal—a helluva good deal," he told Clarence. "The best kind deal I ever saw anyone gettin'."

"—One t'ing I wanna tell you guys, though," he added. "As far as syndicate concerned, we don't know where you guys got diamonds from. Okay with you guys?" He looked at four of them, nodding.

"You don't have to worry about us," Doc assured. "We understand what you mean."

"Well, okay, then. As long as we understand," Ah Hong said, walking over to the screen door with the brief case held snuggly to his side. "I gotta catch cab to airport light 'way before I miss my plane," he said over his shoulder, opening the door and stepping out.

"That wise sonofabitch!" Clarence fumed as soon as the door slammed behind Ah Hong. "Whodahell he think he's dealing with?—bunch of kids?"

"In a way, Ah Hong's right about the diamonds," Doc said. "They can get in trouble for selling us smuggled goods."

" 'At's right," Yosh said, stepping out from the booth and standing between Doc and Clarence. "There's some kind of Territorial law against selling or buying smuggled goods."

"That means we can get in trouble, too," Clarence said, frightened.

"Don't worry about it," Doc said. "As long as no one talks, we're safe." He handed Clarence the bag of diamonds. "You keep them in your safe until we get back from Kahului. We're gonna go down right now and talk to those three rich guys I was telling you and your father about."

"Sure, Doc," Clarence said, winking confidentially. "That goddamn Ah Hong, he's gonna crap in his pants when he finds out we sold the rocks for five hundred a piece the same day."

"To hell with that Pah-ke," Doc said, placing an arm around Clarence.

Yosh stood there grinning that familiar sneering-frowning grin of his.

Sab smiled to himself, thinking of the thousand bucks he was going to have soon.

"We'll be back in couple of hours," Doc said, giving Clarence a warm, friendly pat on the back and heading for the door, Yosh and Sab following right behind.

Outside, Sab walked between Doc and Yosh, hoping Kimi had not seen him coming out of the restaurant. Yosh and Doc remained silent, hurrying to Market, their expressions hard, cold and distant. Doc kept gazing across the street towards the Alexander House Settlement where the cabs were usually parked.

At the intersection, Yosh, turning abruptly to Sab, said: "Look, Doc and me have to go down to Kahului by ourselves. You know how it is, huh? Those guys might not want to get mixed up with someone young as you. Why don't you take in a show? I'll call you early tomorrow morning and tell you how we made out. Okay?" He took out a five from his pocket.

" 'At's all right, Yosh. I got some money. I t'ink I'll go see t'at John Wayne movie."

Doc Kong was already across the street.

Sab turned and began walking away.

"Hey Sab!" Yosh called.

Turning around, Sab noticed Yosh looking at him in a kind of guilt-ridden way which he thought was so uncharacteristic of tough, sharp Yosh Nakata.

"Ah, neve' mind. 'At's all right," Yosh finally said, still looking at him awkwardly. "I'll see you, huh?"

"Yeah, sure, Yosh," Sab jerked his head. "I'll see you."

Yosh turned slowly, then raced across the street to join Doc.

Sab continued on towards the theatre, beaming. Him, getting into a real big deal and coming out smelling like roses. He must be living right. That Yosh, what a guy! he thought, a burst of warm affection racing through him as he pictured his good friend handing over the thousand bucks.

He crossed Market, then walked over to the ticket seller's window. He knew he'd have plenty of time to catch the bus home before anyone found out he had not gone to school.

18

KAMA WAS WAITING furiously at the kitchen table when Saburo finally came home from school—rather, from the John Wayne matinee movie. He had found out about his son's truancy and his so-called business dealings about two hours ago. It was early in the morning, however, when he first had a foreboding that the day would turn out to be one of those nightmarish ones filled with heartaches, pains and sorrows.

It had all begun when he and his wife were having their usual breakfast of coffee and toast, and the President of the Wailuku Okinawan Association had called to suggest that tomorrow would be as good a day as any to announce the marriage of Kenyei and Kimiko. Kama, of course, had immediately agreed with the President and had invited him over for another chicken hekka dinner so they could make the necessary arrangements. But when he had told Tsuyu about it she had said in her subtle, quiet way that perhaps Kimiko was too young to get married and that Kimiko still had ambitions of becoming a school teacher and might not go through with the proposed marriage.

"Not go through with the marriage!" he had protested, alarmed, almost dropping his coffee cup on the table. "I thought we had it all settled."

"Yes, I suppose in a way we thought it had been settled," his wife had said, her voice soft but unquestionably firm, "but we forgot to ask Kimiko first."

"Didn't she say it would be all right with her?"

"No, I think it was you who said it would be all right."

"But what about my promise to Ikehara-san?"

"I guess you'll just have to tell him the truth."

"I've already committed myself."

"You'll have to un-commit yourself, then."

Women! Damnit! Why can't they make up their minds? he had thought frenziedly, cringing when picturing himself facing Ikehara-san and trying to make an excuse. It wasn't only Kimiko who objected to the marriage, but from all indications it seemed even Tsuyu no longer liked the idea. Instead of arguing with her, however, he had remained silent, pondering on what to say to the honorable President of the Wailuku Okinawan Association. To argue with his wife would have been futile, for her decisions concerning the children—whenever she had had any—had always ended up the final one.

"Basan, Ikehara-san is a very influential man," he had finally told her. "We just can't back out on our word."

"Perhaps, we should let Kimiko explain."

"Kimiko! No, that wouldn't do. She might say something embarrassing."

"Well, then, it'll be up to you to think of something before tomorrow night," Tsuyu had said, standing up and leaving him alone at the table to deliberate on the dilemma.

Everything would be so simple if that girl of his would just go ahead and marry Kenyei, he had thought, terribly bewildered, rubbing his craggy, unshaven chin despairingly. What a headache it was to rear children under the influence of the damned American ways.

As if Kimiko's up-in-the-air marriage wasn't enough to drive a man nearly out of his mind, Kama, later in the day received an even greater shock that had almost caused another heart attack.

This time it had been Niro, his number two son, who

was supposed to have been attending school in Honolulu. Niro was the last person in the world he had expected to do a foolhardy thing.

Kama had gone over to the Waihee post office and had been pleasantly surprised to discover that Niro had at last written home; in fact, had written two air mail letters: one to Kimiko in English and the other to him in simple Japanese. Niro had seldom written directly to him (always maintaining it was hard to write in Japanese), and so, greatly overwhelmed by Niro's thoughtfulness, he had driven home as fast as he could and had opened the envelope excitedly.

He nearly fell flat on his face.

He couldn't believe what he had read. Not Niro, not his number two boy. There must be a mix-up, he had told himself, re-reading the letter, then again for the third time. In sheer desperation, he had then hurried over to the vegetable gardens near the pig pens where Tsuyu was hoeing between the rows of young tomato plants.

"Oi! Basan! Basan!" he called, waving the letter at her. "Something terrible has happened. Come here! Quickly!"

"What's wrong!" she cried out, dropping her hoe and waddling over anxiously on the dirt road that went up to the neighbor's place. She had on her baggy gardening clothes and her Mother Hubbard hat which she took off approaching him. "What's the matter?" she asked, lifting her long skirt and wiping the beads of perspiration on her face.

"That Niro!" he said disconcertingly, handing the letter to her, "he must have gone out of his mind."

"What did he do?"

"Read the letter."

"Oh, no!" she cried after reading it. "Why did he do it!" her dirt-covered hand jumping up to her mouth.

"I don't know why he would do such a foolish thing," he said, shaking his head, wincing.

"What's going to happen to him now?" Tsuyu cried, misty eyes looking down at the letter once more.

For the next minute or two, they stood there silently in the middle of the road, Tsuyu, looking at her shoes with tears streaming down her cheeks, and Kama, staring blank-faced up at the towering, sun-bathed Kapuna mountains behind her.

Taking back the letter from Tsuyu and looking at it again, he uttered hopefully: "Niro said the Army is not taking anyone of Japanese ancestry. That's why the Nisei boys at the University left school to volunteer their services as civilians."

"Didn't he mention they are hoping to be called in soon?"

"It still doesn't mean they'll be taken. The 'Merican Army may not want Japanese boys."

"Some of them are already in."

"They probably will be released."

"Why are the Niseis so anxious to volunteer? Don't they know how terribly worried their parents will be?"

"Who knows how young boys feel these days. Especially when they were brought up in a foreign country."

"I still can't believe our Niro would do such a thing."

"He did it because others did it," Kama said. "He's still very young, and easily led. He said thousands of 'Merican soldiers and sailors were killed by the Nihon airplanes; that ships are still on fire in Pea-ru Har-bah. He also said one of his friends who was injured in the attack is in a hospital. He must feel bitter against Japan."

"He's a Nihon-jin, too."

"He must be mixed up, that number two boy of ours."

"Why do people want to destroy one another all the time?" Tsuyu sobbed. "Isn't it enough we must all die some-day from one form of illness or another?"

Kama said nothing, only realized with horror that the war might not turn out to be a remote battlefield for strangers, but one that might involve a son of his—a son who might get killed fighting against his own homeland.

"The boy at least had the decency to write and tell us about it right away," he now said stolidly. "He said that because we had taught him to have honor and pride in himself he did what he felt was the right thing to do. We may not approve of what he did, Basan, but we know the boy is honest with himself. He'll be all right, Basan," he went on, trying to console his distraught wife, head shaking slowly.

[215]

"You think Ichiro might have to join the Japanese Army?" Tsuyu asked. "Will he have to fight in the war, too?"

He looked compassionately at his wife. "Ichiro's situation is a baffling one. He may be a Nihon-jin in Japan; actually he's an 'Merican citizen. I don't know whether they would take him in the Army or not."

They stood there under the hot afternoon sun for another minute then, not saying anything more, Kama turned around and walked back slowly to the house, leaving Tsuyu standing alone crying pitifully to herself.

The terrible happenings of the day, however, did not end with the distressing plight of Kimiko and Niro. At about two-thirty, while Kama was at the pig slop cookery watching the glowing fire, Lin Wo and his sassy half-Kanaka boy had driven into the driveway with a burst of speed in their black Ford sedan, and had immediately begun accusing him of harboring a thief in his family.

At first, he had thought they had come to apologize for their nasty behavior the day the war had started. He was still incensed over the incident, but had been willing to forgive them. Standing up promptly from his squatting position, he had walked down to Lin and his son, intending to welcome them to his home. (Lin had always been a welcome guest of the Gusudas in the past—in spite of the war between China and Japan.)

No sooner had he approached them half-way down the driveway than that dark boy of Lin's began demanding belligerently: "Where's that goddamn boy of yours?" His blood-shot eyes darted around the back yard. "Where's Sab?" he asked, fists clenched tight at his sides, towering over slightly hunched Kama.

"You boy, him no good, no good," old man Lin said, joining his lanky son, head shaking balefully, wry, wrinkled mouth twitching. "Boy, him big crook."

"My boy?" Kama uttered, not having the slightest idea what they were talking about.

"Yeah. Your boy, Sab! Wheredahell is he?" Clarence Wo demanded again.

"Boy go school," he answered.

"School!" Clarence Wo scoffed, his broad nose flaring. "He's no more at school than your pigs are at school. He was over my place all morning with those crooked friends of his."

"No-o," Kama said, taking off his sweat-stained straw hat and holding it at his side. "Him go school. School start again today."

"Whodahell you think you're bull shitting!" Clarence Wo shouted, shoving him hard.

He stumbled backward, almost falling down. "Whassamattah you! Why you come here make trouble!"

Clarence Wo gave Kama another mean shove. "You don't know what trouble is until I catch up with that lousy boy of yours," he said maliciously, his dark brown eyes once more darting around the yard and up at the pig pens. "I'm gonna break every bone in his body when I get hold of him," he ranted on.

"Gusuda-san," old man Lin interrupted, pushing his son away, scowling, "you boy, he come wit' fliends to lestaurant today. He sell me no-good, junk diamonds."

Kama was even more baffled now. "Lin, what you talk abou'?" he questioned, scratching his head, sharp valley of v's forming between his dark brows. "You talk abou' my boy, Saburo?—my numbah one youn' boy?"

"Yeah. Saburo—Sab!" Clarence blurted again. He took another step forward.

"Clalence!" Old man Lin shoved his son away again. "You shut up! You let me talk Gusuda-san."

"But Lin," Kama said, still not knowing what the two were blabbering about, "my boy go school. You make mistake."

"No-o. No mistake, Gusuda-san," old man Lin said, old eyes behind the thick-lensed glasses narrowed into tiny slits, heavily wrinkled, ancient face pulling tight. "I know boy. See him come lestaurant many times."

"I tell you, he go school."

"You mean he neve' come home yet?" Clarence shouted.

"No," Kama said, "still school. —Whassamattah you come make trouble? Su-pose you come make friend, bery good. I make friend, too. You come make trouble, I say gettahell outta here. I no want trouble."

"You goddamn Jap-anee!" Clarence Wo burst out savagely, raising his hand.

"Clalence!" Old man Lin stepped between Kama and his son. "You go back car," he ordered, shoving his son away. "You—you clazy boy! Buy junk diamonds."

After Clarence walked back to the car parked just inside of the county dirt road, old man Lin, speaking in clipped pidgin English, began explaining what had taken place at the restaurant, the upshot of the whole thing being, as far as Kama could make out:

Saburo had been involved in a scheming plot with three other men to rob Lin and his son by pretending to sell them genuine Hong Kong imported diamonds that in reality had turned out to be nothing but worthless zircons.

Lin went on to explain with angry tears that half of the so-called diamonds were to have been sold today to recoup their investment, but when Saburo and his friends had failed to show up as previously arranged, Lin, suspicious, had taken out the bag of diamonds from the safe and had discovered that several of them were terribly disfigured. He had then run over to his friend's jewelry store to have them appraised and had learned with horrible shock that they weren't only chipped badly, but that they were not diamonds at all.

Upon describing the men from whom he had purchased the worthless rocks to his jeweler friend, Lin had learned that the whole transaction had been a swindle from the beginning; that two of the men were notorious Honolulu con men who had swindled other victims in the past.

Lin, greatly alarmed, had then hurried back to his restaurant where he ordered his gullible son to find Yosh and Doc Kong and not to let them out of his sight. In about ten minutes, however, his son had returned, reporting that Yosh and Doc Kong had checked out of their hotel rooms earlier in the morning and couldn't be located anywhere in town. Lin, realizing what they must have planned all along, had then called the Hawaiian Airlines ticket office.

The girl at the ticket office had said that Yoshio Nakata, Gilbert Ah Hong and Richard Kong had all flown to Honolulu on the noon flight.

Lin and his son had then rushed over to Kama's house, hoping to get part of their money back from Saburo, and also to find out the address of the other three men in Honolulu.

Standing there holding his battered hat in both hands, the hot sun bearing down on his head and listening to Lin Wo accusing his son of being a thief, Kama was so overcome with shame and grief his hands trembled, his entire body shuddering.

"You suah, Lin?" he asked feebly, "you suah, t'is my boy you talk abou'?"

"Oh, yes, Gusuda-san," Lin answered vehemently.

It couldn't have been Saburo! he told himself, looking away from old man Lin's accusing eyes. He refused to believe it. Not a son of his. There was no thief in his family. No! No! No!

"Where boy now?" Lin asked. "No come home yet?"

He shook his head. He looked over Lin's head at the distant white clouds in the blue sky, telling himself over and over that what he had been hearing was something out of a horrible nightmare.

"Me catch 'em t'is other t'ree men go Honolulu," Lin threatened with rage. "No worly, me catch 'em. I tele'- hone fliends Honolulu. T'ey find 'em. But I wanna talk you boy, too. Find out he got my money."

"If my boy havo you money, you get back everyt'ing," he said with grim determination. "I no have boy keep money."

Lin regarded him with level eyes for a moment. "You tele'hone me when boy come home?"

"Suah! I te-re-hon you," he said, chin lifted at Lin. "Supose boy have one cent you money, I get 'em back for you."

"All ligh', Gusuda-san," Lin said, his voice suddenly soft and warm. "Me tlust you. No angry wit' you, Gusuda-san. Maybe boy, vely youn'. Don' know what he do. Maybe, he no steal money—only t'is other men fly Honolulu steal my money."

"Me find out, Lin," he said. "Me find out when boy come home."

"All ligh', Gusuda-san."

After looking sort of uncomfortably at Kama, Lin stepped closer. "Gusuda-san," he said warmly, "me solly t'is happen.

[219]

You, me, good fliends long time. I no want make tlouble for boy."

"You call policeman?" he quickly asked, not quite understanding what Lin had meant.

"No. No call policeman," Lin assured, placing his old, wrinkled hand on his shoulder. "I no want boy get tlouble wit' policeman. I only want money back. —No worly. My fliends Honolulu, t'ey get money back for me. If boy got some money, he give back. No call policeman."

Kama took a tight affectionate hold of old Lin's gnarled hand and pumped it vigorously, bowing deeply several times.

Lin turned around slowly and padded over stoop-shouldered to the Ford where his son, glaring over at Kama, was waiting impatiently.

After they had driven out of the driveway, Kama stood looking down at his grubby, slop-stained shoes with painful tears rolling down his weathered face, his whole body still shuddering under the impact of the harsh accusation. What could be more humiliating than to have your own son accused of stealing? he thought with suicidal depression, wiping his misty glasses with his wrinkled shirt tail, sniffling with man's shameless, chest-heaving sobs, finally putting his glasses back on.

He made up his mind that if Saburo—regardless whether Saburo had taken any of Lin's money or not—had ever been involved in the deceitful scheme, he (Kama) would guarantee every penny Lin had lost. And he'd disown the boy, so help him! He'd disown that boy tonight if what Lin had said was true. But first, he'd have to listen to the boy's side of the story. The boy, no doubt, was a little wild and hard to control, but stealing—never! Not a son of his. No son of his would dare disgrace the good name of Gusuda Kama.

After feeding the pigs he had come into the kitchen to wait for Saburo's return, a sake jug sitting on the table before him. God! he wanted to get stinking drunk.

It was only a few minutes after he had reluctantly told the whole mortifying story to his wife who refused to believe a word of it and to Kimiko who had just come home from work that Saburo had at last walked into the house.

[220]

"Saburo!" he called harshly as the boy intended to pass through the kitchen into his bedroom.

"—Sab! where have you been all day?" Kimiko joined in.

Saburo stopped, looked over at them. "School, of course."

"Sit down!" Kama ordered, pointing to a chair at the head of the rectangular table.

Saburo hesitated, then sat down. "What's all this about?" he asked, looking over at Kimiko, then at his mother sitting dumb-struck across from Kama.

"Did you learn much at school today?" Kama asked, eyeing the boy coldly.

The boy looked away with a tight grimace. "What I did wrong this time?" he mumbled. "What you folks tryin' to do? Give me the third degree?"

He kept studying the boy's expression. There was no question now that the boy had not gone to school.

"You played hooky today, didn't you?" Kimiko questioned.

"Who? Me?"

"Yes, you! Who do you suppose I'm talking about! We know all about it; you might as well tell us the truth."

"About what?"

"About you playing hooky and going around with those gamblers in Wailuku. With—with that Yosh Nakata and his bum friends."

"Who told you t'at?"

"Never mind who told me! Mr. Wo and his son were here this afternoon. They told Father all about the crooked way you and your bum friends cheated them."

"What ya mean?—cheated," Saburo said, snickering.

"So you were involved in that dirty scheme!" Kama jumped up to his feet and swung his hand viciously across Saburo's face. The boy toppled backward on the floor with a loud impact, the chair sprawled under him.

"Jisan!" Tsuyu cried, rushing over to Saburo on the floor. "That's enough! Give him a chance to explain." She reached down for the boy's hand and helped him up.

The boy stood up slowly, rubbing the left side of his face which was quickly turning purplish. He continued staring at Kama with blazing, shocked eyes, mouth pouted morosely, not uttering a word, just rubbing his face and flexing his jaw muscles.

"You no-good boy, you!" Kama burst out, stamping his foot hard, feeling his heart pounding behind his eyes, breathing loud, gasping breaths.

Saburo, after sitting down, looked down at the table. When no one said anything for a while he mumbled feebly, almost incoherently: "We neve' cheat the old man. He's gonna make money like everyone else."

"How can you expect anyone to make money with worthless rocks?" Kama said, finally sitting down.

"Those diamonds are worth lotsa money," Saburo said, grinning a sly grin now. "They can be sold for as much as five hundred dollars a piece."

"They're worth nothing! And you and your friends sold them to Lin Wo knowing they were worth nothing."

"But I'm telling you, Otoosan, they're worth lotsa money. I saw them myself."

He studied the boy. He suddenly wondered whether the boy had known about the scheme after all.

"You mean you didn't know your friends were selling zeer-cons to Lin Wo?" His eyes stayed fixed on the boy, breathless.

"Who told you anything about zircons?"

"Those di-ya-mons turned out to be nothing but cheap zeer-cons, Saburo," he informed his son, a surge of emotion almost compelling him to reach over and embrace the boy. The boy was innocent! Thank God! He was innocent. "The three men caught a plane to Honolulu with all the money."

Saburo's face suddenly took on a pale, ashen expression. "Who told you that?"

"Mr. Wo and his son were here right after they found out about it," Kimiko said. "They thought you had taken some of their money."

"Did you?" Kama asked.

"What money? I didn't take a dime."

"How in the world did you ever get mixed up with people like them?" Kimiko asked, making a face.

"Yosh used to be my roommate in Molokai."

"That Yosh Nakata!" Kimiko was fuming. "He's the biggest bum on Market Street. He's never earned an honest dollar in his life."

"He's all right," Saburo mumbled.

"You mean you still think he's a friend of yours—after what he did to you and Mr. Wo?"

Saburo looked down at the table.

"Where did you get the money to buy those di-ya-mons, Saburo?" Tsuyu asked, befuddled, looking over at the boy tenderly.

"It wasn't my money, Okaasan," Saburo answered. "It was Yosh's. He just told me to hold it for him."

"That means you didn't know what they were planning to do all the time," Kama concluded, convinced that his son had not been implicated in the scheme.

"'At's right," Saburo said softly.

Kama sighed deeply, unconsciously forgiving the boy for playing hooky. He lifted the sake cup—his fifth or sixth drink, he didn't know the exact number—and gulped a hefty swallow. "I'll have to call Lin and tell him that you were not involved," he said, smacking his lips and standing up. "I don't want him to keep thinking a son of mine is a thief."

He walked over to the telephone on the wall opposite the table, feeling a little dizzy.

"Ha-ro! Lin?" he said, pressing the cold earpiece to his ear when someone had answered.

"Just-a-minute," the voice said.

Must be one of Lin's half-Kanaka children.

"'A-lo!" old man Lin answered, breathing hard into the telephone.

"T'is Gusuda, Lin."

"Oh, 'a-lo, Gusuda-san," Lin said curtly. "You speak boy?"

"Boy don' know not'ing abou' sellin' no-good, junk di-ya-mons, Lin," he answered. "He all-da-time t'ink di-ya-mons good."

"Oh-h . . ." A pause. "T'en, boy no have money?"

"No, Lin. Only t'is other men. T'ey talk boy make believe di-ya-mons good."

"Oh-h . . ." Another pause. "—No worly, Gusuda-san. Me catch 'em other men."

"T'ey go jail all righ'."

"I fix 'em up. No worly, I fix 'em up plenty good. You tell 'em boy, me no angly wit' him. Him, all ligh'."

[223]

"T'ank you, Lin. You good-u man, too," he said, feeling a strong affection for the old Pah-ke. "Good-u bye, Lin-san."

When he turned around, Saburo was no longer at the table.

While his father was talking with old man Lin, Sab, no longer able to contain himself, had rushed into his bedroom and flung himself face down on the bed, cursing the hell out of Yosh Nakata, Doc Kong and that fat Chinaman, Ah Hong.

Those lousy bastards! Those goddamn crooks!

He kept pounding the mattress, mouth frothing with animal hatred. They conned him! Him—Sab—their friend. And that Yosh, that bastard who was supposed to be his good friend, had sucked him into the deal.

Yosh! How could you? How could you do it?

Five hundred bucks! Down the drain.

After a while, his agony having somewhat subsided, Sab, still lying face down on the bed, couldn't help feeling a certain amount of admiration for the sleek way those three had handled the deal. It sure was hard to believe the whole thing had been a set-up from the beginning. And that Ah Hong, that lousy Chinaman, should get an academy award, he thought, grinning sourly, experiencing a gloating sensation picturing Clarence Wo sick to his stomach for having been taken.

Good for that sonofabitch! he thought vindictively. He may have lost five hundred bucks, but Clarence and his old man lost seventy-five hundred—exactly what they deserved for being so greedy, he told himself, speculating now whether old man Lin planned to call the cops.

As far as Sab was concerned, he knew nothing. Wasn't he a victim, too? Anyway, he doubted very much whether the old man intended to call the cops. The old man would only be admitting he had been willing to enter into an illegal transaction.

He suddenly recalled Yosh wanting to tell him something at the intersection. Maybe, Yosh had wanted to tell him not to worry about the five hundred bucks, he thought with new-found hope and confidence.

Then, almost simultaneously, a cold, chilling thought crept

up from the subdued recesses of his mind. He could hear Yosh's sardonic voice: "Neve' give a sucker a break. A sucker's not only born every day; there's one made every day."

Did Yosh consider him a sucker, too? a fish? he wondered, again feeling sick deep inside. That sonofabitch!

Later in the evening, after everyone had gone to bed, Kama sat alone at the kitchen table in a drunken stupor, slowly spinning a crumpled cigarette between his lips, meditating. The terrifying happenings of the day seemed a nightmare. It just did not seem possible for so many unpleasant events to take place in a span of a single day.

Kimiko not wanting to marry Kenyei . . . There still was the unpleasant task of breaking the news to Ikehara-san when he came over tomorrow night. What would that proud man think? Probably would never speak to Kama again.

Niro quitting school so he could join the American Army . . . Why? Why would the boy want to do a thing like that? If Ichiro should ever be called into the Nihon Army those two might end up shooting at each other.

Where was the sweet taste of victory, of glorious conquest in a war of this sort? he asked himself inebriatedly, heavy eyelids closing and opening, head bobbing up and down. Where was the exalting joy of triumph if one of his sons annihilated the other? The war was becoming like a sumo match between two brothers, the father standing aside not knowing for whom he should cheer banzai.

And there was the youngest boy, Saburo . . . What a deplorable scandal it would have been had Saburo been involved with the three men to rob his friend, Lin! he thought, cringing.

"Saburo!" he mumbled drunkenly, weaving from side to side on the chair, mouth drooling, "let today be a lesson to you. You ought to know now that no one gives you something for nothing."

"SABURO! YOU HEAR ME!" he called out loud, voice slurring. "Life gives you back only what you put into it. You cannot expect to gain anything by trying to take the easy way out. Your duty now is to go to school—not trying to make money. Your time will come—in an honest way.

"—What! You want to end up like your own father?—

No education? Barely able to read and write? End up a drunkard like him?"—he cried, turning his head towards Saburo's bedroom, weaving.

"NO! SABURO!" he shouted throughout the quiet, iron-roofed home, pounding the table. "I don't want any of my boys to become just another Okinawan pig-slop man.

"Life is no different than planting seeds in a garden: If you want turnips you plant turnip seeds; not carrot seeds."

He ran the back of his hand over his watery mouth, suddenly lurched forward and tipped over the sardine-can ashtray, leaving the table strewn with butts and ashes.

After a while, he pushed back his chair, staggered over into his bedroom and fell asleep.

Then, suddenly, as though only a flicker of an eyelash had passed since he vaguely remembered flopping down on the bed, he was wakened by a sharp, excruciating pain flashing across his chest. He found himself lurched forward momentarily before falling backward on the bed again, a vise-like pressure welling up inside his chest. He was breathing in short, clipped breaths; his entire body feeling frozen with ice.

He knew he was having another heart attack, similar to the ones he had before; only, this one much more painful. He lay still and kept pressing his right hand down on the left side of his chest, massaging it slowly, steadily, agonizingly, hoping the sizzling pain would go away. It subsided for a merciful second, then came flashing back, a little fainter this time. Then, it disappeared altogether.

He was no longer feeling drunk; his mind incredibly clear and sharp. He wondered whether he was going to die right there and then. Without anyone to comfort him.

"Basan . . ." he gasped.

He now felt the cool fresh breeze blowing in through the low window above his head, and could hear the gentle, breathless stir of the mango tree leaves in the front yard, the chirping of crickets in the bushes, the far-away barking of dogs and the pounding of the surf down the ocean.

He listened for the crowing of roosters, but could hear none. It wasn't morning yet, he told himself. He tried to get up from the bed; his legs wouldn't function. He opened his eyes. Darkness. He tried to look out the window; his head wouldn't move.

For an instant, just for a flashing eyeblink, before drowsiness assailed him, his perception heightened to such intensity he thought he could actually see every crack on the walls of his small bedroom, every splotchy spot on the roof over his head, even tiny lizards with long tails sleeping peacefully on the two by fours. Slowly, mercifully, sleepiness began shrouding his senses.

In his sleep—as though he wasn't sleeping at all, but just lying there—a frightening vision came to him. He knew he was awake, yet at the same time knew he was more asleep than awake.

The scene was a battle-scarred jungle surroundings on an island where Americans had been in fierce battle with Japanese soldiers. From his vantage point above the tall green trees covered with vines, he could see his number two boy, Niro, in a brown, sweat-stained American Army uniform, a steel helmet on his head and a microphone in his hand. Niro was about to address a group of Japanese soldiers hiding out in a cave about a hundred yards from where he was standing.

"This is Gusuda, Niro," he began in flawless Nihon-go, his voice over the speaker echoing throughout the thick jungles, causing birds to flutter up, frightened, in the sky. "You men up there in that cave! You are the last group of Japanese soldiers on the island. The rest of you have either been killed or have surrendered. I ask you as a fellow Nihon-jin to give up the senseless fighting. You will not be mistreated. I repeat: You will not be mistreated."

While Kama watched Niro in his brave role, his vision suddenly switched over towards the dozen heavily bearded, emaciated-looking Japanese soldiers lying on their bellies at the mouth of the cave. They were watching Niro, an exposed, inviting target. As he looked closer he saw one of them aiming his rifle at Niro, ready to fire.

"No!" he yelled, "don't shoot!" He discovered with horror that the soldier was none other than his oldest son, Ichiro. "Ichiro!" he cried out frantically, squirming helplessly on the bed, "don't shoot! It's Niro, your own brother!"

But Ichiro could not hear him. He pulled the trigger. The

blast roared throughout the jungle. Niro, the microphone jumping out of his hand, toppled backward from the murderous impact of the bullet, his feet flying up, his head landing on a rock with a sickening thud.

"Oh, no!" Kama moaned, lurching forward, the knife-slashing pain racing through him again, his entire left side throbbing gruesomely. "Basan . . ." he gasped, mouth wide open, not knowing whether he had actually called her or not.

He lay in silence, wondering fearfully whether what he had envisioned would be the ultimate fate of his sons. Please God, he pleaded, sobbing, please spare them. They are so young; they had harmed no one.

He could once more hear the sad, lonely barking of dogs in the stillness, and could feel himself breathing in choppy, gusty breaths. When would the next attack come?

He thought he had heard the crowing of a rooster. He listened carefully and heard it again. It must be morning, he sighed, tasting bitter, alcohol-sour froth on the corners of his mouth. If he could only hold on for a few more hours; at least be able to see Tsuyu and the two children before he died, he prayed. Again, he heard the rooster defying the silence of early morning.

Is this the end for him? he asked himself, not so much with fear as with unconsumed regret and sadness. There were so many dreams and promises yet to be fulfilled: He wanted to see his oldest boy again; he wanted to send Tsuyu back to Okinawa for a visit—she had been so young when she left there.

"Tsuyu . . ."

He yearned to feel the touch of her warm, comforting hands, smell the clean, fresh scent of her vibrant body and hear her soft, gentle breaths against his ear.

And in deep revery, he remembered his mother . . . As the years came tumbling back he saw her standing at the narrow trail near their home, her raggedly patched, dark kimono fluttering against the early-morning wind. She was waving goodbye to him with tears streaming down her tired, wrinkled cheeks. When her lonely, sad face came closer he reached up, but she was gone.

Okaasan . . . Okaasan . . .

Now, he prayed for a last wish. A wish to see all of his

children with Tsuyu beside him and marvel at how well they had turned out despite a low, humble beginning. Oh, God, he entreated, tears rolling down the sides of his wizened face, if You would only grant me this last wish. Please . . .

The third attack was more vicious than the two preceding ones. The white-hot pain felt as though a knife was being plunged into his chest and arm, his heart beating savagely.

He tried to call Tsuyu again; his eyes snapped shut; his head jerked to one side with an electrifying shock; and his arms went limp on his chest.

19

After his father was finally buried at the barren, unkept Japanese cemetery, across the train tracks in Wailuku, Sab, fighting back sobs, slid under the steering wheel of the pickup and drove up Market Street, then turned right and headed for home. Beside him was his mother, and on the other side was Kimi, both in black dresses, handkerchiefs dabbing their eyes. Sitting behind on soda pop crates were Ishi and Tengan, stone sober, solemn and stunned.

It was a dreary Saturday afternoon, the mountains completely covered by black clouds, and the ocean front being pummeled by a steady downpour, fast developing into a tropical storm. Sab continued driving slowly around the short bend until coming to the open road bordered by wind-buffeted cane fields. He picked up speed, feeling the damp, wet-dry mountain breeze blowing in through the window. Gripping tight on the wheel, he suddenly remembered that time, about five years ago, when he and his father had gone on a pig-buying trip over to Lahaina on the other side of the mountains.

His father, as usual, had combined business with pleasure and had gotten very drunk with several of his Okinawan friends by nightfall. When it had been time to come home, his father had asked Sab to drive. From Lahaina, it had meant going through four miles of treacherous curves winding around sheer two- and three-hundred-foot pali cliffs that dropped down into the jagged coast line.

When they came alongside the calm, sandy beach, Sab, hoping his father would take over from there, had brought the pickup to a gradual stop. The evening was nice and cool, the full moon glittering silver-orange over the wide expanse of low-tide water.

"Why have you stopped, Saburo?" his father questioned, lifting his head from the backrest and looking outside.

"We're at the Pali, Otoosan," he said, looking helplessly at his father.

"It's no different than any other road."

"There's lotsa curves."

"Drive a little slower. One curve is no different from the other. You take them one at a time."

"It's dark, too."

"You have the lights on, don't you? Night is no different from day if you can see where you're going."

"You sure I can make it, Otoosan?"

"Don't let the curves and darkness frighten you, Boy. You have to drive through them someday, anyway. When you see the lighthouse beam you'll know you're on the other side of the mountains."

"Well, all right, Otoosan," he finally muttered, half-fortified by his father's words.

He craned his neck over the high dashboard and slowly began driving up the steep hill to the first curve, his hands sweating on the wheel. Taking the first curve cautiously, and sighing deeply when he knew he had made it, he took the next one looking straight ahead following the light beams. He refused to think of the dark cliffs alongside the narrow road, and found himself maneuvering around the rest of the curves with greater confidence. Sometimes, he even dared himself to look out towards the twin islands of Molokini and Kahoolawe basking under the glowing moonlight.

At last, the lighthouse beam beckoned!

"Otoosan! I made it! I drove through the Lahaina Pali!"

"I knew you could make it, Boy," his father said, proud.

"It wasn't hard, was it? Remember, Saburo, when you take the curves one at a time, it is never hard."

Now at the long, Wailuku-Waihee slope, Sab shifted into neutral and turned off the ignition to save gas. He realized his mother had been talking to him.

"—Drinking isn't good, Saburo, but your father knew no other pleasure in life. To him, drinking was like you going to a movie, or to a foot-u-ball-u game. When you think of your father, think of him as a man whose only goal in life was to provide his family with a good living. If you, with all your advantages, can accomplish as much as your father did, I will be very proud of you. And I know your father would have been proud of you, too."

Sab listened to his mother, recalling his father's words: "When you take the curves one at a time, it is never hard." It suddenly dawned on him that life itself was a road full of curves. Perhaps, that was what his father had been trying to tell him that night.

Glancing over at his mother, Sab said: "Don't worry, Okaasan. I'll look after everything like Otoosan did."

"Yes, Saburo," his mother said softly, sobbingly, "you're the man-of-the-house now." Turning to Kimi, she said: "I thought there would be more people at the funeral; your father had so many friends on Maui."

"It's because of the war, Okaasan," Kimi said. "The Provost Marshal forbids large Japanese gatherings. I couldn't even locate a Buddhist priest. They're all held by the FBI."

"It doesn't matter too much now. I'm sure your father understands."

Feeling the pickup bouncing up the dip, Sab could remember the countless times he and his father had driven down the slope together with pig slops in the back. From now on, he would have to look after the pigs and chickens, and help his mother earn whatever they could from the vegetable gardens, he told himself.

Geez! he wished he hadn't lost the five hundred bucks the other day. It sure would have been handy. He could have helped pay for his father's funeral. A tight grin formed at the corners of his mouth as he thought of the article he had read in this morning's Honolulu Advertiser. It had said that three gamblers—Yosh, Doc Kong and Ah Hong —had been robbed and beaten up severely in a downtown hotel room. When discovered by a bell hop, they were still unconscious with head and facial wounds. They were taken by ambulances to Queens Hospital where preliminary examination showed that they suffered concussions caused by repeated blows of a blunt instrument. The article said that the three men were robbed of approximately ten thousand dollars. It further stated they were being held by the police for withholding information concerning identification of the assailants.

Good for those three crooks! Sab thought vengefully, glad now he had not taken any of old man Lin's money. As for his five hundred dollars—well, there would always be another day, he told himself not too cheerfully. As soon as he got hold of some cash he planned to get into a big crap game and clean up the gang. His mother wouldn't have to work hard in the garden, then.

Kimi, watching her mother wiping her eyes, suddenly realized that although her mother and father had never manifested affection for one another, there, nevertheless, had been a beautiful, tender love between them. How odd it was, she thought, that the greatness in a man could only be recognized after his death. Her father, in his own way, had indeed been a great man. Despite his backward upbringing he had taught himself to read and write, and had also managed to send his oldest son to one of the best colleges in Japan.

How she hoped that when she and her George got married someday they would share the same kind of warm, tender love her mother and father had experienced. She wished that George, somehow, had been able to meet her father. She knew they would have liked each other; that her father's resentment against George would have been replaced by understanding and compassion. George, oh, George, how she prayed the war would end soon so they could be together again.

The letter she had received from him yesterday morning had indicated he might be away for a long time; that the war might last way longer than they had expected. It was his first letter, telling her of the horrible destruction of Pearl Harbor, Hickam Field and parts of Schofield Barracks. He said that big battleships and cruisers and hundreds of smaller ships were capsized in the harbors, and that ugly black smoke was still spiraling into the skies as far as the eyes could see. Ambulances with bodies were still screaming down the streets near the shipyards; fire engines from Honolulu continually fighting erupting flames. The number of servicemen killed may go into the thousands; the number of civilian casualties still undetermined.

When the Maui volunteers reached Schofield Barracks they were shocked to discover that the Niseis in the 298th Infantry Regiment were being guarded by haole soldiers. "How do you like that?" George had said, "American soldiers suspected as enemy spies." He went on to say that everyone seemed so confused they no longer trusted one another; only concerned of what will happen to themselves in case of an all-out invasion. He also mentioned that he used to feel terribly guilty guarding the Japanese internees on Maui while in the Home Guard, because some of them were fathers of guys with whom he had played basketball at Baldwin. "Kimi, what's happening to all of us?" he had asked. "Where's the warmth and friendliness the islands are known for?"

Oh, George, Kimi prayed silently now, eyes flowing, please don't let the war change you. Please be the same wonderful George she loved so much. Please God, please keep him. Bring him back to her safe and sound.

Was Gusuda-san's funeral over by now? Kenyei Shiroma asked himself, hearing the gong of a church clock striking twice from the not too distant background. Chagrined, he lowered his head over his thighs, throat tightening, feeling his eyes welling up with warm tears as he bit hard into his thumb. The man had been like a father to him, and he had not been able to attend his funeral. What would Mrs. Gusuda—and Kimiko—think? Probably would never forgive him.

It was all Ishi's and Tengan's fault. Those two lousy drunks! he thought furiously, fists clenched tight at his sides. They had gotten drunk last night, trying to forget Gusuda-san's death, and had forgotten to shut the blacked-out window in their room. What made Kenyei even more furious was to think of those two being released right away, and he had been held responsible for the violation.

Why hadn't he acted like they had when the four big
aole MP's had burst into the house and hauled them
ff to the Provost Marshal's office: Yes-yes-ing everybody;
ot understanding a single word spoken to them; not even
nowing their own names.

Wait till he got home. This time, he would show them
o mercy. He'd kick them out of his house. Enough was
nough! as Gusuda-san had once told them.

He glanced up at the high, steel-barred window back of
he dimly lit cell and noted that the afternoon sun had
disappeared. The skies beyond the canopy of green foliage
vere now a dark, cloudy gloominess. Bringing his head back
lown again while sitting there on the edge of the canvas
ot, he wondered when he would be released. The cell
next to his was occupied by a young Kanaka and a Japanese
boy who reeked of stale beer and unwashed bodies. They
had been hauled in early this morning, and had been disturbing everyone on the basement floor of the Wailuku
Police Building with their loud singing and talking. The two
cells on the other side of the corridor, formerly occupied
by four Japanese school teachers, were now empty.

"Hey, Guard!" the Kanaka boy called the fat Porlegee
policeman sitting on a chair at the backdoor reading a
comic book. "How about some kau kau. We neve' eat not'ing
since last night."

The guard continued reading.

"Goddamnit! If you no goin' give us some grub, then give
us some smoke."

"Shut up!" the guard said, slowly moving his chair around
and facing the other direction.

"T'at bastard!" the Japanese boy grumbled, slumping back
on his cot, kicking his feet down hard on the canvas.

"Hey, brother!" the Kanaka boy now called through the
bars. "You get any smoke?"

Kenyei looked up.

"How about givin' us some smoke, huh?"

He got up from his cot, took out his pack of Chester-
fields from his denim shirt pocket, and slipped it between
the bars.

The boy's eyes locked with Kenyei's for a second,
looked down at the pack, then back at Kenyei again, fingers

working out half a dozen cigarettes. "Hey, t'anks, huh?" he said. "We neve' have no smoke for long time." He handed the pack back. "What you in heah for?"

Kenyei squeezed the pack; only couple of cigarettes left. "Me forget black-out."

"They locked you up for t'at?"

"You, heah, what for?" he asked, curious.

The boy grinned a devilish grin. "We got drunk last night. The cops said we went into some restaurant, started a big fight, then tried to steal some beer. Funny t'ing, we no remembah not'ing about it." The boy burst out laughing.

Kenyei backed away to his cot and sat down again, suddenly more depressed. He was being forced to associate with common criminals. Him! Shiroma, Kenyei, talking to thieves.

After a while, restless, he got up and stepped over to the high gray concrete wall below the window and stood there for a moment, again wondering how long he would be locked up. If he were kept there several days, what would happen to his taro patches? They needed water and had to be cultivated. And Kimiko? What would happen to her? They were supposed to have announced their engagement last night. Akisamiyo! Everything was so mixed-up and confusing.

Even the defeat of America did not seem as promising as it had been a few days ago. Japan, somehow, did not seem capable of ending the war as fast as they had first hoped. The haole FBI man who interrogated him this morning in faultless Nihon-go seemed neither despondent nor frightened over what the mighty Nihon airplanes had done to Pearl Harbor. Was this the attitude of all the Americans? he asked himself, very bewildered.

He walked back to his cot, sat down, and stared at his dull, mud-covered shoes. In a way, he should be glad he was in the police jail, he thought, and not in the old armory behind the Police Building where the Japanese school teachers, priests, and other Japanese community leaders were locked up. Being in the police jail meant he was not a suspected spy, and would be released soon.

A dark Kanaka policeman and a tall, well-dressed Japanese man in a charcoal-gray tropical suit walked up to his cell. The policeman fumbled with a bunch of keys and, finding the right one, opened the steel door and let the Japanese man in, then locked the door again.

The man gazed over at Kenyei, bowed expressionlessly, then sat down silently on the edge of the other cot. He was about Kenyei's age, appeared to be a Buddhist priest or a school teacher.

Unable to stand the disturbing silence, Kenyei stepped over to his fellow patriot. "Sensei," he addressed respectfully, "please have one of my cigarettes."

"Ah-h, arigato, arigato." The man fingered out a cigarette and returned the pack.

Kenyei quickly struck a match.

"Arigato, arigato."

He stepped back and sat down on his own cot, gazing over at the silent patriot. The man seemed quite young for a community leader. "Sensei, when do you think the war is going to be over?" he asked.

The man sucked a deep drag, looked over fleetingly at Kenyei, at the fat guard, and back to Kenyei again. "Soon. Real soon."

"You think they will be landing troops?"

The man nodded silently.

"Then, it'll be just a matter of few days before—"

The man quickly put a finger up to his mouth and shook his head.

Kenyei leaned closer, whispered: "I heard over the short-wave station that the Philippines and Hong Kong might fall any day."

"You have a short-wave radio?" the man questioned softly.

"A very good one. Very powerful. I listen to the Nihon stations every night. Sometimes, even during the day.

"What news have you heard lately from Japan, Sensei?"

"Very encouraging. Very encouraging."

Kenyei smiled a big, broad, toothy smile, eyes beaming. Wait till he got home and told everyone who he met in jail! They certainly would be amazed to discover he had shared confidential information with someone in direct contact with the Nihon force!

"Sensei," he whispered, leaning over again, "I heard Maui might be captured soon."

"Who told you that?"

"My uncle, Ikehara-san."

"What's his first name?"

"Kansuke—Ikehara, Kansuke."

"Where did he get his information?"

"He's got a short-wave radio hidden under his house. Not only that, he has a long list of names of people willing to contribute to the big welcoming celebration we're planning to have."

"That's wonderful. Is your name on the list?"

"Oh, yes, Sensei. It's going to be a personal triumph for me when Nihon troops march into Maui."

"Oh-h? . . ."

Kenyei looked over at the guard for a second. "You see, I was once a corporal in the Nihon Army."

"A corporal!"

"Oh, yes. Were you ever in the Nihon Army, too?"

"No," the man shook his head.

"But you must have been educated there. Anyone can tell that just talking to you."

The man smiled a slow smile. He got up from his cot and walked over silently to the door. "Guard!"

The Porlegee guard dropped his comic book on the concrete floor and hurried over. He let the man out, locked the door again, then went back to his comic book. The man walked up the stairs alone.

Well, that was strange, Kenyei thought, watching the tall man disappearing up to the main floor of the Police Building. He must have powerful influence to order the guard around.

Shortly, two big haole MP's with steel helmets lowered over their cold blue eyes and bayoneted rifles on their shoulders came up to his cell. They were escorted by the same Kanaka policeman who had brought the Japanese man down a while ago. "Cmon, you're going with the MP's," the policeman said gruffly, opening the door.

"Go where?"

"Never mind—where! Let's go," one of the MP's ordered, towering over Kenyei. "C'mon, c'mon . . ."

The two giant MP's escorted him through the backdoor and down to the old armory fifty yards behind the Police Building. It was beginning to drizzle outside. Kenyei, alarmed, double-stepped on the gravelly ground to keep up with the long, loose strides of the big MP's.

On either side of the weather-beaten, wooden-floored entrance of the armory were monstrous machine guns, each manned by two haole soldiers. The MP guard to Kenyei's right handed a piece of paper to one of the soldiers, waited, took back the paper, then led Kenyei into the armory.

Kenyei was astounded to see the entire basketball-court floor occupied by dozens of well-dressed, elderly Japanese men sitting around canvas cots passing the time reading, talking or playing Go Japanese checkers. There were several stone-faced haole sentries with rifles walking back and forth on the platforms high above the main floor.

As he stood there, still bewildered, he heard someone calling him.

It was Fukunaga-sensei, the Waihee Japanese school teacher.

"Did they just bring you in, Shiroma-san?" the lanky, pale-faced teacher asked with a grave look.

"I don't know why they brought me here. I was in the police jail minding my own business when—"

"Did a Nisei policeman come to your cell?" the teacher questioned suspiciously.

"Nisei Policeman? No. No Nisei policeman came to my cell. Only the two MP's who came to—

"Akisamiyo!" He stared at the teacher, horrified. "You mean—you mean that— Oh, no!"

"Oh, yes!" the teacher exclaimed. "That Nisei is a traitor! He turned in over a dozen of us, even the father of his own wife—Yamamoto-san," pointing to a slight, gray-haired man playing Go with another elderly patriot. "That's Yamamoto-san. He owns a restaurant in Wailuku."

Still speechless, Kenyei slowly sank down on a cot beside him, eyes shut tight, head going from side to side.

20

As DUSK SETTLED in Honolulu that same day, Niro was sitting on the edge of his bed talking solemnly to Ed Oshima with whom he was now living above the School Street Market. Ed's former roommate, Hank Endo, was living in Roy Ito's apartment on Hotel Street while Roy was convalescing in Queens Hospital.

When he had received the telegram from Kimi yesterday morning, he had hurried down to the Hawaiian Airline ticket office but was told there were no seats on flights to Maui for several days. Desperate, he had then sent a telegram back to Kimi telling her he couldn't make it in time for the funeral but would be home as soon as possible. Ever since December seventh, so many unpredictable events had taken place that even his father's death seemed lost in the general confusion. It was as though everyone in Honolulu was struggling to free themselves from a terrifying nightmare.

"When you think you can make it home?" Ed, dressed only in shorts, asked, looking over at him from the edge of the other bed in the stuffy, confined room.

"I have to check with the airlines Monday morning," he

answered, gazing down at his shoes, then out through the half-opened, blacked-out window. It was very quiet outside, hardly any cars passing usually busy School Street, the sun already beyond the Heights, and the skies rapidly turning silver-gray.

"Damn war. It's screwing up things more and more. Look at my hands," Ed said, bringing them up before Niro's eyes. "I got them from digging those damn trenches at Fort Shafter."

"You didn't have to volunteer."

"And be called a traitor or a no-good Jap?" Ed made a sour face.

"You think I enjoy what I'm doing?"

"We must've dug ten miles of trenches by now. And those bastards down the Fort treat us like we were prisoners or something. They have guards following us everywhere. Even to the toilets."

"You the one who said we gonna show everyone what great Americans we are."

Ed looked down at his blistered hands again, grinning. "How was I to know they gonna treat us like this?"

"At least, they not using us for targets."

"Aw-w . . ." Ed scoffed. "Things gonna get better. Sooner or later they gonna realize we're valuable."

"For what?"

"For, well, for officer material."

"What's the matter with you! I told you, we'd be lucky they take us in as buck-ass privates. You heard the guy yourself down the recruiting office: 'We'll call you when we want you, Jap Boy.' "

Ed fingered a blister delicately.

"I didn't ask to be an interpreter for the lousy MP's," Niro went on bitterly. "I rather be digging trenches."

"Who told you to tell them you could speak good Japanese?"

"They saw it in my records. They found out I went to the tenth grade in Japanese school."

"That's what you get for over-educating yourself."

"Aw, bull shit. I should've told them you could speak better Japanese than me."

"You better not tell them that, you sonofabitch!" Ed said, sitting up straight, eyes fiery. "I don't wanna have anything to do with sending people to concentration camps."

"You accusing me of that! I only do what they tell me down at the Provost Marshal's office. They could've asked you to do the same thing."

"One of these days you're gonna have to interrogate someone you know."

"What can I do? except go along with the military."

After a moment of silence, Ed looked side-eyed across the narrow space. "Lemme ask you something. What would you do if your old man was alive and was contacting Japan with a short-wave radio?"

"What if YOUR old man was doing it?"

"I'm asking you."

"I'd get a sledge hammer and wreck the set."

"Then what?"

Niro pondered.

"You wouldn't turn him in?" Ed questioned.

"Would you?"

"I don't know. I'm glad my old man's not a spy."

"You telling me your old man don't care who wins the war?"

Ed grinned. "As long as he don't act pupule like that old gardener did on December seventh, he'll be all right. —By the way, what happened to your old buddy that raised the Japanese flag on the Buddhist Temple the other day?"

"Aw-w, kiss my okole."

"He's your buddy, huh? You saved his life when you talked him into dropping the flag and giving himself up."

"If I neve' go up the roof the MP's would've shot him down."

"The papers said you did a heroic act."

"The old man was harmless. Besides, I had no choice. The Major ordered me up there."

"What they gonna do to the old man?"

"Nothing."

"After what he did!"

"Whatdahell you expect them to do? Shoot him? He was in the Kaneohe pupule house couple of times before."

"That's exactly where that goddamn Tojo belong for starting this crazy war."

"Why don't you write him and complain about your blisters."

Ed examined his blisters again.

"Next time you do any volunteering for me I want a written guarantee my constitutional rights won't be violated."

"Yeah, sure. I'll even have President Roosevelt sign it. How's that?"

After another round of silence, Niro stood up and tucked his aloha shirt into his khaki trousers.

"Where you going?"

"Down Nuuanu. I'm supposed to meet Detective Campbell and couple of MP's from Headquarters. They said something about raiding a home up the valley."

Ed grimaced.

"You think I wanna? They said they might need an interpreter."

He walked out the door and down the back stairways to School Street. It was nearly dark, a refreshing evening breeze coming down from Pacific Heights. Walking across Fort and passing the now empty playground, he saw two MP's and Detective Campbell waiting on an open jeep.

"Damnit! Gusuda," the detective fumed. "Where you been? We don't have all night. C'mon."

He ran up to the jeep and hopped on the back beside the detective. The two steel-helmeted, broad-shouldered haole MP's with automatics in hip holsters gave him disdainful glances. The driver was a Private; the other a Sergeant. Both dressed in neatly starched Army khakis. The detective, a brawny, curly-headed haole-Hawaiian, was wearing a dark blue suit.

The driver quickly shifted into gear and gunned the jeep forward, the three of them lurching back against their seats. The Nuuanu wind was chilly. Niro, leaning forward, stuck his hands into his pocket, his mop of hair ruffled over his forehead. The two grim-faced MP's up front remained silent, busily chewing gum, cold eyes looking straight ahead through the windshield.

"Gusuda, I don't want you to say anything when we get there," Detective Campbell ordered, cupping a hand over his mouth close to Niro's ear to make himself audible over the din of the roaring engine and the strong wind blowing against their faces. "If the people can't understand English I'll ask you to interpret for me. Okay?"

Niro nodded.

They went past Kuakini and Bates Streets, then just before coming to Iolani School grounds, the driver slowed down and brought the jeep to a gradual stop alongside the curb.

"T'is it, Campbell?" he asked, turning his head, mouth moving up and down.

Campbell studied the dusky surroundings: the tall palm trees fringing the street, the row of houses on the other side, and finally the house beyond the growth of low hibiscus hedges on their side of the street. "Yeah, this looks like it."

"Well, c'mon, let's go get 'em," the Sergeant said, adjusting the helmet on his head and jumping out of the jeep. He unfastened the button of the holster and yanked out his automatic.

The driver killed the engine; a hushed silence descended around them. High above their heads, on tall, dark trees, tropical birds were chattering last refrains. The homes around them were completely blacked-out; Iolani School, a block up, a dome of cathedral silence.

"Sergeant," Campbell whispered, sticking his hand into his coat and bringing out his pistol, "there may be no need for rough stuff."

"Listen, Campbell," the Sergeant hissed back, eyeing the detective coldly, "this here is a military matter. If these Japs are spies we know how to handle them. You just tag along. Let me do the thinking. —C'mon, Peterson, getdahell outa the jeep."

The driver took out his automatic and jumped out. Campbell and Niro followed.

The Sergeant led them silently to the wooden gate, pushed it open slowly, glanced back at the three of them, then walked stealthily up to the front steps. The dark yard was as silent as the shadows of the Matsu trees bordering a miniature lake. The house was a low structure, the eaves like a Buddhist Temple's. All the windows were shut tight, no lights showing. Approaching the two steps of the long veranda, they could hear Japanese music. The Sergeant looked back over his shoulder once more, nodded knowingly, then jerked his head at the door.

"Ready!" he hissed, bringing up his automatic.

The driver and the detective nodded, holding their weapons tight.

"Let's go!" the Sergeant cried out, charging across the veranda and crushing his massive shoulder against the thin wooden door.

The door burst wide open. The Sergeant almost stumbled on the floor of the semi-dark living room. The detective and the driver rushed in, Niro right behind.

"Get your hands up!" the Sergeant bellowed, stabbing his automatic at a frail-looking, middle-aged Japanese man in sleeping kimono, and at two pajama-clad girls, about eight and ten. The man, alarmed, jumped up from a low couch and threw up his hands over his head. The two frightened children wrapped their arms around him. A small phonograph on the floor kept on playing soft Japanese music.

"What's happened!" a feminine voice cried forth in Japanese from the kitchen doorway.

The Sergeant whirled around. "Get your hands up and stand next to him," he ordered, waving the automatic.

The slight woman, with an apron around a cotton dress, shuffled over quickly beside the children and her husband.

"What's happened?" she sobbed.

"Anyone else in the house?" the Sergeant demanded.

The man shook his head. One of the children flung her arms around her mother, whimpering; the other clung on to her father, head buried against his chest.

"You understand English?" the Sergeant questioned, pointing the automatic at the man's face.

The man nodded timidly, hands high over his head.

"Where's your short-wave radio set?"

"Radio set?" the man said, eyes wide.

"C'mon, don't stall me. We know you got one," the Sergeant snarled viciously.

"Wait a minute, Sergeant," Campbell interrupted, stepping beside the MP. "Let me ask him a few questions."

"Campbell, I thought I told you not to meddle with military matters," the Sergeant said angrily. "This ain't your goddamn business."

The detective stepped back, looked over at Niro and shrugged helplessly. He placed his pistol back into his chest holster.

"Peterson, search the house for that radio set," the Sergeant ordered. "And I don't give a damn you wreck the joint finding it. Understand?"

"Right, Sarge." The driver stepped into the kitchen, and in a few seconds loud scattering noises came from the back.

"Okay if I question him now, Sergeant?" Campbell asked.

"You better search that kimono of his first," the Sergeant said.

The burly detective shrugged again. He slid his hands over the man's kimono.

"You want me to search the children, too?"

The Sergeant frowned. He dropped the automatic to his side. "You better search the woman."

"Aw, now, Sergeant . . ."

"She might be carrying a knife in her apron." The Sergeant raised his left hand to the fear-stricken woman who stepped closer to her husband.

"Sergeant!"

The Sergeant froze, gazed over at the detective.

"I'm warning you. Don't carry this too far."

The Sergeant considered, then moved back reluctantly, dropping his hand.

After exchanging tense, smouldering looks with the Sergeant, Campbell, taking out a pad from his shirt pocket, turned to face the man. "Your name Hitoshi Abe?"

"Hitoshi Abe? Oh, no. Kiyoshi Ohashi."

The detective turned his head. "Who gave you the information, Sergeant?"

"Somebody called in last night; reported hearing wireless sounds. Said the man who lived here was President of the Bank of Tokyo and could be a dangerous spy."

The detective winced. "What you do for a living, Mr. Ohashi?"

"Me? I, gardener for Mr. Richardson, big shot, bank down town."

"Hey, Sarge," the driver said, stalking back into the living room, "there ain't no radio set in this heah house. I've searched everywhere."

The Sergeant placed his automatic back into his holster. He avoided everyone's eyes.

"I guess we made another boner, huh?" Campbell told the Sergeant.

The Sergeant made a deep grunting noise in his throat.

Niro glanced over at Mr. Ohashi, at his wife, at the two whimpering children, then quickly looked down at the floor. He swallowed with difficulty.

"No, Campbell, I don't think we made a boner," the Sergeant at last said, studying the phonograph at his feet with hard, cold eyes. "These people ain't got no business listening to Jap music." He picked up the record off the phonograph and crushed it over his knee. As he bent down to grab a handful of the other records Niro rushed forward.

"Wait a minute, Sergeant," he urged, taking hold of the Sergeant's arm, "those are just children's songs."

"Take your goddamn hands off me, Jap Boy!" the Sergeant threatened, shoving Niro away. He smashed the records brutally over his knee and dropped them on the floor.

The two children looked up at the tall Sergeant with tears streaming down their cheeks, then down at their broken records.

"I'll show 'em they can't listen to no Jap music from now on," the Sergeant roared, tramping on the rest of the records, watching the agonizing expressions of the children with a hard-bitten, stony grin. After he had crushed all the records, he gave the phonograph a vicious kick, then stormed out the front door, the driver following behind.

The detective stood there for a second or two shaking his head, gazed over squeamishly at Mr. and Mrs. Ohashi, then saying nothing, followed the two MP's out.

Niro looked down at the broken records, over at the children, then slowly up at Mr. and Mrs. Ohashi who were eyeing him with utter contempt. He wanted to say something to them, anything, but couldn't find the words. Mr. Ohashi suddenly stepped up to him and spat into his face.

Shocked, Niro jerked his head back, stared into the dark, hate-filled eyes of the slight man. He wiped his face slowly, turned around and walked out the door, feeling stripped of the dignity and honor he wrote his father about only three days ago.

Riding back down Nuuanu on the open jeep, head hung

low, eyes misty, he wondered distressedly how long all the distrust, hatred and intolerance that had started on December seventh would go on. As he lifted his head and gazed up front, he quickly noted the Hawaiian full moon rising from the dark ocean and a colorful rainbow arched high over the quiet city—an old legendary omen of victory. He hoped and prayed that the propitious sign meant the quick return of the warm spirit of Aloha once enjoyed by everyone in the islands.

ABOUT THE AUTHOR

JON SHIROTA was born in Peahi, Maui, Hawaii. The son of Japanese-American parents, he was fourteen years old when the Japanese bombed Pearl Harbor. Following the war he attended Brigham Young University. After graduating in 1952, he decided to explore America; he spent several years tramping around the country taking whatever work he could find. Finally, when he had had his fill of the free life, he began work as a Treasury Agent for the Internal Revenue Service in Hollywood, California.

Mr. Shirota has been writing ever since he was a small child. In 1959 he wrote to the famous Lowney Handy Colony in Marshall, Illinois, which had produced James Jones and Tom Chamales. He worked with Mrs. Handy by correspondence until 1963, when he moved to the colony and finished *Lucky Come Hawaii*. He now lives in Los Angeles, California.

Mr. Shirota is one of the very few Japanese-American writers to be published in the United States.